ESCAPE

RUNE AND FLASH BOOK 2

ESCAPE: RUNE AND FLASH BOOK 2 Copyright © 2024 by Joe Canzano. All rights reserved. Printed in the United States of America. No part of this book may be used or reproduced in any manner whatsoever without written permission except in the case of brief quotations embodied in critical articles and reviews. For contact information visit Happy Joe Control at www.happyjoe.net.

Happy Joe Control books may be purchased for educational, business, or promotional use. For contact information visit Happy Joe Control at www.happyjoe.net.

ISBN: 979-8-9859132-2-4

Library of Congress Control Number: 2024925114

Cover design by Veronica Scott

ESCAPE

RUNE AND FLASH BOOK 2

JOE CANZANO

www.happyjoe.net

Chapter 1

They had to keep moving. There was no better plan.

They were plowing through the dense forest, stepping around broken logs and ducking under whip-like branches. Luckily, Markla was small and quick like a squirrel. She tossed back her tangled black hair and glanced at Rune. What was he thinking? Would he have regrets? Somewhere not too far away was the smoking carcass of the Dream Center and the battle they'd left behind, at least for now.

"Let's stop at my house," Rune said. "We'll get supplies. Also, I can see my mother."

"That's a bad idea, Rune. They're going to be after us."

"But why? Our side won."

"They destroyed the streaming stations but the government is still there, and lots of people will still support them. Also, Aldo was Gin's brother."

Aldo, who she'd killed. Was it smart to remind him? Probably not. She glanced at Rune and tried to stay calm.

He was quiet. Then he finally said, "Okay, but they'll need time to figure things out. They have bigger stuff to worry about. We'll have a little time, an opportunity."

Opportunity? Markla almost laughed. How much opportunity was there for a sixteen-year-old girl who'd murdered three people? Her thoughts were interrupted by the ocean-like roar of several police hover-ships skimming low over the trees.

Markla grabbed Rune's arm and pulled him toward some foliage. They peered up through the scraggily branches as the crab-like ships scurried across the sky. They were coming from the direction of Liberta, the capital of Sparkla that was just across the Bay of Gems. They were heading toward the prison.

"We need food," Rune said. "Right now all we've got is the stuff in your backpack."

"Your house is the first place they'll look."

"Maybe, but we'll be gone before they get there. Besides, they don't know what happened to Aldo. Anyone could've killed him."

Maybe, Markla thought. After all, a battle had been raging, and she and Rune might be viewed as just a couple of escaped prisoners, and Aldo was the kind of dead guy who'd generate a long list of suspects. So Rune and Markla wouldn't necessarily be blamed—unless, of course, the events in that room had been recorded.

"It's still a bad idea," she said. "What's your mom going to say when you tell her you're running away from home? I can't see that going too well." She looked at him again, and she liked what she saw—with that dark hair blowing around his handsome face, and those earth-brown eyes. But those same eyes told her his thoughts were unchanged.

"Okay, let's do it," she said. "But we need to be quick."

Rune grinned. "We'll be like two bolts of lightening. Come on."

They'd reached a path in the woods now, and they could move faster. Rune was in the lead, but he kept glancing back, and Markla knew he was looking out for her. For a second, the thought made her tingle a bit. I have no regrets, she thought. *The world turned me into who I am.* Then she shook her head, like maybe she could push some of the horror out of her mind. But she knew it would always be there, along with other things she could never erase.

Rune's house backed up to the woods, and as they approached the sun-bleached wooden shed at the edge of the backyard, Markla's mind flashed with passionate images of her and Rune together, and once again she felt something electric ripple through her. Then they ran through the yard to a side door and burst into the cluttered kitchen, and there was Rune's mother Maya.

Markla had a vague memory of Maya bringing Rune to school at the age of seven. She looked the same—pretty in a discombobulated way. Today she was wearing a fuzzy purple bathrobe, and she looked like something furry that was being electrocuted. Every dyed hair on her blonde head was falling in a different direction, and her eyes were rimmed with red, and now her mouth dropped open.

"Rune!" she said, and she lunged forward and hugged him.

Rune said nothing but hugged her back. And now Maya started crying.

"Your father is dead!" she wailed. "They killed him."

"I know," Rune said, and he squeezed his mother harder. "It'll be all right." But she kept sobbing—and then she stopped and stared.

"Markla Flash," she said, and her voice was like an ice-pick. "Rune, what are you doing with her?"

"Dad was fighting the government," Rune said. "And I was helping him, and we have to go. I came to say goodbye."

Maya looked stunned. "What? That's ridiculous! You can't go with her! She's the one who sucked you into this mess!"

Yeah, Markla thought, that was true, and she felt sick to her stomach. But she said nothing.

"No," Rune said. "Dad was fighting for a good cause, and so was Markla—and so was I."

"She's a murderer, Rune! She's part of an evil cult. You need to stay here, and she needs to leave. I should call the police."

Markla squirmed a bit but Rune put his arm around her shoulder. "I'm going with Markla," he said. "It's what I want to do."

For a long second Maya studied Rune, and then Markla—and

then she swore softly. And then there was a humming sound outside.

Markla snapped her head toward a window. "They're here!" she said. Two dark-blue police hover-cars were pulling up in front of the house. "Rune, let's go!"

"No!" Maya said, and she reached out and grabbed Rune's hand. "You won't have a chance. Follow me—quick!"

Markla hesitated. Rune said, "She's right—we're trapped. I just saw two knobbers running around the back. Come on."

Markla gritted her teeth and followed Rune and Maya as they raced through the living room and into a bedroom. This is a bad plan, she thought. Then Maya pulled open a closet door. "Hide in here," Maya said. "Hurry!"

Markla looked at the closet and then at Maya—and no, she wasn't going in there. And now her heart was pounding, and black memories were rampaging through her head. Her own mother was staring down at her, and a door was closing, and Markla felt crushed by a suffocating space.

Rune once again put his arm around her. "Markla, it'll be all right. It'll be fine."

Markla could barely speak. "Okay," she whispered. She took a few deep breaths and plunged into the closet behind him. They pushed through some clothes and stood behind a rack of heavy coats. But there weren't enough coats, and it was hard to be completely hidden. Then Maya closed the door.

They were in total blackness now but she felt Rune's fingers on her hand, and then he grasped her palm. Suddenly, she felt better—but then she felt rage. I need to be stronger, she thought. She recalled the dagger strapped to her belt. She wasn't going down without a fight. Then Rune squeezed her hand and spoke in a low voice, "Don't worry. My mom's got this."

Really? From what little Rune had said about Maya, Markla

found it hard to believe he was so optimistic. But then Rune was always optimistic, and it was good to have someone like that in her life.

Through the door, Markla heard footsteps and voices.

"I'm sorry about Blog," a deep voice said. "But we need to look around." The wooden floor creaked as heavy footsteps entered the bedroom. Markla heard Maya talking in a low voice, and she strained her ears to hear but she couldn't make out the words.

The footsteps came closer. There was more creaking, and someone was coming toward the closet, and someone was standing in front of it—and Markla felt the hair on her neck rising. This was such a stupid place to hide. Anyone who opened the door would see her, and was that Maya's plan? Of course! Why had she fallen for this?

Her free hand slid the dagger from its sheath and pressed it close to her thigh. Her movements were smooth, and Rune didn't notice. Then the door swung open, and Markla caught her breath. There was a man standing there, and he scanned the forest of coats—and he glanced at Rune, and then he stared directly into Markla's eyes. She stared back but remained still. She was ready to strike.

When he reaches for me, I'm going to fight!

He didn't reach. Instead, he closed the door.

"Okay," he said. "I guess there's no one here."

"I told you that," Maya said. "Now can you please leave?"

Markla heard the officers walking away, and the voices became more muffled. A wave of relief washed over her, and she returned the weapon to her belt. Then she whispered, "What just happened, Rune?"

"I'm not sure."

There was a squeaking sound, and the closet door swung open again. But this time it was Maya standing there, and she was alone.

"They're gone," Maya said. "That was Mano, a friend of your father's. Blog had lots of friends."

For an instant, Rune smiled. "Yeah," he said. "Dad had friends. We have to go."

"You're going to leave me here all alone? Isn't Markla the one they really want?"

"No. Some things happened at the prison, and they're looking for both of us. We need to go."

Maya paused and wiped away a tear. "All right," she said. "You should take some supplies. I'll get a few things together."

"That would be great."

She looked at Rune with her watery eyes and flashed Markla a stare like a blade. Then she headed into the kitchen.

"Your Mom hates me," Markla said.

"She doesn't hate you. She doesn't know you."

Markla shook her head. "Maybe she knows me better than you think. Hey, your father was the king knobber. I'm sure he had a bunch of guns. Can we get one?"

Rune hesitated. "Why do we want a gun?"

"Because the people chasing us have guns, and I'm not going back to the Dream Prison."

"I don't want to shoot anyone."

"I don't either. But I'm not going back to the Dream Prison, even if the person I shoot is myself."

They locked eyes. Markla didn't want Rune to be uncomfortable but she wanted a gun. She did.

"Don't talk like that," Rune said. "I'll get a gun."

"Get two."

Rune walked fast into another part of the house with Markla close behind.

The guns were in his father's office. Markla scanned the vast collection of awards, medals, and pictures scattered across the walls—all things related to Blog's life. She noticed how Rune seemed to avoid looking at them as he went to a walnut-colored cabinet in the corner, and her heart went out to him. Inside the cabinet was an assortment of weapons.

Rune stared at the collection but he didn't touch. "Look," Markla said. She picked up a couple of magazines and slid out a few shells. "Some of these are loaded with rubber bullets, and this one's got tranquilizer pellets." She grabbed a snub-nosed black pistol and offered it to him. "You can also load the pellet shells into this. They're less accurate, unless you're really close—but they'll put people to sleep fast." Rune hesitated but then took the weapon along with a few magazines loaded with the pellet shells. Markla returned her attention to the cabinet, where she eyed a lightweight rifle but decided it would still be too hard to carry and conceal—but hey, here was a Max 92, a fat handgun capable of firing shells with exploding bullets. She grabbed it along with some ammunition. She could feel Rune's eyes on her as she snapped a magazine into place and then stuffed the extra ammunition into her backpack. She didn't meet his gaze.

"I'm not a psychopathic killer," she said. "I just want to be ready. The police aren't the only ones chasing us. It's 20 Eyes, too. They monitor the communications, and they're going to be after me because of Dru."

"Dru—yeah, someone killed him. Aldo said it was you."

"Aldo was right," she said, and then she stopped moving. "Do you see what you're getting yourself into?"

"Yeah, and I don't care. I'm sure Dru deserved it."

For a moment, she was quiet. "We need the flyboard. Let's get it and go."

Right now, Rune only had one flyboard here—and it was his backup board, having lost the other one when he'd been arrested. The plan was to try and steal another one from somewhere.

Meanwhile, Maya had loaded all kinds of stuff onto the kitchen table, mostly packages of food but other things as well. As Rune and Markla surveyed the supplies, Maya walked in. She was no longer crying, and she no longer seemed scared. In fact, she seemed quite together, moving fast and with a purpose. She was carrying a denim jacket and a well-worn backpack.

"This backpack was in the closet, Rune. It was your father's, and I put a few things in there that might be useful. Markla, I put a few things in there for you, too, stuff a boy wouldn't think about. And you'll also need jackets because it's going to get cold. Markla, this one is mine, and it's going to be big on you, but it's all I've got. Check the pockets. I put something important in there." She handed Markla the jacket.

"Thank you," Markla said.

Then Maya pulled out a container about the size of a bar of soap and handed it to Rune. "You'll need this," she said.

"What's in here?"

"Cash. Blog had a stash in the house. Just take it."

"Thanks," he said. Cash wasn't used much anymore. It was something many people in the government wanted to eliminate since any transaction could easily be done by GoBug. But every GoBug transaction could also be tracked, and so there were some who wanted to keep cash viable, and Rune wasn't shocked his father had been one of them.

Maya pointed at some cucumber-like containers on the kitchen counter. "There's some stuff here from your father's military days, and also some camping supplies." She stared at the guns. "Do you really need those?"

"It's just a precaution!" Rune blurted. "Markla quit 20 Eyes, so she might need some protection until we get to the border, that's all. I need my flyboard."

Maya frowned and looked away. Rune put on the backpack

and then ran toward his bedroom. Markla was now alone with Maya.

Markla could feel the tension in the air, and she could feel guilt gnawing at her insides. Then Maya took a step toward her, and Markla braced herself—and Maya hugged her.

"You crazy girl," Maya whispered. "My son loves you, do you know that? I think he always has… You make sure he stays alive. Promise me you'll do that. Promise me!"

Markla felt like the room was spinning. "I'll do that, Maya," she said. "I promise."

Chapter 2

The plan was to get to Sliver, an industrial town filled with lumber yards and solar-powered factories. The huge hover-trains that carried freight all stopped there. The idea was to sneak onto a hover-train and mix in with the cargo. They'd let the train carry them to the border somewhere south of here and then sneak across. But it was a long walk to Sliver.

We'll make it, Rune thought. *How hard can it be?*

They'd already crossed the bridge over the Rainy Wish river, and they'd gone past the outskirts of Turnaround. Now they were in the woods again with the autumn sun sinking like an orange boulder and the air getting cool. Rune was thinking they might have been more comfortable at his mom's house tonight but he didn't want to put Maya in any more danger, and besides, Markla had insisted on leaving.

He glanced at Markla and felt a ripple of anxiety. There were some wild and tangled places in her mind. She was capable of doing the most extreme things—and could he do the same? He had some doubts.

Like that situation with Aldo. Aldo, who'd been responsible for the death of his father. Aldo, who Markla had unceremoniously slaughtered. It should've been me who killed him, he thought. *But I couldn't do it!*

They kept walking until it was almost dark, and they came to a gurgling stream that was wide and deep. "This is a good spot," Markla said. "We can sleep here and get an early start tomorrow."

The water in Sparkla bubbled clean and clear, and Markla had no problem filling up her canteen. But Rune wanted to use a few purification pills from Blog's camping supplies.

"You don't need them," Markla said. "I do it all the time." Then she laughed. "Then again, maybe I'm stupid all the time."

They couldn't make a fire because it would be spotted for sure but they had some self-heating packets of protein-fortified rice and beans, and it tasted like a feast. Then Rune rummaged through his backpack, taking stock of their supplies—and then he went through Markla's backpack, doing the same thing, and he found her wooden flute.

"Hey, you still have this?" he said, and he examined it. It was primitive compared to the ones he'd seen made of silver. "Let's play! I'll find something to bang on."

She shook her head. "I think we should probably be quiet. Besides, I don't know any songs. I just improvise."

He laughed. "Why is that? You don't like playing songs people know?"

"It's not like that," she said, and she laughed, too. "I just like to pick my own notes. It makes me feel…calm."

Right. Somehow this made sense.

"Markla, when we get to Narna, we're going to play."

She smiled. "Okay, we'll do that."

"Is that a promise?"

"Yeah, it is… But right now, we've got other issues. It's going to be cool tonight."

They were sitting on the ground, and he moved closer to her. He put his arm around her. "That's true," he said. "But luckily we've got the SuperSeal sleeping bag. And we've got each other."

"Yeah," she said, and she kissed him, and his whole body tingled. Then she raised her eyebrows and said, "Rune, look at this." She reached into the pocket of the baggy denim jacket she was wearing and removed a tiny container. "Can you believe it? Your mother gave me birth control pills."

Rune stared at the box in her hand. "She's been a good mom," he said in a deadpan voice. "The best one I ever had."

Markla laughed. "I couldn't even get my mother to give me

a chocolate bar. I remember asking when I was little, and she said it would make me fat."

"But you're so thin."

"I know. It was just one more way she wanted to torture me. Anyway, I'm going to take one of these, okay?"

Rune smiled. "Okay." They were soon wrapped in each other's arms, moving together on the floor of the forest. At times she held him so tightly, like she was desperate for something—but later she was soft and brimming with affection. She was filled with a sweet kind of passion few people would suspect, and Rune never wanted to let her go.

He woke up in the morning, and he shivered from the cold. He reached out his hand but she wasn't there. He popped his head out of the sleeping bag and scanned the forest. The sun was still below the horizon, but the sky was changing from black to indigo to violet—and now he saw her silhouette a short distance away, kneeling down and fiddling with her radio. Rune guessed she was doing a frequency scan, trying to see if anyone was chasing them. She stood up and clipped the device onto her belt, and he waved to her.

He wanted her to come lie down again in the sleeping bag, and he wondered how long the effect of those pills lasted—but she was all business now, and he understood. They had to get moving.

"Rune, I already ate. You should eat something, and we should go."

Rune ate some more rice and took a quick bath in the cold stream. Then they were off.

Rune was carrying the flyboard under his arm. "We need to get another board," he said. "It'll make things so much easier."

Markla shrugged. "I like walking in the woods. I guess it would be better if we weren't both fugitives."

"Yeah, but you're my favorite fugitive."

"Thanks," she said with a short laugh.

He studied the sky, now filled with the fiery rising sun. "Are you sure we're going the right way?" he said. "If I could turn on my GoBug for two seconds, this would be so easy." Then he pulled the almond-sized device from his pocket and stared at it with affection. He itched to place it behind his ear and once again see all the mindstreams of the world glowing before his eyes. "Two seconds," he said. "I could put the power crystal back in and plug into a script that would tell us exactly where we are. Two seconds."

"In two seconds the knobbers would track us down."

"Well, yeah. But does that crazy thing in your hand really work? Can't they track that, too?"

In her palm, Markla was holding a round metal container. Rune had never seen anything like it. It had a needle in the center that kept moving.

"It's a compass, Rune. It's an ancient device, and no one can track it, and it tells us our direction."

"Does it have a setting for 'Sliver?' "

"No. It has a setting for 'north.' "

"What? That's it? How is it powered?"

"It's not powered. But I can tell we're going northwest, and that's what we want." Then Markla lowered her voice and did an impression of a demon. "It speaks to the Earth."

Rune laughed. Of course Markla would have such a device. With her black hair, messy like a pile of snakes, and her moccasins, and her dagger, and her generally primitive styling, Markla absolutely resembled a creature of the Earth. But it's not like she had no interest in modern things. She'd been quite interested in his father's guns, and the thought made him sweat a bit.

"Do you really think 20 Eyes will be after us?"

"Yeah."

"But how will they know it was you—the thing with Dru? And how will they find us out here?"

"They'll know. Blu Baroke more or less saw me do it, and besides, everyone knew I was involved with Dru." She paused and then said, "They also monitor police communication, and they have spies, lots of them."

Rune wasn't sure what to say. He knew she'd joined the dreaded subversive group 20 Eyes because they'd given her something she'd never had—a family. But then it had all fallen apart, and would they really bother coming after her? He set his jaw. Let them come. This time, he wouldn't just watch while Markla did the hard stuff. *This time, I'll do what needs to be done.*

Suddenly, she stopped walking. "Wait," she whispered.

He shot her a glance, and his heart started to pound. Someone was coming.

She ducked down low behind a tree, and Rune got beside her. There were few bushes or shrubs here—they were in the deep woods, and it was mostly trees, leaves, and pieces of other broken trees. Rune put the flyboard on the ground and pressed close to Markla. There's no need to panic, he thought. After all, anyone could be hiking out here, and no one would know them. We should just act like two people casually out for a walk. That would be a decent plan.

But Markla was pulling out the big handgun.

"What are you doing?" Rune hissed. "We should act natural."

"I am acting natural."

"Markla—no! You're acting paranoid. Let's wait and see who they are."

But there was a cold and scary look in her eyes, and for an instant Rune's mind flashed with the memory of Aldo and that knife in his back. He put his hand on her arm.

"I'm just being careful!" she snapped. "I'm fine."

He paused, and then he nodded his head. "Okay."

Then he watched her swap the magazine with exploding bullets for another one—with real bullets.

"What are you doing now?" he said.

"We don't want any fiery explosions, Rune. Fire is a bad thing in a forest."

"Yeah, but why are you using real bullets? What about the rubber ones?"

She hesitated. "Not for this. Trust me."

He wasn't sure how to respond, so he once again said, "Okay." But it suddenly seemed much hotter in the woods; he was sweating. He turned his attention back to the trees.

There was no kind of clearing here. They were behind a tall oak, standing on a bed of leaves, and they were surrounded by more oak trees—and through the forest came the sounds of people. Whoever was coming was not making it a secret. They were swishing through the leaves on the ground, and they were talking loudly, and they were getting closer. And then a bird called out, and there was another sound—and now Rune felt a chill go down his spine. It was the sound of a voice coming from Markla's radio. Someone was sending a transmission, and who used radios? The people who'd been working with his father. And the people in 20 Eyes.

Now it sounded like someone was speaking into a radio. "They came this way. We're on it. They're close."

Impossible! Rune thought.

Now Markla gave him a sharp look, and raised her eyebrows, and said one word, "gun."

Right, Rune thought. He tried to stay calm as he grabbed his backpack, fumbled around, and found the weapon. It felt cold and heavy in his hand.

He knew how to fire it. It was something his father had insisted he learn, and for an instant Rune thought about Blog, and what would he say if he were here? He would be agreeing with Markla, and Rune frowned at the thought. The idea of shooting at a person seemed out of the question—although the cartridges were only loaded with tranquilizer pellets. The pellets were small, like grains of sand. They were coated with a chemical that would burn through most clothing on impact and put someone to sleep as soon as a pellet touched human skin. They also had a limited range.

Suddenly, Markla's radio was crackling with a voice. "Little Wildcat, are you out there? This is 'The Fish' and 'The Bear.' We've come to help."

Rune squinted into the forest, and heard the sound of foot-steps coming closer, snapping branches and crunching dry leaves.

"Markla, are you 'Little Wildcat?' "

"Yeah," she said. "Rune, go to a different tree, maybe one over there."

She pointed to a tree a bit farther away from the direction of the pursuers.

"I'm staying with you."

"But it's better if we're shooting from two different places. I mean if it comes to that."

Right. Why hadn't he thought of that? Rune gritted his teeth and darted out from behind the tree. But he didn't move farther from the approaching pursuers. Instead, he moved a bit closer, off to Markla's right but still closer to where they'd be arriving. They'll have to get through me first, he thought. *And that's not going to happen!*

Then they appeared. They were two guys at least a few years older than Rune, and they were both dressed in camouflage clothing and carrying rifles. They were also wearing armored vests, and one of them was holding a radio. Rune heard Markla shout, "That's close enough, Halo! I have a gun, so stop walking."

They stopped. They were about forty paces from Rune with quite a few trees in the way.

The taller of the two guys, presumably Halo, said, "Markla, we want to help you."

"I don't need your help."

"But you're one of us! We know the knobbers killed Dru. They're putting lies on the mindstreams, trying to divide us. They're using LiveDreams to create phony clips of stuff that never happened… We can help you get out of Sparkla. It's what Dru would've wanted."

Rune sighed with relief. So they don't know who killed Dru, he thought. This was a lucky break.

"The police didn't kill Dru," Markla said. "I did. Now go away."

Rune felt his head spin; Halo and his companion looked at each other. Halo jerked the rifle to his eye—and then there was an explosion of gunfire.

Halo was struck in the chest. He gave a shout as he tumbled backwards. Meanwhile, his friend dove for cover behind a tree, and Markla blasted the tree, and the guy swore, and then Halo was moving—apparently his body armor had saved him. He was crawling fast but Markla kept shooting. He yelped as he was hit in the leg—but he managed to drag himself behind the tree with his friend. Neither one had fired a shot.

But Markla kept firing, shooting again and again at a branch high above them. There was a cracking noise as the branch broke and crashed to the ground. There was a scream—someone had either been shot or hit by the branch. Then Markla stopped to reload, and Rune hesitated, and he slid out from behind his tree.

"Markla, don't shoot!" he shouted. "They're down!"

He ran toward where she'd been firing. He was waving his

hands in the air, though one hand still held his pistol. He was watching the area carefully.

Markla stepped out from behind her tree, aiming her pistol.

"Rune, what are you doing? Get out of the way!"

"They're down!" Rune said again. And then Halo popped up in front of him.

Rune caught his breath. Halo had a look of terror in his eyes—but then he was fumbling with his rifle. Rune shot him in the neck.

Halo yelped as the pellets knocked him to the ground. In an instant, he was unconscious. Then Rune heard a sound, and he whirled—and it was the other guy, pinned under the branch. He was flailing around, trying to get free. Rune fired again, and he heard a grunt as the pellets struck the guy's hand, and then he stopped moving.

Markla raced through the woods. Then she was standing beside Rune, and she was looking back and forth at the two wounded people. Her eyes were wild—but then they were calm.

"Good job, Rune. Grab the rifles."

"But this guy is shot in the leg. Won't he bleed to death?"

Markla knelt down and examined Halo. "No," she said. "I'm a terrible shot, and I only grazed him. If I'd hit him with this thing his leg would be in two pieces. Just get the rifles. These guys can take care of themselves."

Rune hesitated, but then he collected Halo's rifle while Markla snatched the gun from the other guy. Markla also searched them both. One of them had a GoBug and she pulled it apart, removed the power crystal, and smashed the device with a rock. She also found two black daggers exactly like her own, and she stuffed those into her knapsack. Then she grabbed Halo's radio.

"Let's go," she said. "This way."

Once again, they were wading fast through the woods, stepping over roots and ducking under branches.

They didn't talk, but they soon came to the stream again in a spot that looked fairly deep. "Give me the rifle," Markla said. Then she tossed both rifles into the water and watched them sink down.

Rune shook his head. "Why did you tell them you killed Dru?"

"Because I wanted them to know—and Rune, they already knew. Trust me, they're sneaky."

"But you don't know for sure. They sounded like they wanted to help."

"No. They were going to kill us."

"I think you should've waited a bit."

She stared at him, and he stared right back, and then the radio she'd taken from Halo crackled to life. A male voice was speaking.

"Hey, Bear, are you there? Any sign of that cat?"

Markla handed the radio to Rune. "Here, talk," she said. "Tell them 'no sign.' "

Right! Rune thought. He pushed down the transmitter button and said, "No sign."

"What?" the voice said. "I thought you were getting close?"

"No sign of her now."

There was a pause. "Well, keep looking. According to what we intercepted, she's probably in the woods with Blog's kid… And we can't let her get away—not after what she did to Dru."

Rune caught his breath, while Markla just shrugged. Then she motioned for him to continue.

"Okay," Rune said. "We'll keep looking."

"Good. And remember, don't kill her. We want her alive. She's going to suffer."

"Right."

The transmission ended, and Rune once again stared into Markla's eyes.

"Well, you were right," he said. "So maybe we didn't make a mistake."

"No, we did," she said, and she gave him a little smile. "We left them alive." She studied his reaction, and then she laughed. "I'm joking," she said. "Well, maybe."

Rune said nothing. Then he said, "We beat them up pretty good. They won't catch us."

"Yeah, but all the shooting might attract attention. We better run."

Once again, they started running. Soon enough, they heard the sound of a hover-ship.

Chapter 3

Tanna Xantha stormed down a hallway of the capitol building. The building was a sparkling mint-colored cube that overlooked the shimmering Bay of Gems, and she eyed her reflection in every glass door. She smiled a bit because she looked so sleek and sexy today in black leggings with a matching shirt. Her hair, also black, was tied in a ponytail that hung down her back like a shiny snake.

Tanna was moving fast but she always moved fast, and who were all these security people trying to keep her from seeing her father? They acted like she was a child but she wasn't. She was seventeen years old, and they had no right to treat her like this.

Okay, so a few radicals had destroyed the streaming stations, ravaged the Dream Center, and temporarily crippled the government's ability to broadcast LiveDream propaganda. But they hadn't taken over the government. In fact, they hadn't even attacked this building located in Liberta, right across the bay from Cooly Strip where the Dream Prison stood. These rebels were a bunch of amateurs.

One of them had killed Uncle Aldo but she'd never liked Uncle Aldo. However, he'd once told her that "in disaster there's opportunity," and his death was an opportunity, and she was going to grab it. His murder had been recorded by a surveillance camera and the identity of the killer was known—and so Tanna had a plan. She just needed to get past all these jug-headed stormtroopers and talk to her dad.

The last stormtrooper in her way was about her age, and he was planted in front of the heavy wooden door that led to the president's office. This guy was sturdy like a tree, and as Tanna approached and saw who it was she relaxed. Meanwhile, he smiled and gave a nod of his big head.

"Hi, Tanna," he said. "I don't think you should go in there. Your father's busy."

"I'm busy too, Stillo."

He grinned and stepped aside. "Don't tell him I was so easy."

She returned his smile. "I'm sorry. I didn't mean to be rude. But I need to get things done."

She opened the door and saw her father pacing around the room, using a GoBug behind his ear to conference with someone. Since she had access to his conference stream, she immediately connected and joined the three-dimensional display. It seemed to glow in front of her eyes. Unfortunately, she was looking at Stroll Nadum, the new Centurion and head of the national police—and why was he wearing a helmet to a meeting with the president? Tanna tried not to laugh. Maybe he was trying to show he was in battle, but together with his sunglasses and black handlebar mustache, it almost seemed like he was disguised.

Well, he should be disguised, she thought. *After the way the security forces failed at the Dream Prison, he should be wearing a bag over his head.*

Gin glared at Tanna because she hadn't been asked to join but then he turned his attention back to Stroll.

Stroll coughed a few times. "The streaming stations will be up and running soon," he said. "Unless we get another attack."

"That's very profound," Gin said. "And what are we doing to prevent another attack?"

"We're locating the rebels. We have good intelligence concerning their identities, and we're compiling lists."

"And what about my brother's killers? Did you check Blog's house?"

Now Stroll squirmed a bit. "They weren't there, or maybe they left before we got there—or maybe they never went. We're searching for them."

Gin rolled his eyes, and Tanna did the same. It was obvious that the best people had been fighting with Blog, and they were still out there fighting, and now they were left with this?

"You're being outwitted by a couple of kids!" Gin said. "Find them!" Then he snapped off the stream and spoke partly to himself in a low voice, "Aldo was my best advisor, and I miss him." Then he went to the cooler in the corner to fill his stainless steel cup with a gloppy protein drink. He took a swig and looked at Tanna.

"No," he said.

"What? I didn't say anything."

"Whatever you're thinking, the answer is 'no.' "

She threw up her hands. "I want to go after the people who killed Uncle Aldo! I just graduated, and I'm not a kid anymore, and I can form my own team from people at the academy."

Gin laughed. He had a loud, booming kind of laugh. "It's great that you want to be involved with law enforcement, and you did well with the training because you're good at everything, just like me—but there are lots of people ahead of you in line. You need to be patient."

"No one in that line had their uncle brutally murdered!"

"Yes, but you don't have the experience. Besides, you're a LiveDream writer—not a police officer."

"I'm in training to be a special agent! I've helped arrest people."

"Tanna, I have a country to run. We're trying to suppress a serious insurrection, and with the streaming stations down, people are turning to the indie stations that the rebels left operating, and they're seeing and hearing lots of propaganda. We won't be able to get our own propaganda up and running for days—maybe longer. So that's my top priority, and I need to figure out the best way to deal with it."

"Why don't you destroy the indie stations? Then everyone will be equally blind."

Gin hesitated. "Not a bad idea, but people wouldn't stand for that. Unfortunately, this is still a democracy, and they'd vote me out."

"But how would they know? You could blame it on the same rebels that knocked out our stuff. And we have the resources to rebuild faster than the indies, so we could get our stuff back out there a lot faster and spread that story. In fact, we can start creating the LiveDreams right now that show whatever we want to show, and they'll be ready to go as soon as the streaming stations are up and running."

Gin paused and took another sip of his protein drink. "When did you get so devious?"

Tanna shrugged. "I was always this way but you were too busy working out to notice. And Mom was too busy doing LiveDreams and shopping." Then she laughed, trying to make a joke out of it—but it was all true, and it was probably silly to care but sometimes she wanted to say it. Then she said, "Anyway, while you're busy doing this stuff, I can go after the people who killed Uncle Aldo. I'm smarter than that dumb Centurion. He looks like he's got a dead rat stuck to his face."

Gin laughed and shook his head. "You're not ready for that kind of thing, Tanna. The girl we're talking about was in 20 Eyes, and this is no LiveDream training session. She's dangerous."

Tanna took a deep breath, trying to control her anger.

Markla Flash? Who is that little runt compared to me?

"I have a plan for that, too," she snapped. "If Markla was in 20 Eyes, she monitors the radio, right? I'll send a special broadcast to her."

"And she's going to listen to you?"

"Yeah, because there's more to the plan."

As she told him the rest, he raised his eyebrows. Don't gloat too much, she thought. But then again a little was okay. After all, he was finally paying attention to her.

"Tanna, did you just think this up now? Aldo would've been proud of you."

"Good. You need to put me in charge of a special team. I already have them picked out. They're people from the academy—people I know. They're young and smart. Not like your idiot police force."

"Tanna—"

"I already created the documents. I'll GoBug them to you. And I'll get busy with the Markla situation."

Chapter 4

Markla peered at the sky and swore.

The hover-ship was close, circling like a black bat over the spot where they'd fought with 20 Eyes. Maybe it was looking for a place to land but there was no place. Then it was dropping down, crashing through the branches of a gigantic tree.

"Okay," Markla said. "Maybe the toads will waste a few minutes checking out those guys on the ground. But they'll still be after us pretty quick."

"Yeah," Rune said. "I don't think we can keep outrunning them."

There was a roar, and five more hover-ships appeared. Markla held her breath as they moved overhead and fanned out in a circular pattern. Then like the first ship, they started dropping to the ground.

"Five ships," Rune said. "We're really popular. They've got us surrounded."

Markla reached into her backpack and pulled out one of Blog's olive green canisters.

She already knew what was inside because she'd checked before leaving the house. She removed several brownish orbs, each about the size of a walnut. She'd never used these in a real situation but she'd used them in a 20 Eyes LiveDream training session. Despite their war against technology, she'd had many such sessions, where someone had loaded a LiveDream into her mind and she'd seemingly gone to a place filled with guns, bombs, and knives—and then she'd practiced how to use them.

These small orbs had been in one of the LiveDreams. Now they felt exactly the same in her hands.

Rune's eyes were wide. "No!" he said. "That's crazy! If we start flinging bombs, they'll kill us. There's got to be a better way."

Markla gave a short laugh. "Rune, do I look like a 'bomb flinger?' Wait—don't answer that. Seriously, I don't want to fling any bombs. These have timers, and I have an idea. Here, help me plant them. I'm setting them to blow up in about ten minutes."

"But where do you want them?"

"Anywhere between here and where we're going. Put them in pairs—like this."

She dug into the earth and buried one of the bombs. Then she moved a bit, less than a step, and buried another one. "With each pair, set one to blow up about 60 seconds after the first one."

"So we're going to kill these knobbers?" Rune said. She could hear his voice warbling a bit.

"These aren't meant to kill, Rune. It's something I learned in the Eyes—if you have a bomb just strong enough to injure somebody, others come to help. So now those others are busy helping, and you take two or three people out of the fight instead of just one. So don't worry about that."

"I'm not worried!" he blurted.

But she could tell he was worried. She kept digging.

They soon ran out of bombs but now they were close to the first hover-ship. Markla got down low and peered from behind a tree. The hover-ship resembled a creepy arachnid. She could feel Rune pressing against her as she examined the ship through a pair of vision magnifiers.

The ramp was down, and four troopers dressed in black were marching out. Then a cargo door on the side slid open and three hover-bikes appeared. Also an H-dog tracking device, floating like a big bug covered with spines and eyes. It was about the size of a large loaf of bread.

Rune grabbed her arm. "Maybe we should run."

"Where are we going to go?" she said. "They'll catch us like they did last time. We need to get a ride." She kept studying the ship with the magnifiers. "Have you ever been inside one of these things?"

Rune hesitated. "Yeah, they're small. It would be like trying to hide in a bathtub with three other people."

She handed him the magnifiers. "What about inside the cargo area?"

Rune narrowed his eyes and scanned the space. "Not unless you can make us invisible. We could fit, but they'd see us when they put the bikes back."

"What about the roof?"

"What?"

"The top of the ship. Can we get on top of it and hold on?"

Rune paused again, and then his eyes lit up. "Hey, that might work. But the H-dog is still around."

"We have a flyboard. That might confuse it a bit since it can't track us when we're on the board."

"We only have one," he said, and then he stopped talking and grinned. "We can do it!"

She grinned back at him. "Let's circle around to the other side."

They raced in a wide arc through the trees, trying to stay quiet and not stumble over rocks and downed branches. Finally, they were facing the back of the ship.

Meanwhile, the police officers were getting on the bikes. The H-dog was moving now, starting to do a sweep and presumably searching for the pre-programmed scent of Markla or Rune. And then the first bomb went off.

"Get down!" someone shouted. The troopers dove to the ground and ducked behind trees.

"Over there! Fan out!"

They leaped up with their rifles ready and started spreading out while scanning for their attacker. Meanwhile, the H-dog headed fast toward the explosion. The cops on the hover-bikes followed behind.

"Let's go!" Markla said. "You first."

Markla felt her heart pounding as Rune crouched down on the flyboard and quickly zipped across the open area between the trees and the hover-ship. Was there anyone inside? Maybe, but there were no windows on the back. Rune hopped off the board and turned it around and shoved it back in her direction.

It was a perfect push. Markla stopped the flyboard with her hand and then quickly hopped on. As she was gliding over the ground, the air was rocked by another explosion as the second bomb in the pair went off. Then she heard shouts and saw the H-dog coming through the trees. For an instant, she was seized by panic—but wait! It wasn't moving like it usually did, maybe because it was on fire, and maybe because it had been right near the second blast. The device was warbling and smoking like a flying piece of firewood—and then it was crashing into a tree and falling to the ground.

Her heart leaped. Technology is great, she thought. But it's nothing compared to good luck.

She smiled. *Also, a good plan. We're going to get out of this. And I'm going to keep Rune alive.*

In an instant she was beside him, examining the hull of the ship.

There were rungs on the outside that were meant to make it easy for someone to get on top, probably for maintenance. Markla scrambled up. Then Rune followed, climbing with just one hand. In the other he held the flyboard. The hover-ship was wide. If they stayed flat, lying in the center, no one on the ground would be able to see them.

They ended up on their stomachs, staring at each other and still wearing their backpacks. Rune was also lying on top of the flyboard. Markla found a strip of metal bolted in place right near their heads that they could grab on to, and Rune clutched the strip with his left hand and put his right arm around Markla. Meanwhile, she grabbed the strip in her right hand and wrapped her other arm around Rune. They exchanged worried smiles.

Another two bombs exploded—and now they could hear the confusion among the police. Was someone shooting at them? Were they under attack? They were yelling and shouting and still diving for cover. Apparently, someone had been hurt when a bomb had blown up under a hover-bike, and the injured officer was being brought back to the hover-ship. More hover-bikes were approaching as troopers from other hover-ships hurried over. A few random shots were fired. Then they heard someone say, "Hold your fire. Hold your fire!"

Another bomb went off. Another H-dog was coming, and it was scanning the ground. It was moving around the ship but it wasn't coming right up to it. An officer said, "These were charges that were planted. They're definitely around here, and we'll track them down. But we need to get Filo to a hospital quick—so go."

There was a little more commotion, and then Markla felt a bump as the ramp to the hover-ship closed. They were taking off—perfect. As the engines came to life, Rune squeezed her and smiled again.

"Hang on, Markla."

Once again she smiled back at him. I will, she thought. *I've been hanging on my whole life.*

Chapter 5

Tanna knew the four older people in the team didn't like her but her dad had insisted she bring them along. They resented her being in charge because she was only seventeen and because she was the president's daughter—but really, shouldn't it be about who was more capable? And she clearly had them all beat in that category. The most brilliant people in school rarely become police officers.

But she'd had all the police training, and she'd done well. She also regularly used LiveDream simulations to practice fighting maneuvers, and she was getting pretty respectable. At any rate, she was better at fighting than she was at getting along with others. Yeah, she could improve with that. Maybe in the spring she'd go to Sparkla University but right now she was going to get some great experience as a Special Tactical Agent.

It was late morning when the four hover-cars arrived at the target house. She'd used a special police order to access the positioning information of the GoBugs owned by the two suspects; both devices had just been used, and the suspects were home. The cars did not sound their sirens.

Tanna looked at the little house and laughed. It was a faded shade of green and featured crooked front steps, a broken window held together by tape, and a backyard filled with knee-high weeds. The solar tiles on the roof were partially obscured by an overgrown maple tree, and there was a scraggily gray cat sitting out front. This place looked like an abandoned building. No wonder Markla Flash had turned out so badly.

"Moony, you and Star go around the back. Jonna, you and Gray go around the other side. My team will hit the front door."

"What about the woods?" Star said, because the house was adjacent to the woods on one side, and this wasn't just an insignificant patch of trees; the house sat on the outskirts of the forest. "The Eyes like to hide in the trees. They have spies in the police. They could know we're coming."

"I'm not worried about that," Tanna said. "We're pretty sure this girl killed the local 20 Eyes captain, so I don't think they're hiding in the forest looking to protect her house. But yeah, you and Moony check the woods. Jonna and Gray, help them out. Just in case."

Tanna smirked. This was a perfect plan to get these old knobbers out of the way so her team could do the important stuff, the stuff that would make her look good.

She motioned for her three-person team to move toward the front door, and she checked her weapon one last time—and then the air exploded with gunfire.

There was a shout, and Moony went down. Tanna froze—what was going on? Then she felt Star grab her arm and yank her behind one of the vehicles. There was more gunfire, and the car was pummeled with shots, and two other people from her team screamed. Now they were on the ground.

"Fire!" Tanna blurted. But the officers were already doing that—blasting into the woods where they could see nothing but bushes and trees. Star was shouting directions. Then one of the other cars was hit by an exploding bullet, and it blew up and knocked Tanna to the ground. Pieces of shattered glass flew through the air and a ball of fire unfurled toward the sky.

Tanna's hands were shaking. She fumbled with her Magvox Auto rifle, and she tried to catch her breath—and then she leaped up and pumped a hail of shots into the woods. But she saw no one there and ducked back down. She fumbled some more and jumped up again and fired the grenade launcher, and there was a whooshing sound, and the grenade sailed into the woods—and it bounced off a tree and came flying back toward the street. It skipped on the ground a few times and rolled under one of the other police cars and blew up. Tanna cringed and swore.

Jonna was on her GoBug, calling for help—and Tanna was furious.

I've got to do something!

She gave a shout and rushed out from behind the car. She was screaming and shooting as she ran. Star called out to her but Tanna didn't respond. She just kept running and blasting. She had to salvage this disaster.

Tanna reached the forest. She shouted again and ran in among the trees and stumbled on a root and crashed through some foliage. She fired a few blind shots and fell down but leaped to her feet with her gun up and ready. She heard Star calling out to her again, telling her to come back—but she kept going.

"Come out!" she screamed. "Come out and show yourselves, you cowards!"

Where were they? It occurred to her that the gunfire had stopped, and now it was quiet, and there was no one here. But she walked deeper into the woods and kept going. She told herself that she wasn't scared. But wait, where was her team? Why weren't they following her? *What am I doing?* She stopped walking, and she felt a chill in her spine—and she heard the sound of a shot.

There was a sharp sting in her leg, like she'd been bitten by an insect.

"Ugh!" she said, and then she was on the ground. She gasped and tried to grab her weapon but her arms wouldn't move. She felt a sense of panic and she tried to stand but her legs wouldn't move, either. She'd been paralyzed by some kind of dart! And now someone was kneeling down beside her—someone in a black mask. She felt a sharp blade at her throat.

Tanna caught her breath.

It was a guy, and he was big and shaggy like a bear, and his voice was low. He said, "What are you, some kind of super knobber, charging in here alone? You're Gin's daughter, right? We could've shot your dumb ass but we didn't, and I should cut your throat but I won't—because you need to hear something. Markla Flash is none of your business. We take care of our own problems, understand? Tell your team of idiots the same thing."

Tanna couldn't speak. Finally, she whispered, "Okay, I'll do that. Please, don't kill me."

The guy gave a grunt and rolled her over, and she felt a flash of fear, and there was a knee on her back. She sensed at least two people around her, and in an instant her hands and feet were bound with tape—and her mouth was sealed shut. And then they were gone.

She writhed around on the ground, trying to scream.

Where was everyone? Why weren't they charging in here to save her? She guessed they'd find her eventually but what about the mission?

They better not do it without me, she thought. *They better not get all the credit!*

Chapter 6

The wind was worse than Rune had expected, like it wanted to rip them from the metal skin of the ship.

He squinted into the torrent of air and squeezed Markla hard. But the wind was really blasting them, pushing them backwards on the slippery surface of the hover-ship as it rushed toward a hospital, and they didn't have much to hold on to—just a bolted band of metal, and they were barely gripping it with their fingertips.

"Just a little longer," he thought. *Just hang on a little longer!*

His head was a jumble of ideas. Where were they going? It wouldn't be Sliver. The local ships were blue and white, and this one was black, and it had probably come from the capital city of Liberta located just across the Bay of Gems. There was a hospital complex there, and Rune guessed that's where they'd end up.

But that might be fine. If they ended up in Liberta, maybe they wouldn't need Sliver. There was a train station there, and while it wasn't nearly as discreet as the one in Sliver, he was sure they'd still be able to hop on top of a freight train and escape. We'll be free, he thought. *We'll be free*!

They couldn't move nearer to the edge or sit up but they could see the distant view from either side, and it was all trees and dense forest, and the leaves were turning colors, and it was a splotchy blanket of yellow and tangerine. Liberta sat on the bay but they were traveling over land to get there. They wouldn't see the water until they reached their destination.

Suddenly there was a lurch, and the wind stopped. Rune looked at Markla, and they both gave a sigh of relief. The ship was hovering now, and then it began to descend. On Rune's side, a city came into view with buildings topped by sparkling green tiles designed to collect sunlight. Most of the structures were no more than two or three stories high; Sparkla had plenty of space and there was no need to build tall towers. On Markla's side there were no buildings, only the rippling turquoise ocean.

There was a bump as the hover-ship landed.

"We're in Liberta," Rune whispered. "What now?"

But Markla was already moving, making sure her backpack was still secure. "We wait until they unload the guy," she said. "Then we jump off. I doubt this ship will stay here long, and we don't want to end up back in the woods or at the police station."

Rune glanced around. The hospital was looming above them, and he felt a jolt of panic as he realized that anyone looking from an upper story window might see them. Then he heard the clanking sound of the ramp descending, and there were some voices—and then the ramp was closing again.

Markla was on the side that didn't face the building. She peeked her head up, looked around, and then slid toward the edge.

"Come on!" she said. "Let's go."

She grabbed a few of the rungs built onto the ship and dropped down. Rune tightened the strap on his backpack, grabbed the flyboard, and followed her over the edge. He also laughed to himself. Following Markla over the edge was a normal thing to do.

He landed on his feet beside her and quickly surveyed the scene. They were in a landing area adjacent to a parking lot. There was a low fence around the landing zone but nothing too dramatic. There was the hospital right there and a rolling green lawn. As the engines of the ship roared to life once again, Markla raced toward a gate in the fence with Rune close behind. As soon as she went through the opening, she stopped running and he did the same. Then he tried to appear casual as he looked around. Had anyone seen them?

He held his breath. There were scattered people in the parking area, walking to and from the hospital, but they were in the distance and seemed indifferent. No one was looking directly at them. They followed a sidewalk out to a main street and they were in downtown Liberta.

"We made it," Rune said, and he stopped and gave Markla a big hug. "We are so amazing."

Markla just laughed and hugged him back. Then she looked around with wide eyes. "So, this is Liberta," she said. "It's bigger than I thought."

Rune smiled. For a couple of reasons, he liked this friendly-looking city. The bustling street was broad and clean and lined with storefronts, cafés, and trees. There were flowery trees and plants everywhere, and while the buildings were all made of reddish brick, the predominant color was leafy green, and walking down the street was like walking through a garden. But nothing in this garden was paved. The sidewalks and streets were made from specially packed soil, so while the place was pretty and environmentally friendly, it was also perfect for riding a flyboard, and what else really mattered?

The hover-cars floated by, and Markla grabbed his arm at the sound of a siren and the sight of a police car. But it was moving fast and continued on without incident, just like the many pedestrians who were scurrying around seemingly lost in their own thoughts.

"Yeah, this is Liberta," Rune said. "Haven't you been here? Everyone's been here."

Liberta wasn't far from Cooly Strip where he and Markla had grown up. It was a short ride across the bay.

"Not me," Markla said. "Never."

Rune looked at her and laughed. "Really?"

"Yeah, really," she said, and she seemed embarrassed. "My mother never took me anywhere, and I never went on my own. I guess that's why all the kids at school thought I was a Basic, right?"

"No one thought that."

"Rune, I know what they said."

Rune grinned. "Yeah, okay, but I never thought that, and I wouldn't have cared, anyway. No Basic ever rode a flyboard like you."

She gave a grim smile. "This city has a train station, right? Let's find it and catch a ride."

"Yeah, but it's not a train yard like the one in Sliver. It's a station for passengers so we'll need to be a lot more careful."

"There's got to be a spot where freight trains stop. Every city needs freight, right? We're almost free, Rune."

"I had the same thought. We're almost there."

Rune suddenly felt light, like he was walking on air. As they strolled past a bakery and a bush bursting with purple flowers, Markla's radio beeped and she stopped walking.

"Someone's broadcasting," she said. "Let me check it out."

She did a frequency sweep, and they heard a girl's voice. The broadcast was crackling a bit but her voice cut through the street sounds like a blade.

"Markla Flash, are you listening? Markla, can you hear me?"

Rune felt his stomach tighten, and without thinking he reached out and grabbed Markla's arm.

"This is Tanna Xantha, and you murdered my uncle—and we've arrested your mother and your brother upon suspicion of conspiracy. If you and Rune don't surrender immediately, they're both going to be charged. This message will repeat for three days. Respond."

Rune stopped breathing. Then his head started spinning. He looked at Markla, and her face was blank—like her brain had been erased.

She let the message play again and then turned it off. She took a step toward the brick wall of the bakery and slumped down to the sidewalk. She sat still with her back against the building and said nothing.

People kept walking by but it all faded from Rune's mind. He sat down beside her. He wanted to say something comforting or insightful—or maybe just useful. But no words came.

Finally he said, "It'll be all right," and he squeezed her hand. "We'll think of a plan."

Markla stayed quiet for a full minute. Then she spoke in a soft voice.

"I'll turn myself in. That's my plan."

"No!" Rune blurted. "That's not a plan."

She shook her head. "It's all my fault Tommi's in trouble, and I dragged you into this, too. I hurt everyone around me. I don't deserve to escape."

She blinked a few times and a tear streamed down her cheek.

"Markla, that's not true. We'll think of something—we always do."

"No," she said. "Forget it. I don't want you getting killed because of me. It's time I pay for the things I've done."

"That's ridiculous!" Rune said. "You don't need to pay for anything. We have three days, right? That's plenty of time to think of a strategy. Besides, do you really think they'll let Tommi go if you give yourself up? They're lying."

Rune looked around. People kept walking by, and it didn't seem like anyone cared about what they were saying. Then he spied a store next to the bakery, a national chain called RVS that sold everything from soap to shaving cream to communication devices.

"Wait here," he said, and he leaped to his feet. "I'm going shopping."

She stared up at him with watery eyes.

"You're not going to leave me, are you?"

"What? No—of course not. Why would you say that?"

"Everyone leaves me," she said, and her voice was low. "My real mother, my stepfather, 20 Eyes—all gone."

"I'm not going anywhere! I just want to buy something, and the police are looking for two people together. I'll be right back. Don't move!"

She shrugged. "I'll be here if you come back."

"Markla, I'm coming right back!"

He shook his head and bolted down the sidewalk. He'd never seen her like this. It was like she was in a daze, and he hated to leave her for even an instant. But he also knew she wouldn't approve of his purchase. In under two minutes he was walking out of the store, and he breathed a sigh of relief when he saw that Markla was still there, slumped against the building.

"I got it," he said, and he held it up to her eyes. It was a GoBug—but it was a *blank*. "They're perfectly safe. Top criminals use them—the best of the worst. Even people in 20 Eyes use them. My dad told me that once."

He knew she wouldn't like it. Normally, when someone purchased a GoBug, they also purchased a *stream pass* that allowed it to connect to the streams, and they paid for that pass through a company that offered it, and then their name was registered to that device. But there were blank GoBugs that had no regular stream pass. They came with pre-purchased amounts of stream-time, and anyone could use them to connect—and if Rune were to connect using a fake name, then technically it could not be traced to him.

He also knew that Markla had used blank GoBugs as a student at the North Point Dream Academy—because GoBugs were a critical part of the creation and operation of LiveDreams. He'd never asked her about the details, but she'd used them.

Markla wiped her eyes. "They can still trace it," she said. "They have algorithms that can analyze the streams and see who's searching for what, and who those people are talking to—and then the Electronic Brains can guess that a particular blank is you. And even though it's blank, those EBs can trace the signal and find you."

Rune shrugged. "So I'll keep the searches general, and I won't contact any registered users on any normal streams. Right now, I feel like we're blind, and we're going to need information, and then we need a plan."

"I don't want you doing anything crazy. I don't want you getting caught because of me."

He squatted down and stared at her. "We need another flyboard, and there's a place down the street. I've seen it on the streams, and I always wanted to check it out." He reached out and took her hand, and he said "Please."

She looked at him through red-rimmed eyes, and his heart went out to her, and then she stood up.

"Okay. Let's go."

Great! Rune thought. *She'll be fine. She just needs a little time.*

Fly Born was the name of the place, and they walked there in under a minute. It was located on the corner of the main street and a smaller street. As they approached, Rune noticed a metal door that opened to the side street. But it was obviously locked from the outside so he went around to the main entrance.

"I'll only be a minute," he said.

She gave him a sad little smile. "Don't rush because of me, Rune. I know you like to shop. You always had the best clothes."

"Hey, style is important. I can't be the most unfashionable fugitive in Sparkla."

"You won't be. Not as long as I'm around."

Rune laughed, glad she still had her sense of humor. It was also true, she'd always been the least fashionable kid in school—but for some reason, this had always been one more thing that had made her so interesting. Even though he was somewhat fashionable.

Rune strode into Fly Born, trying to look nonchalant. There was a counter directly ahead, and the flyboards were displayed on the walls. They had all the top brands.

There was a doorway behind the counter that led to a back room, and out walked a lanky guy with bronze skin and long black hair.

"Looking for a board?" he said.

"Yeah, that black Eagle Six."

Rune gave him the cash, and the guy handed him the board—and then his heart almost stopped. Through the wide front window, he saw two guys outside, and they were talking to Markla. They weren't wearing uniforms but now one of them was flashing a badge, and Markla started to move—and the other guy pulled out a gun. The first guy shoved her to the ground, and he was trying to cuff her but she was fighting. Then a siren whooped, and a hover-car pulled up in front of the place.

Rune swore and pulled out his weapon. "Where's the side door—show me! Fast!"

The guys eyes got wide. "Don't shoot! It's right through here." The guy pointed to the doorway behind the counter.

Rune tried to control his rage. They were not going to take Markla from him—no way! He bolted behind the counter, raced through a room cluttered with flyboards, and burst through the metal door that led to the side street around the corner. Then he ran around the corner to the front of the building and started shooting.

He was only firing rubber bullets but his aim was good. He shot the guy struggling with Markla, and the guy went down. He hit the other guy in the chest. A knobber from the police car knelt down and fired at him—but right before he did, Rune saw Markla take off. His heart leaped as she jumped up and bolted down the street. She had the flyboard in her hand.

Rune ducked back around the corner just as a flurry of shots slammed into the brick wall. Then he gritted his teeth and stepped on his new board. He felt it rise above the ground and grab on to his feet. Markla had a board with her, but she'd also need a second or two to put it down and set herself. He was going to get her those seconds.

Rune zoomed out from behind the building. He knew that knobber was right there—but Rune was ready. He came out shooting and whizzed into the middle of the street, in a wide arc on the opposite side of the police car. Horns blared and hover-cars slammed to a stop. Rune kept shooting while trying to steer. The trooper stayed down behind the police car, and then Rune was back on the sidewalk and speeding down another side street where Markla had gone. The officer fired a few more rounds and Rune felt something blow past his left ear.

He swerved around a few people, trying to keep Markla in sight—and there she was. She was on the flyboard, sailing past hover-cars, zig-zagging around pedestrians, and moving fast down the middle of the road. He was right behind her. Obviously, she'd changed her mind about turning herself in. She spun the board around, coming to a dead stop. It was a sweet move.

"Rune, where are we going?"

He wasn't sure. "Follow me!" he said.

He turned down another street, and then he heard sirens wailing in the distance—and then there was an explosion. It was a deep boom, and it shook the city. He heard distant screams and shouts.

That wasn't for us, he thought. Are the rebels still hitting targets here? Or maybe 20 Eyes? Either way, it was to their advantage. It might distract the people who were after them.

They reached the campus of Sparkla University, a mix of stately stone buildings and newer ones made of blue and green crystal. In front of the buildings were outdoor tables made of stone and people hanging around looking confused. He saw lots of kids staring with "bug eyes"—the look someone gets when watching GoBug images. How many streams were still operating? Had an alert been broadcast? He glanced around fast. To his left was a road, and beside the road was a boardwalk that stretched out over the bay.

Now Markla was hovering beside him. "Rune, we can't stay here. I have an idea—come on."

She spun the board around a few times and headed down the boardwalk. Rune squinted into the wind and followed her. He didn't know what she was thinking but the boardwalk was the perfect place to ride a flyboard. The wind ripped through his hair, and he felt like he was flying.

The boardwalk was lined with colorful shops and concessions, and they rocketed past them, and then five or six restaurants, and then the hotels—and then there was nothing. The boardwalk ended, and they were staring down at the water lapping against a hard slope of craggy rocks. Along the slope was the road, and then a forest of pine trees. Rune noted that the road curved sharply, putting it out of sight of the city. Markla crossed the road and headed into the woods, navigating around the trees while riding above the ground on a bed of pine needles. Rune suddenly felt pretty good. This seemed like a reasonable plan—back in the woods. But then she stopped and turned the board to face him.

"Rune, let's double back and go under the boardwalk."

"What?"

"There are cameras everywhere and people using GoBug 'eye-capture,' and anyone could've seen us riding down the boardwalk. But I think we're out of camera range now, so if we get to the bottom of the rocks and then flyboard over the bay, we can get under the boardwalk. I'm guessing there are sand or rocks underneath it, right? We can hide there."

Rune's mind was racing. "But they might see us climbing down. They'll see us riding over the water."

"We'll use the boards to get down quick, and we'll only be over the water for a few seconds. Hopefully, they'll be looking for us in the woods. I think it's worth the risk."

Rune shook his head—and then he grinned. Yeah, it was a risky plan, but risky was pretty much their thing.

The rocks were huge slabs, black and slippery, and full of hard angles. It was terrible terrain for a flyboard. A flyboard attempted to float at a fixed height by constantly calculating the distance from the ground—so smooth was better than jagged. A jagged surface like this would give a very bumpy ride as the board constantly struggled to recalculate, and even though the board gripped the rider's feet, the grip was only so strong. So it would be easy to fall off and land hard on those rocks. It would be easy to break a bone.

It was a test—a challenge. Rune wasn't worried about himself but he was concerned about Markla. He couldn't stand the thought of her getting hurt.

"Are you ready?" she said.

"I don't want you to get hurt."

She gave him a little smile and took off down the rocky slope.

Rune watched her for an instant—and then he gave a whoop and followed her.

It was a wild ride. The boards were bouncing and swaying and swerving—up and down, up and down— Rune was see-sawing like a ship in a squall, and then rocking from side to side, and then almost falling off. It took all his skill to stay on the board. And what about Markla?

He'd always respected her ability with a flyboard, but deep

down inside, he'd never thought she was his equal—until now. She reached the bottom before Rune, and a few seconds later she was over the shimmering Bay of Gems. The turquoise water was smooth like oil, and she was riding fast. Rune could barely catch his breath before he was over the water, too. Once upon a time, he'd considered riding over water to be a dicey thing to do, but after that trip down the rocks it was an easy trick. Markla kept her board low, almost touching the water, and it shot a glistening spray into the air as she headed under the boardwalk. Rune was still behind her.

His first instinct was to duck but there was more headroom than he'd expected. Then as they moved closer to the land the headroom shrunk considerably. Yet there was a decent stretch of sand that was not submerged, and there was enough room to stand. Markla came to a stop.

She jumped off the board and laughed. "Can you believe we did that?" she said.

"No." He wrapped her in his arms. "We should have our own stream, and show people the way to ride."

"Yeah, that's what we'll call it! 'The Way To Ride.' Then she paused and said, "We're in trouble, Rune. They're going to kill us."

"They won't. It's not our destiny."

"I don't believe in destiny."

"That's okay. I believe enough for both of us."

They tossed their backpacks on the sand and sat down. Then Rune pulled out the blank GoBug he'd purchased. "Now it's my turn to have an idea," he said.

She eyed the device and gave him a sideways glance. "I hate it already. But go ahead."

He grinned and placed the device behind his ear and signed on with his smasher account—a phony identity he used to communicate with other anonymous people on the streams who traded illegal scripts.

The streaming world lit up before his eyes—a three dimensional vision that could only be seen in his mind. He saw the glowing lists of streams he could join, and he noticed the ones that were missing. The biggest ones were all gone, the ones sent out by the government and large commercial conglomerates. But there were lots of less popular ones that were still operating—the indie streams that had always existed, some of them outside the regulation of the law. He found a news stream he'd seen before and connected to it. It was a stream called "A Better Shade of Entropy."

Two people were talking about something called "rovers." Then there was a clip, and Rune frowned—it was a recorded image of Gin Xantha, apparently from a few hours ago, blabbing about a vote that had somehow been held last night.

Gin was smiling as always. Did he look like Aldo? Rune saw little family resemblance.

"It's wonderful how Sparkla has united during this crisis," Gin said. "It was nothing short of miraculous, the way we patched together a series of indie streams run by heroic volunteers in order to have a national vote—and so even in a time of emergency, our system of direct democracy perseveres."

Then the clip vanished, and a man and a woman were live on the stream discussing Gin's words.

"It was an illegal vote," the woman said. "Because of the communication disruption, no one even knew it was happening. It wasn't verified or certified. This is a disgrace."

"Right," the man replied. "But it probably would've passed anyway because people are scared."

"They should be scared. Gin Xantha is using these subversive attacks to justify the use of more extreme measures we don't want."

"But is that true? People seem to want them. So maybe they should really be scared of each other."

"Sad! Anyway, now that the vote has passed, the rovers will be released later today, and we're not even sure what they're capable of—but if you see any swarms of little flying spheres, know that someone is watching you. We're pretty sure they can scan anything around them and identify a person by DNA."

A three dimensional image appeared, and Rune felt a flash of fear. The image resembled a group of metallic peas, maybe six or seven, and they hovered in the air. Apparently, they travelled in swarms, but when grouped together they looked like the single eye of a sinister insect.

Rune disconnected the stream. He thought about his father, and the things he'd been fighting for, and how he'd never told his family about any of it. I never really knew him, Rune thought. *But I know him now. And he was right!*

Rune looked at Markla. "Look out for little round things in the air," he said. "They're called 'rovers.' The government is releasing them today, and they might be able to scan for DNA."

He told her the rest of what he'd just heard.

"More spy machinery for the toads," she said. "Face scans weren't good enough? I guess they want to be sure about who they're torturing."

Rune was back on his blank GoBug. And suddenly he noticed something.

He had a message.

Chapter 7

Markla could tell it was something serious. She could see it in his face.

"Rune, what does it say?"

"Maybe we should read it together."

He reached into his jacket and removed another GoBug. As she frowned, he handed it to her. "I bought two blanks," he said. "I think you should be in this stream with me. You can connect using my fake account. I know you hate these things but it's not like you've never used one."

It was true. She'd never owned a GoBug with a stream pass. But she'd used blanks because they'd been necessary when she'd been a LiveDream writer at the North Point Dream Academy. GoBugs were an integral part of the creation and operation process, and since she'd supposedly been infiltrating the school for 20 Eyes, Dru had bought her a bunch of blank ones.

Dru, who was dead—because of her. A gory image flashed through her mind, the same bloody image that often went through her mind, and she forced it away. Then she looked at the device in her hand—and now her mind did more than flash with a picture; it was like her mind shattered. For an instant, she was back in the Dream Prison, and she was terrorized by a nightmare, and the nightmare had been pulled from a part of her brain she'd walled off years ago.

She wanted to scream but she did not. She wanted to cry but she did not. She turned her head so Rune couldn't see her face, and she took a deep breath.

I'm under a boardwalk! she thought. *I'm under a boardwalk with Rune! That's where I am!*

Rune was craning his neck a bit, trying to see her face. "Markla, are you all right?" He moved closer to her and grabbed her arm. "What's wrong? What is it?"

"Rune, I can't do it," she said in a soft voice. "I just can't."

I hate myself, she thought. *I hate who I am.*

He hesitated. "It's okay," he said. And he put his arm around her. "I'll check it out myself."

His arm felt good around her shoulder, but in her stomach she felt sick. Sick and weak.

She gritted her teeth and slid the device behind her ear.

"I'm on," she said.

He squeezed her a bit. "Are you sure?"

"Yeah, I'm fine. Let's go."

"Okay," he said, and he kept his arm around her. "Don't worry about anything. My smasher account has no connection to my old LiveDream account. It's on an EB outside the streams of government and commercial EBs, a stream controlled by anonymous smashers."

"Can the smashers be trusted?" she blurted. "Just because they fight the government doesn't make them heroes. I learned that when I was in 20 Eyes."

He shrugged. "I don't trust them all. I got this account from a smasher on a stream I found with a script I got from someone else. When you connect, you'll be in a part of the streaming world we call 'The Outland.' He grinned. "You'll fit right in."

"That would be a first."

He just laughed.

She could see the stream now, sitting like a black canvas in front of her eyes—and yeah, there was a message for Rune. The subject line was glowing in frosty green.

It said, "I know who you are."

She studied it, and she blinked. Before she could comment, Rune said, "Don't worry, I know this guy. His name is 'Gort' and I've traded scripts with him lots of times."

"Have you ever met him?"

"No, of course not. Smashers are anonymous."

"Then you don't know him."

Rune didn't reply. Instead, he issued a thought command to open the message, and the green faded, and a wider image of darkness seemed to surround her. It was like a hemisphere of onyx and a sea of stars on a beautiful clear night. Then she heard a male voice but of course this meant nothing. It was easy to alter any voice.

"Hello, Rune," the voice said. "Contact me."

Markla banged her hands down on the sand. "I knew it!" she said. "How does he know your name? We cannot use GoBugs. Disconnect it and throw it into the ocean."

"Yeah, maybe I should," he said.

But he didn't. Instead, he issued another thought command, and the starry night sky vanished, and now Markla was staring at a guy with light brown skin and kinky dark hair. He had chiseled features and a gold tattoo of a curved blade, like a half-moon, under his left eye. But again, it was probably a filter. Gort could look and sound like anyone.

Markla noticed Rune was broadcasting a simple avatar for his own image, a picture of a crow—and he had her connection shielded, so Gort didn't even know she was connected.

Rune hesitated. Then he said, "Hi, Gort. I'm Crow Flier. How do you know my real name?"

"I've known it for over a year."

"Really? Then why tell me about it now?"

"Because your name didn't pop up on any news streams until now."

"Oh. So how did you identify me?"

Gort smiled. "You left a trail, Rune, and I traced it."

"But the data trail isn't traceable."

Gort gave a short laugh. "Everything is traceable if you know how to do it. Everything that happens leaves a trail, whether it's smoke from burnt toast or a scrap of traceable data when you sign on to a stream."

"Then the government could smash into these accounts."

"Yeah, they can—and they do. But then we come up with new blocking scripts, and then they come up with new ways around them, and it goes on and on. But we can also smash into their streams, and we do it all the time. Anyway, your Dad was involved with FS."

"FS?"

"Free Sparkla."

"Was that on the news?"

"No, but I rarely watch the regular news streams. I only monitor smashed streams from the government and the police. Is Markla Flash with you?"

"No," Rune said.

"Yes," Markla said. "I'm right here."

Rune sighed. "She's right here."

Gort grinned. "It's good to meet you, Markla."

"It's good to meet you, too—sort of. Did they really arrest my family?"

"Yeah, according to the police streams—your mother and your brother. They were arrested this morning."

So it was true, Markla thought. And her heart sank. She said, "Why did you contact Rune?"

"Because I thought I could help," he said. "Let's just say that I hate the government, and that's why I'm a smasher." Then he looked at Rune. "I knew your father, Rune—not well, but I knew him. I supplied the FS people with information lots of times. There are a lot more people against Gin than he realizes, and it's the main reason he's going to fail. Arresting Markla's family won't help him at all." Gort paused, and then he said, "Do you two want to rescue them?"

There was a moment of silence. Then Rune practically shouted, "Yeah, of course we do!"

Markla felt a twinge of anxiety, like an electric shock. "How?" she said.

Gort grinned again. "I just sent you the location where they're being held, and it's right here in the capitol. They were transferred from Cooley Strip about an hour ago. Apparently, Tanna Xantha has taken quite an interest in you, Markla. Check out what I sent, especially the script."

Markla didn't look at anything. Instead, she waited for Rune to give his opinion. When she saw his mouth hanging open, she decided to look at the information herself—and she caught her breath because it was amazing. There was a three dimensional blueprint of the police station, and there was a script that allowed them to access the entire security system inside the building. Rune, who was never intimidated by any script, was already switching around between the various electric eyes inside. And he was smiling.

"Is this real?" he said.

"Yeah," Gort said with obvious pride. "It took me a while to smash into this, but it'll be worth it."

Markla stared at the images Rune brought up. There was an interrogation room, and a room filled with weapons, and lots of police rushing around—and there were a small number of holding cells. "Where's my brother?" she said. "Can we find him?"

"Yeah," Rune said. "I see him."

She kept staring, and now she felt light-headed. Tommi was sitting alone in a drab gray cell with no windows. The image indicated the camera was on the ceiling.

Markla felt her heart breaking, and for a moment she had trouble breathing. "Tommi," she whispered. "I'm sorry. I'm so sorry."

"We'll get him out," Gort said.

Rune switched to a few other cameras. "Let's see if we can find your mother."

"I don't care about her," Markla spat. "She can rot."

Despite her complaint, Rune found Sharli Flash soon enough. She was in a cell, and she looked like she was asleep.

"Drunk as always," Markla said. "I've seen enough. Turn it off!"

She felt like there was a giant stone on her chest, and now she was staring into the darkness under the boardwalk, and she didn't see a thing. Meanwhile, Rune was still looking at the images and talking to Gort. She heard their voices but they seemed far away.

"How do we get Tommi out?" Rune said.

Gort said, "The government thinks all this technology makes them stronger, and in some ways it does—but in other ways it makes them weaker. All their information is on the streams, and I can do more than just access these cameras. Everything inside the building is controlled by an EB, and I can access it. So here's the plan: We turn off all the alarms and other security. Do you see that door in the back? I can unlock it from here. You go in, and the cells are right there, and they're all connected to an EB that verifies identify with an eye scan—but you won't need an eye scan because my smashing skills are amazing. I open the doors and you get them out of there, and that's it."

"Great plan!" Rune said.

Markla shook her head. "No," she said. "It's half a plan. Once we're outside, how do we get away? Everyone will be after us."

"They're already after us," Rune said.

"Yeah, but we lost them—at least for now. We'll need a plan after we come out."

Gort nodded. "She's right. I'll send a hover-car. It'll be there before you go in."

"Great!" Rune said.

"No, not great," Markla said. "A hover-car can be followed and tracked, and they'll cut off every road. We'll never get away by car."

Gort nodded. "You're right. The car will be a self-driver, and it'll be a decoy. The car will go on its way, and you'll make your way to a hover-ship—and while they're chasing the car, you'll take the hover-ship straight to the border. I'll make sure there are some supplies on the hover-ship."

Rune started to speak but then he stopped and looked at Markla.

"What do you think?" he said.

Once again she shook her head—because she had no intention of getting Rune killed. *I promised his mother I'd keep him alive—I did.* Then she said, "I think there are lots of knobbers in there, and they've all had lots of training. We might need to shoot someone."

Rune hesitated. "We have guns," he said. "They have rubber bullets and sleep pellets. We don't even need to hurt anybody."

"Yeah, maybe," Markla said. "But it might not go that way."

Gort laughed. "Don't worry, Markla. This will be easy. It'll be perfect."

Markla frowned. "I'm not saying it can't work, and I want to rescue my brother. But nothing ever goes perfectly because it just doesn't."

"We'll be ready," Gort said. "Now get some rest. I can have everything set up by tomorrow night. There are lots of people who want to help, Markla. Lots of people."

Gort ended the connection, and Markla was quiet.

In her mind, she saw a picture of her brother. He'd been a happier kid than her—for some reason they'd left him alone. For some reason, she'd always been the one they'd picked on.

Rune was rummaging in his knapsack where he found an

apple. He offered it to her. "You should eat something," he said. "You need to stay strong."

She studied the bay. The water was calm and shiny like glass but she wondered what lurked beneath it. "I always thought it was my fault," she said. "The stuff my mother and her boyfriend did to me. I thought I deserved it."

"It was never your fault. You were a little kid."

"It's a trap, Rune. Think about it. This guy is leading us into a detention center, and how is he arranging all this stuff? How do you know everything we saw wasn't some phony LiveDream?"

Rune bit into his apple. "I don't think so. I accessed over twelve cameras, and I was switching between them pretty fast. It would be complicated to have LiveDreams ready for every camera. And I think he can arrange things because there are lots of people against the government—a lot. I think this is real, and I think Gort is for real, too."

"I don't trust him."

"Why not?"

"Because I don't trust anyone—except you."

Rune smiled and once again put his arm around her. "Wow. I'm flattered."

She hesitated. Then she said, "There's something you should know, Rune… I have flashbacks—they're like nightmares, only worse. And they can happen in the daytime, do you understand? And I looked into it, and I read about it, and there are things that trigger them. If I feel trapped or like I have no choice, like my mother made me feel, like the guy at the Dream Station made me feel, like Aldo made me feel… I lose control… I can't cure it." Her voice trailed off.

Rune squeezed her a little harder. "It's okay," he said. "I saw it, remember? It's not your fault. None of it."

She realized her heart was beating fast. When she spoke

again her voice was low, and she asked the same question she'd asked before. The one that was often on her mind.

"Are you going to leave me?" she said.

"Never. No chance."

He kissed her on the cheek, and then she was wrapped in his arms, and they were together on the sand, and they were fumbling with their clothes. Was she really in the mood for this?

Yeah, she was.

Chapter 8

Diano Drogo felt shaky. She'd had little sleep as usual but this was a more extreme situation. As her footsteps echoed through the halls of the capitol building, she heard an explosion outside, and it didn't help her mood. She'd been called into a meeting with Gin Xantha, the President of Sparkla, and she was afraid it would go badly. There were obvious reasons for this.

After all, wasn't it her fault that Gin's brother was dead? She'd handed Markla the murder weapon. Had she wanted Markla to kill Aldo? She'd known that crazy girl was capable of it.

But how much did Gin know? The Dream Center had been under attack. Rune and Markla had been freed but was there any evidence it had been done by her? It could've been done by someone else. In fact, it was possible no one had even known they were strapped to those chairs except for a couple of Aldo's helpers, and Diana knew they'd been killed during the battle. It's possible Aldo hadn't told anyone.

I should confess, she thought. *I'll feel better if I confess.*

A bulky guard smiled at her, and a heavy door was opened, and now she was standing in front of Gin Xantha. He was sitting behind his desk, smiling just like he did in all the mindstreams she'd seen. Sitting beside him was a girl Diana recognized as his seventeen-year-old daughter Tanna. She smiled, too, but it was a slippery smile. She was stunning in a slithery way.

Gin rose and held out his hand, and Diana stepped forward and shook it. Of course, he had a firm grip.

"Diana, it's good to meet you," he said. "This is my daughter Tanna. Aldo told me great things about you."

"I'm sorry for your loss," she said.

"Thanks. But we need to move on. And the first thing I want to do is talk about MindCore. With Aldo gone, you're the leading expert."

"Me?" she said, and her heart skipped a beat. "I'm not an expert."

"Didn't you help with the design?"

"Yes, but I'm not an engineer. I'm a dream designer. I'm a teacher."

"I don't need an engineer. The thing is already built, and I need someone who knows how to work it—and who can teach others."

She shrugged, and she started to say, "It's pretty simple," but then she stopped herself. "What do you want me to do?" she said. "Who do you want me to teach?"

"I want you to teach my daughter. She's going to be doing some special work for us."

Diana looked at Tanna. "Oh. Are you a LiveDream writer, Tanna?"

"It's one of the things I do. I was over at Kinly."

Kinly was a private academy located in the northern part of Sparkla. It was a place where rich kids went. But they never wrote the best dreams, at least not from what Diana had seen. Maybe they just didn't need to imagine as much.

Gin said, "She's going to be concentrating on LiveDreams. It's the only thing she'll be doing for now."

Tanna turned to her father and scowled. "I can do lots of other things, too. What happened yesterday wasn't my fault."

"This isn't the time, Tanna. Besides, if you really want to get into it, I saw the reports."

"I had everything under control."

"Really? You had to be rescued. You were bound and gagged in the woods."

"You sent me out there with a bunch of idiots! And they left me there."

"I can't imagine why—and besides, you picked half of those

idiots, and the ones you picked are the ones who ended up dead… Diana, excuse us, this is about another issue."

"It's about everything," Tanna said. "I had a plan, and it was perfect. It just wasn't executed properly."

Gin threw up his hands. "When you're in charge, the execution is your responsibility! You led a squad of people into a 20 Eyes attack. We lost three people, and you're lucky to be alive."

"The plan is still good, and you know it."

"Yeah, maybe. But someone else is going to carry it out." Gin sighed. "Tanna, you're right—it's not your fault. It's my fault. I never should've let you lead an arrest team. You're smart and capable but you're not ready."

"I am ready," Tanna said. "I can catch Markla and Rune. It's my idea, so I should get to do it."

Gin shook his head and turned his attention back to Diana. "So, like I was saying, Diana, I'd like you to teach my daughter about MindCore. She's had a lot of training in LiveDream writing, and I'd like you to start today."

Diana felt a storm of uncertainty swirling around in her head. It had been there for a long time, and would it ever go away?

She forced a smile onto her face. "I'll be happy to help," she said.

Chapter 9

The evening turned cool, like autumn in Sparkla was supposed to be, and Markla shivered in her denim jacket. But then she was also sweating, and she hated the feeling. She was lying on her back under the boardwalk, and she turned her head to look at Rune lying beside her.

"Is it time yet?" she said. And was she really asking again?

"No," Rune said. "But soon. Are you worried?"

"Yeah. There's too much stuff we can't control. It's like the night I was arrested."

Her voice trailed off, and she recalled the night 20 Eyes had raided the Serenity Six Dream Station and she'd been left behind. She caught her breath, and for an instant she felt her attacker's body on top of her, and she was trying to squeeze out from under his crushing weight, and she was clutching her dagger, and her hand was slick with blood.

"Markla, it's not like that. This is going to go fine."

She started to answer and then stopped. She vaguely considered how the same dagger was strapped to her belt right now—the same weapon she'd used two other times. Why hadn't she thrown it away?

There's something wrong with me, she thought. *He'll figure it out eventually.*

"I hope you're right," she said. "I know I've messed up Tommi's life, and I can't change that. But maybe I can do this one thing."

Rune hesitated and then said, "What about your mom? You say you don't care about her, but what is Tommi going to think if we leave her behind?"

Markla grabbed at the sand and squeezed it. "I know," she said. "We can't really leave her. But Rune, I'm not going out of my way to save her, okay? And I don't want you to go out of your way, either. She's useless to the government. When they realize I don't care about her, they'll let her go."

Rune was quiet for another few seconds. Then he said, "Was there ever a time when you liked her? Before all that stuff happened?"

Markla gave a sarcastic laugh. "When would that be? Before I was six? She's not my real mother, Rune—but she's Tommi's real mother, and he called her 'mom,' so I did, too. Supposedly, I was 'so lucky' to be adopted by Sharli but I never remember feeling that way, and I never will. I don't know why I'm talking about this now. I'm sorry."

"Don't be! It's good that you're telling me."

"Is it? Anyway, it doesn't matter. I can't change the past. I can't change what's in my head. It's there forever."

Rune stared at the boardwalk above them. "Maybe not," he said. "Maybe in time it'll get better."

He wants to say the perfect thing, she thought. *But there are no magic words.*

She reached over and took his hand. "Rune, I'm glad you're here with me, okay?"

He looked at her and smiled. "I'm glad I'm here with you, too."

"Is it time?"

"Yeah, it's time. Let's do it."

Right, she thought. And she pushed everything else out of her mind and thought about the toads, and what they'd done—and how she was going to try and fix it.

They were at the far end of the boardwalk, near the rocks and the tall trees. But now they got on their flyboards and rode in the other direction, under the full-length of the wooden structure, to the opposite end where it met the beach near downtown Liberta. It was dark but there was a silvery glow of reflected light coming from the ocean, and they moved fast over the sand and seashells. They quickly reached the end and rode out onto the beach, and the moon was like a big gold coin, and the surf was roaring in and washing up on the sand, and the flyboards flew over the lip of the ocean, and Markla took a moment to realize how beautiful it all was. Then she thought about the pistol in her knapsack and the dagger on her belt.

Rune had the blank GoBug behind his ear now. He stopped moving and got off his board.

"Markla, sign in," he said. "We need to be seeing and hearing the same stuff."

She didn't want to, of course. But he was right, so she put the blank he'd given her behind her own ear, and then they signed into the stream. Instantly, they heard Gort, and his voice was bubbly.

"All right," he said. "Everything looks good. Make your way to the station. They're still looking for you but they've got lots of other priorities, and I can see the whole police force from here. I can even see the rovers and where they're swarming. Don't worry, you've got one amazing smasher on your side! Do you both have the 'dissolve' command? Not like we'll need it but just in case?"

"Yeah," Rune said. "We've both got it."

The dissolve command would not only disconnect the GoBug from its connection to Gort—but it would also wipe out any information regarding any stream connection. It was used in case of capture. Gort, of course, could dissolve the connection on Rune and Markla's GoBugs from his end if necessary, in case one of them were suddenly killed.

"I'll send you a route," Gort said.

Now in front of their eyes, Markla and Rune saw the city— along with a bright blue line telling them where to go. It was like someone had painted it right into their vision.

"Great," Rune said. "We're on our way. We're ready."

Rune got back on his board. He raised his eyebrows at Markla, and he started moving. She followed close behind.

Once again, she thought back to that disastrous night at the Dream Station, and she tried to recall whether she'd been scared. *I was scared and excited,* she thought. *And now? More anxious than scared but not too excited—not yet.*

She stayed low on her board, right behind Rune, and she realized why she wasn't as confident as he was—because she'd been through this before, and she knew lots of things could go wrong, especially when they were relying on an unknown person using too much technology. Rune loved the tech stuff; he was hypnotized by it. She liked to say she didn't hate it but she did. *It's just the way I'm wired,* she thought—and she laughed.

I'm not wired. I'm more or less organic.

She needed to stop worrying. She was still wearing the backpack she'd retrieved from the Dream Center—the one she'd been wearing when she'd been about to flee Sparkla with Rune. And she still had the dagger. The dagger was very low-tech but it always worked, and the idea made her laugh grimly to herself. Maybe that's why she'd never gotten rid of it.

They slid through a few shadowy backstreets lined with trees and circumvented the bustling downtown. But soon enough they reached the police station.

It was a white building, plain like a big square box, but it was bursting with bright lights. It was three stories high, and Rune and Markla circled around to the back. Behind the station was a parking area ringed by a black iron fence. The station backed up to a residential neighborhood, and Rune and Markla ended up across the street from the parking lot, in front of someone's house, standing behind a group of sizable oak trees.

"That fence is old-style," Rune said. "But there's the gate, just like in the images Gort sent."

The gate was heavy and automated. It was built into the back part of the fence across a driveway that went to the street, and it was probably meant to bring large vehicles into the parking area. There were no human guards at the gate, but it was probably monitored at all times.

Gort's voice boomed inside their heads. "The fence is supposed to be decorative, although I suppose it does keep people out. But there's a surveillance ring inside the fence—a beam of invisible light. Anything that breaks the ring sets off an alarm. So don't be fooled."

His words stuck in Markla's mind. Were they being fooled right now? They'd find out soon enough.

"What about the car?" she said. "What about the hover-ship?"

Gort gave a smug laugh. "The green four-door Seacrest right there on the street is a self-driver. It'll take off as soon as you come out. The hover-ship is in a lot four blocks away, like I said it would be. I've sent you the location. I'll also send a route when you come out… Do you want to go over the plan again?"

"No," Markla said.

They'd gone over it many times during the afternoon, and she was tired of it, and the scene looked as expected. This was the police station Gort had shown them, and they'd seen the inside over and over again, and they knew the hallways, and where the guards were, and the location of the holding cells.

"We're ready," Rune said and his voice was strong.

He's so cool under pressure, Markla thought. *And he thinks I am, too—and he's so wrong.*

She took a deep breath. They'd done fine during a simulation Gort had set up using the GoBug. But he'd also written a LiveDream script for that simulation. Real life was not controlled by a LiveDream. Real life was about surprise and chaos and disaster, and things were about to get very real.

"Get in position!" Gort said. Rune looked at Markla, and he motioned with his head toward the gate.

The plan was to leave the flyboards near the gate. Tommi knew how to ride. Sharli had no clue but they only had two boards. Rune had proposed an idea where Tommi and Markla got on the boards, and he escorted Sharli to the ship—but Markla had shot that down. It was going to be her and Rune on the boards, and they were all going to stay together, and if Sharli couldn't keep up, too bad. Luckily, they only had to go four blocks to the hover-ship.

"Night vision on!" Gort said, and the GoBug caused their vision to suddenly change—and it was like having night vision goggles, only it was done by a script that interfaced the GoBug with their eyes. Everything seemed to glow.

"Ready?"

Rune looked at Markla again. Then he whirled around and hugged her.

"Don't worry, this will be easy," he said.

Markla just nodded. Then Rune pulled out his pistol, the one loaded with cartridges of sleep pellets. She'd loaded her weapon the same way because she didn't want to hurt anyone, not this time, and maybe not ever again. Also, after the incident in the woods with the guys from 20 Eyes, she didn't want Rune to think she was a maniac. But despite these thoughts, the front pocket of her denim jacket held an additional magazine, one that Rune didn't know about. Just in case.

"Let's do it," Rune said. "Go ahead, Gort."

They watched the police station, and they waited—and it went dark. Just like that, every light on the outside and inside went out.

"Wow," Rune said, and with a clanking sound the gate began to slide open. The power was off where they didn't want it, and it was on where they needed it, and for a moment Markla was impressed. This stuff couldn't be done with a bomb or a blade.

The gate was barely open as they slipped through and raced across the parking lot, and now Markla forgot the past, and her hair was blowing in the breeze again, and she was excited to be fighting the toads. Now she was going to save her brother and her heart was pounding.

Rune grabbed the handle to the back door, and it was unlocked. They rushed inside.

They were in a dark hallway, and they could see nothing. Then a light went on, a single bulb like a reddish eye near the end of the hall. People were shouting, and Markla sensed confusion. Gort's voice crackled in their heads.

"Straight ahead and to the right. Knobber coming as you turn."

They moved fast, and they turned, and there was a shadowy shape right there—and Rune fired a shot. There was a grunt, and the man went down.

"Good job! Holding area in front of you!"

They stormed into a room adjacent to the holding cells. There were two ways into this room—the way they'd just come, and another doorway straight ahead that led down a long hallway. To the right was a door that led to the holding cells.

"All set!" Rune said. "Markla, go!"

Rune was going to guard the entrance while she freed the prisoners.

"You're clear," Gort said. "No one in there!"

Markla ran into the cell area, a hallway with a bunch of metal doors. There was another red light at the far end but even with her night vision it was mostly shadows and darkness. She didn't hesitate. The first door was Tommi's cell, and there was a clicking noise—and it opened. She grabbed the door, and where was he? It was like a black hole in there and she couldn't see a thing.

"Tommi?" she hissed.

"Markla?"

"I'm here! Come on, we're going."

He crashed into her, hugging her hard, and for an instant she was shocked. Then she said, "This way!"

"What about mom?"

Right—mom. She was in the next cell, and Markla opened the door.

"Mom, are you in here? It's Markla. Come on, let's go."

"What?"

"Mom, let's go! We've come to rescue you!"

Tommi said, "Come on, Mom!"

Suddenly Sharli was standing right in front of Markla. Markla caught her breath, and she looked into Sharli's eyes, and she saw—bewilderment. And then a siren sounded. It was coming from outside.

Rune shouted, "Come on, Markla! Let's go!"

She ran to him, and Tommi and Sharli followed—and then there was gunfire.

"Get down!" Rune said.

But Markla was already down—and she yanked Tommi down, too, and then fired a salvo of shots.

More people were shouting now, and more people were shooting. Rune was blasting into the darkness with his sleep shells but the return fire was like a storm. Bullets were slamming into the walls and ricocheting around the room.

This is not going to work, Markla thought. Sharli screamed and ran back into the holding area—and then Tommi ran after her.

Markla swore. Rune kept shooting. The siren kept blaring, and there was a lot more yelling in the distance, and Gort was saying something, and Markla fumbled in the dark and yanked the magazine from her gun. She tossed it onto the floor and snapped in that other one she'd brought.

She shoved Rune out of the way. "Watch out!" she said. She fired.

The shell rocketed down the hallway, hit something, and exploded. The building shook, and there was a scream. Then she fired two more rounds and there were two more explosions. Pieces of the roof rained down, and in the distance she saw flames. There was a loud sound, like something bursting—and water came pouring down from the sprinkler system. Apparently, it was not disabled. She grabbed Rune's shirt.

"Where's Tommy?" They were in a downpour, yet smoke was still swirling all around.

Tommi was beside her. "Mom won't leave the cell!" he shouted.

"Come on!" she said. "We're going without her."

"You want to leave her? We can't do that."

"Yes, we can."

"No, we can't. I'll get her!"

Markla grabbed him by the arm. "No—stay with Rune. I'll get her." Then she swore and dashed back down the hall. She was furious. Why am I doing this? she thought. Well, she was doing it for Tommi. She stared into her mother's dark cell and saw Sharli standing there, not moving.

"Mom, come on. We're leaving."

"I'm not going anywhere."

"Do you have to be so difficult?" Markla shouted. "We need to go now." She grabbed her mother's arm and yanked.

Sharli struggled to get free. "Let go of me! I'm not going anywhere with you. You were never any good, Markla. Never!" She pulled herself free—and then she backhanded Markla across the face.

Markla was stunned. Then she just saw blind rage in front of her eyes, like everything was red.

She let out a yell and shoved her mother as hard as she could, and Sharli fell to the hard floor. In the distance, she heard Rune shouting. She heard a few more shots being fired.

"Goodbye, Mom," Markla said. She whirled around and then raced back to Rune. Tommi stared at her and she said, "Mom is staying. Forget it."

He saw the look in her eyes, and this time he didn't object. Then they all ran down the hall toward the exit.

Markla was in front with Tommi close behind. Rune was in the rear, and he turned to fire a few more shots into the rain and smoky darkness. They reached the back door and ran out into the parking area.

The lights were out in the parking lot, and Markla saw a red line in front of her eyes—the route they were supposed to follow. But now her mind was distracted, thinking about her mother. Thinking about everything. Forget about her, she thought. *Concentrate!*

How long had the attack taken? Markla had no idea. It was like time had stopped but it had probably only been a few minutes. They were sopping wet as they ran through the parking lot toward the gate.

Gort was talking. "Bad news," he said. "Knobbers on the way—at least three cars. You've got to get through that gate quick."

They were moving fast, but three police cars came roaring down the street, sirens blaring. And then two more from the other direction.

Two of the cars barreled through the gate but before the officers got out Rune, Markla and Tommi ran right past them. Markla could've touched a police car, she was that close to it. Then they were through the gate and the troopers were leaping from the cars. On the street, three cars had come to a stop and more officers were spilling out.

Markla jumped on her flyboard—and she saw Rune handing his flyboard to Tommi.

"No!" Markla said. "We stay together."

"There they are!" someone shouted.

"We can't!" Rune said. "Tommi, follow Markla. I can run, and I have Gort! Go! Go!"

Tommi fired up the board. Rune blasted several shots at the police car but they were only sleep pellets and did no damage. Markla swerved away from the gunfire, ducked down and zipped across the street. Tommi went in another direction as more gunfire filled the air.

Markla was incensed. She felt like her chest would explode. She saw Rune run through the front yard of a house and disappear. Then the self-driving car on the street started driving—but it didn't head down the road. Obviously, the decoy plan wasn't going to work, so Gort was changing it. Instead, the car smashed into one of the police cars. Then it spun around and tried to ram several officers. They were blasting the car.

"Tommi, stay behind me," Markla said. The best thing to do was head to the hover ship and hope for the best.

Rune will make it, she thought. *He will!*

She flew down the street with Tommi right behind her. Unfortunately, Tommi wasn't too good on a flyboard, and Markla knew it, and it was another concern.

"Tommi, look out!"

He swerved around a tree—and then crashed right into another one.

"Tommi!"

He was sprawled in the street. The board keep going and headed down the road. Tommi wasn't moving, and Markla leaped from her board and ran to him. Then a police car appeared—and it stopped right on top of her flyboard.

She was watching the car, and she was pulling Tommi to his feet.

"Tommi, can you move?"

He shook his head and looked at her with wild eyes. "I'm fine! Let's run!"

She didn't want to run but she saw two cops jumping out of the car, and another car was coming, and they had no choice.

"Follow me!" she said, and she took off. She spoke to Rune with the GoBug.

"Rune, we're on our way! Rune? Rune?"

There was no answer.

The red line was still there, and she followed it. They zigzagged through a few backyards, and then came out on a side street. She wasn't thinking anymore and it seemed like the best thing to do. I've got to focus, she thought. But she still called Rune a few more times—and she still got no answer, and then they reached their destination.

It was a small parking area for hover-cars and other vehicles. She stopped and looked around—no knobbers yet.

"Gort, where is Rune?" she snapped. "I don't think getting on the ship is a good idea. We have no decoy car, and they're after us, and now they'll just track the ship."

For an instant, there was no response, and she felt her heart racing. Then Gort was back on, and he was talking fast, "The knobbers are surrounding the area. I'm looking at the surveillance, and the hover-ship is still your best chance. I've got the surveillance in the lot turned off and I can jam some of their tracking—this has been planned. Get on the ship!"

"Where is Rune?"

"I don't know but get on the ship."

"Not without Rune!"

"You need to go! You need to get on now!"

Tommi was tugging her arm. He couldn't hear the GoBug conversation, but he said, "Markla, what are we doing? We can go back and find Rune!"

"No!" she blurted. She didn't want Tommi doing that.

Then Gort said, "Get on, and we'll try to pick him up on the way."

"Why can't we wait for him?"

"Too many police around. *Will you please listen to me!* I can see what's going on. We'll take off, find Rune, and pick him up."

She swore. "All right! *But we better find him!* Come on, Tommy."

She ran to ship that was marked in red before her eyes. It wasn't very big but it could seat four. She got in, and Tommi followed her and she hated this plan because she'd never flown a hover-ship, and she didn't know how to do it manually, and they would need to rely on Gort or a programmed flight path—and she would never leave Rune, never. But she couldn't risk Tommi, either. They had to go

Gort can find him, she thought. *And we can land and pick him up.*

The ship lifted off. It started flying low—and then with a whooshing sound it was flying fast over the buildings and out toward the forest.

"Wait!" Markla said. "Where are we going? What about Rune? Gort! Stop the ship! What's going on?"

She was banging on the window.

"Markla, calm down," Gort said. "We aren't giving up on Rune, but there's a problem, and it's important that you don't get yourself killed."

"Problem? What problem?"

She suddenly found herself gripping the seat hard.

She heard Gort sigh. "Rune isn't hurt. But he was captured."

For an instant, Markla felt light-headed. And then she was screaming.

"What? Are you serious? Turn this ship around! Turn this ship around now or I'll do it myself!"

"Markla, there's nothing you can do. I'm still getting information, and it's information you'll want. Do not cut me off!"

"You lied to me! I want to get off this ship. I want to go back right now!"

"You can't. You'll just get yourself killed, and I don't want that to happen. You'll get Tommi killed, too."

"I never trusted you!"

"Well, maybe you should start trusting me because I'm the best chance you've got! Isn't your brother sitting right there next to you?"

Markla felt like her chest was going explode; she was gasping for air.

Calm down, she thought. *Calm down, Markla. You can do it!*

Gort was still talking. "Markla! Markla, are you there?"

She took a few more breaths. "I'm here," she said. Then she paused and said, "What do you know about Rune?"

"He's fine. He's not even unconscious. They just arrested him, and we'll get him out. Don't worry."

"Gort, I want to go back."

"You'll go back. But now isn't a good time, okay? Right now you need to get Tommi to safety. Then we'll figure something out."

"Gort, I can't leave, Rune. I just can't do it."

"Yeah, I know that. But Rune will be okay. The rebels have operatives in the police force. I don't necessarily know them, but I know they're in there, and they might protect Blog's son, so don't worry about Rune. We'll figure something out. But I have to disconnect now, okay? I have a situation here."

Markla stared out the window. The hover-ship was moving

fast, and it was over the forest now, and the treetops were just a blur. There was no city in site. At this rate, they would reach Narna soon.

"All right," she said. "I'll keep the GoBug for now and use this account. Send me a message when you know more."

Gort disconnected.

Markla looked over at Tommi who was staring at her with wide eyes.

"Markla, you saved me," he said.

"I messed up your life."

"No, you didn't. You made it better. You've always made it better."

She banged her head back on the seat and said nothing.

Chapter 10

Jorro, also known as Gort, was fumbling around, switching between his GoBug and various scripts on his portable EB. He glanced at the cluttered bedroom of the tiny three-bedroom apartment he shared with two other students at Sparkla University, and he felt glad no one else was home. All his communication was sent via GoBug, using his thoughts—but yet, he'd found himself shouting along with them.

He had to sign off. He had to make sure no one tracked him. He took a deep breath—that was enough Markla Flash for now.

That girl is difficult, he thought. But then again, she'd been a member of a murderous subversive group, and she'd stabbed a few people to death, so what had he expected? And she was no more difficult than his girlfriend, who kept calling with great persistence.

Of course, his girlfriend had no idea he was Gort, smasher extraordinaire and enemy of the government. She only knew his real name, Jorro. He finally connected to her stream, and there she was looking sexy and annoyed. Tanna Xantha often looked sexy and annoyed.

"Why weren't you answering?" she said. Her dark eyes were like pretty spikes.

"I was in the middle of something."

He briefly switched to another stream—okay, still no pursuit of the hover-ship.

"Are you watching the news streams?"

"No."

"Well, that's fine, because most of them are still down. But you monitor other streams, right? Sometimes I think you care more about your GoBug than you do about me… There was a raid on the police station about twenty minutes ago. Markla

Flash tried to free her brother and her mother. Can you believe it?"

Jorro opened his eyes extra wide. "Really?" he said. "So what happened?"

He checked the other stream again. Still no news about the hover-ship.

"The brother is free, he got away along with Markla—at least for now. But guess what? Rune Roko was captured."

"Oh. Well, that's good."

"It's better than good! We don't know how someone smashed into the station EB and controlled a bunch of stuff but I'm sure we'll track that person down. No smasher is that good."

"Right," Jorro said—and he suddenly felt warm.

"Anyway, I look at their mistakes as an opportunity. I'm going to get Markla Flash—just watch me."

"You've got a real vendetta against that girl, don't you?"

"Of course I do! She's a subversive animal who killed my uncle. I'll admit, I never liked him much, but no one liked him—and anyway, I didn't dislike him all the time. I mostly felt sorry for him, and catching Markla will make me look good." She hesitated, and then said, "I need to make up for my mistakes, Jorro. The arrest team I put together was a disaster, and it was all my fault. My father was right. I wasn't ready, and three people died, and I can't even think about it."

She was quiet for a second, and Jorro could tell she was upset. He knew she hated to make mistakes—especially if they made her look bad. He also knew she'd get over it quick.

"Don't be so hard on yourself," he said, and he eyed another open mindstream. Still no news. "Sometimes things just go wrong. Did her mom tell you anything useful?"

"No. Markla's mom is a piece of trash, just like her. You should've seen their house—what a dump."

"Maybe there were circumstances."

"I read Markla's profile, and there were circumstances—but everyone has issues, Jorro. People think I have it so easy because my family has money, and I'm smart, and I'm good-looking. But it's not easy. I've worked hard."

"I see."

"What? You don't agree?" Her eyes flashed with anger.

"No—no! You do work hard. But no one ever abused you, right?"

"I would never let anyone abuse me."

"It's never that simple."

"Oh, really? Are you sympathizing with a subversive?"

"No, not at all," he said, and he forced a quick smile onto his face. "I'll be happy to help if I can."

"All right. You're back on my good side."

"You don't have a bad side, Tanna. You look great from every angle."

She laughed. "Jorro, you might actually be able to help. I know you're still in school, but you're pretty amazing, right? I've seen the stuff you've created. I can put in a good word for you. You could be on my special team."

"What special team?"

"The one I'm forming to help my father. It's an all-purpose kind of team. We're learning MindCore, and we're getting involved with other stuff, too. If you're on the team, maybe you can help track down the saboteur." Suddenly she looked at him, and her look was softer than usual. Those dark brown eyes were almost sad. "There aren't a lot of people I can trust, Jorro. So many people are jealous of me. But I like you, and I'd like to trust you."

He swallowed hard. "Thanks, Tanna. I like you, too. If I can help, that would be great."

Her face lit up. "I'll put your name in for approval. Why don't you come over tonight?"

"I don't know. I have lots of studying to do."

"You can study me," she said, and she flashed her most seductive smile. "I'm very interesting."

He laughed. "Okay, but I have a few things to finish up. I'll be over later."

She smiled again and signed off. Jorro immediately connected to another stream.

As soon as it appeared, he felt a wave of relief. Rune had dissolved the connection on his GoBug completely, so there was no way to trace it, and the police were not aware of Markla's hover-ship—and that was because it didn't exist on their scans. All their scanning information went through a central EB, and since he was controlling that EB they didn't see it. Of course, they would soon regain control, but by then Markla and Tommi would be in Narna.

Hopefully, he'd wiped his electronic tracks clean. But he felt himself sweating because there was always a trail. It might be difficult to find but someone might find it. Something would be revealed.

His mind wandered, thinking back to his days as a kid, thinking about his parents, and how his mother had given him his first GoBug when she'd been a brilliant engineer working for the wrong people—people who'd totally taken advantage of her.

He put the GoBug down on the table. He'd go see Tanna later. She could be nasty and self-absorbed at times but she was also smart, and she was more fun than most people realized. The girl had lots of personality. Also, she might give him some good information about Rune and Markla.

Chapter 11

Markla knew she should be scanning the sky for police but she wasn't. She should be checking in with Gort again but she didn't. She looked at the readouts on the screens in front of her but they all seemed foggy and far away. There was no sign of pursuit—not yet. She guessed they'd reach Narna in half an hour.

And what about Rune? He was the main thing on her mind. Then she glanced over at Tommi, who was staring out the window with a blank expression. He's probably traumatized, she thought, and now she felt sick.

Meanwhile, the moon was bright, and the stars dotted the sky with a thousand specks of white and gold. This was a small hover-ship, approximately the size of a car, with four seats and a rear storage compartment that was accessed from outside the vehicle. They were flying low over the trees, and the ragged treetops were rushing by, and she hardly noticed.

I need to think about Tommi's safety, she thought. Where were they going to end up? Where would they stay? What would they eat? Hopefully there was something in the storage compartment but she couldn't check that until they landed.

Now Tommi looked at her with those eyes of his, soft like the eyes of a deer. He'd always been a gentle kid, and for some reason this made her feel even worse. She was the one who'd always been so hard.

"Are you worried about Rune?" he said. "I thought that guy said he was okay."

"He's not okay," Markla said. "And it's all my fault, Tommi. I'm the reason you were arrested, and I'm the reason Rune is sitting in a prison cell."

"But you got me out. Maybe we can get him out, too."

She frowned and didn't answer. She wanted to talk and make

him feel at ease but she'd never been much of a talker, and she didn't feel at ease herself. She wanted to scream and cry but she couldn't—and maybe it was a good thing. She wasn't sure if she could handle her feelings right now.

She guessed a therapist would feel differently but she'd never been to a therapist. Still, she'd read a few things about mental conditions—in fact, more than a few things. She'd tried to fix herself. Then she'd joined a subversive group and killed a few people.

I'm broken, Markla thought. *I'll always be broken.*

She was tired but there was no way she could sleep, and then she thought about Gort, and how she should call him. But calling Gort was risky. Markla wasn't the most high-tech person on the planet, but she'd been a dream writer, and a flyboard rider, and she was far from ignorant. She knew the GoBugs connected people to mindstreams via Dream Stations and satellites. The GoBug she'd gotten from Rune was unregistered, and the account was fake—but still, how many GoBugs would be sending signals on this trajectory, heading out of Sparkla and into Narna? How many GoBugs even existed in Narna, and could those GoBugs be differentiated from a GoBug originally coded in Sparkla?

This is why she hated GoBugs. Despite what Rune and Gort said, they could be tracked. Everything could be tracked, and the only safe thing to do was to not use these devices at all. But here was her essential problem—she had no other way to communicate with Gort about Rune. Without the GoBug she was blind.

She wanted to hurl it out the window, and under any other circumstances she would have. But without the GoBug, she had no chance of knowing what was happening to Rune, and so she couldn't get rid of it. But she could shut it down temporarily.

She removed the device from the pocket of her jacket, and then she removed the power crystal.

Now, what about the hover-ship? If it was being tracked, she couldn't do anything about it. Hopefully Gort was on top of that, and when it landed they could get as far away from it as possible.

She looked at the readouts again, and there was still no sign of pursuit. Okay, great, but where were they going? Gort had told her and Rune little about their destination. He'd said it was better for them to not know, in case something went wrong and they were captured—and now this seemed like a good strategy, since Rune would be unable to tell anyone about their destination other than it was in Narna, and Narna was big. MindCore could not extract a memory that didn't exist.

But what *could* MindCore do? Was it operational after the attack on the Dream Center, and would Rune end up in MindCore again? What would someone see?

If it still functioned, they would see everything. They would be able to extract the memory of every conversation she and Rune had ever had—as well as the conversation between Rune and his mother, and the episode in the woods with 20 Eyes, and the entire conversation with Gort. They could potentially see every memory in Rune's mind.

Suddenly she felt hot around her collar, like she was overheating. And then she thought about her intimate moments with Rune, and she felt her blood go cold. She didn't want anyone to see those. Those moments only belonged to her and Rune, and it infuriated her to think that someone would be able to watch them.

"Markla, are you all right?" Tommi said.

Markla shook her head, and she almost laughed. All her life, people had asked her this question.

"I'm fine, Tommi," she said. "Don't worry about me."

But there was rage burning inside her. These people had to be stopped.

Chapter 12

Rune barely noticed the handcuffs. He was on the lawn in somebody's backyard, flat on his stomach while sirens screamed nearby. Someone had shoved his face into the grass, but he was straining his eyes and ears, trying to gather information. Had anyone been hurt? What had happened to Markla's mother? And most of all, where were Markla and Tommi?

He heard a lot of talking and swearing and people barking orders but not a word about Markla. He told himself to stay calm. But now his thoughts were racing with grim images—interrogation, torture, and prison.

I'll escape, he thought. *They'll never hold me!*

Suddenly a knobber grabbed his arm and yanked him to his feet. He was a bulky guy and tall like a giant.

"All right, kid," he said. "You're leaving."

"Where's Markla?" Rune asked.

"I don't know, and I don't care. Now move."

He was thrown into a hover-car, and when a different officer got in Rune repeated the question. But he got no answer. They started driving, and Rune had no idea where they were going but he wondered if Gort was monitoring the police communications. He wondered if Markla still had that GoBug. He tried not to worry but he was totally worried.

Markla was a smart girl. In fact, she was one of the cleverest people he'd ever met. But she had a fiery temper and some ferocious demons in her head, and sometimes it was an explosive combination. His father had warned him. He'd said she was likely to do something extreme—like stab Aldo in the back. They'd never really discussed it but he'd replayed that bloody moment in his mind a hundred times. She did what I couldn't do, he thought. And what would Blog have said? That I needed a girl to set things right?

But I'll find her. I already miss her so much!

His own GoBug had been taken away, but it was a blank, and he'd dissolved the data, and everything should be fine—unless they put him in MindCore. Luckily, he didn't know where Markla had gone. So they could never get that from him.

The hover-car didn't go far. They went to another police station on the other side of town where he was tossed into a gray stone cell with no windows and a heavy metal door. There was a gloomy light on the ceiling, and a steel bunk and a toilet, and that was all. Well, he'd been in this kind of cell before, and he wasn't scared. He was getting to be a real pro.

He paced back and forth, waiting for someone to come. But no one did.

How much time passed? It was hard to say. Eventually, he decided to lay down on the rock-hard bed, and he fell asleep. He woke up once, and it was pitch black, and for an instant he felt dazed and hungry—where was he? For a moment, he was back in his bed in his parent's house, and was it time for school? But then reality crashed down around him, and now he sensed it was the middle of the night. Then he drifted off to sleep again and finally jerked himself awake because a light was blaring in his eyes, and the door was opening, and a police officer was stomping into the cell.

"Come on, kid. Time to talk."

Rune said nothing as he was led to a cramped room with no windows, a small table, and two metal chairs. They sat him down, and then the officer stood in the corner as Stroll Nadum entered.

Wow, this guy, Rune thought. He knew Stroll was the new Centurion of Sparkla, and he recalled his father mentioning him a few times, usually accompanied by the phrase "ass clown." So Rune braced himself for something clownish.

Stroll was tall and spindly, and he had a thick handlebar

mustache. He wore a helmet like a stormtrooper, and heavy black combat boots, and an ivory-handled sidearm. Rune guessed he was trying to look imposing—but despite the seriousness of the situation, Rune found himself struggling not to laugh.

Stroll's eyes flashed with anger, and he shook his head with obvious disgust. "What would your father think of you now, Rune? Breaking into a police station and shooting at police officers."

"Don't talk about my father!" Rune snapped. "He was fighting people like you."

Stroll shrugged and looked smug. "Well, you lost your fight, and that's why you're here. You're lucky no one was really hurt."

No one was hurt? Instantly, Rune's heart felt lighter.

"It's good to be lucky," Rune said.

Stroll leaned toward him a bit, and the ends of his curvy mustache seemed to twitch. "Who were you working with, Rune? Who smashed into our grid? I know you're not going to tell me but I'll get the information whether you cooperate or not." Then he paused and added, "Have you ever heard of something called *Mindcalm?* I think you've already seen it."

"You mean 'MindCore?' "

Stroll hesitated. "Right. Isn't that what I said?"

"No. You said something stupid. But I thought MindCore was destroyed."

"One of the units was destroyed," Strom said, and he puffed out his chest. "But we have another one here in the capitol, and we're putting you in it. The days when people can refuse to talk are over. We can reach right into your brain and pull out whatever we want. And we'll be pulling soon."

Now Rune felt a flash of panic—because it was true.They would be able to access his memories, and what would they see? Every conversation he'd ever had, and every word he'd ever said.

"You don't need to do that," Rune said. "Take me to Markla, and maybe I'll tell you something. I just want to see her."

Stroll laughed. "I'm afraid that's impossible, Rune—because she got away. Her and her brother. But we still have her mother!"

She got away! Rune couldn't help but smile.

"What are you smiling at?" Stroll said. "Where did she go? What was your destination?" Stroll seemed furious. "Do you think I'm an idiot, Rune? Well, I'm not. We'll see how you feel after you've been through the mind-calmer."

"I guess so," Rune said. "I'd hate to be too calm."

Stroll sneered. "You little punk. I should smash your face into pulp, how about that?" And he held his fist in front of Rune's nose. "But I don't need to do that because we have your old teacher on our side—Diana Drogo. And she knows how to work that machine, doesn't she? So get ready for a rough time. We'll see who's laughing in a few days."

Diana! For an instant, Rune's mind was blank. But then his heart flooded with hope.

Meanwhile, Stroll sneered again and left the room.

Rune sighed with relief. All in all this hadn't been a bad interrogation.

Chapter 13

Markla's stomach tightened as the hover ship began its decent. It wasn't flying too high so the drop was short, but it wasn't the drop that made her queasy. They'd reached their destination, and now she'd need to start making decisions.

They were landing in a clearing in the heart of a dense forest. The landing gear descended, and the vehicle set down with a light bump right near the edge of the tree line. They'd reached Narna.

She stared at the black forest and thought about how thrilling this moment would've been if Rune were here. But he was somewhere far away, and now she wondered how much he knew about her escape—and was he worrying about her? *Because I'm so worried about him.*

She tried to focus on Tommi; at least they'd done that. He's free, and he needs me to be strong, she thought. He was smiling and leaping out of the ship, and Markla followed. The instant she stepped outside, she felt a cool breeze in her face, like a puff of extra oxygen, and she welcomed it. She was still wearing her denim jacket, and she looked up at the sky. It was a beautiful night, like something from a painting, with a shower of stars and a fat yellow moon. Everything was perfect, except for that one thing—and it made her feel like she wanted to cry. But she did not.

"Where are we?" Tommi said. "We're in the middle of nowhere."

"Yeah, I know. Narna is supposed to be a lot like nowhere."

She went back into the hover-ship and retrieved the flyboards, and then she opened the storage compartment and was startled to discover three backpacks filled with supplies. This was a happy find. Obviously, Gort had quite a few friends. She wanted to thank him, but of course she'd disconnected her GoBug, at least for now.

Tommi started rummaging through the storage area.

"Lots of insta-meals," he said. "Also a tent and some camping stuff." He laughed. "I thought you said this guy didn't know you, Markla."

She laughed, too. It's true, she'd spent lots of time outdoors, mainly to avoid Sharli.

She stood beside Tommi and examined every item carefully, especially the backpacks. She was wary of tracking devices because it was her nature to be wary, but if Gort had wanted them captured he could've made it happen back at the police station. So this stuff was probably safe.

Tommy was putting on one of the backpacks. "What part of nowhere are we looking for, Markla?"

"I'm not sure," she said with a shrug. "This looks like a perfectly good part but let's get as much as we can carry and get away from the ship. We'll set up camp in the woods and think about a plan."

"Do you have more guns? Do you have a knife?"

"I only have one gun. But I have another dagger."

She had two, actually—the two she'd taken from the guys in 20 Eyes. She hated to give him a weapon. But she did.

She didn't intend to go anywhere tonight. They were tired, and stomping through the tangled woods in the dark wasn't on the agenda. So they took the tent and most of the supplies across the clearing, to a spot where they could still see the ship, and then they went into the woods just a bit and set up camp.

Tommy seemed to approve. "This is good," he said. "Now if someone comes to investigate the ship, we can watch. We can see the intruders."

"That's the idea," Markla said. "But around here we're the intruders."

Tommi laughed and they set up the tent. There was a heating

orb in with the supplies, and that was convenient because it was going to be cool tonight, and Markla didn't want to make a fire.

"Get some sleep," Markla said. "We have a lot to do tomorrow."

"Like what?"

"I don't know yet. But we'll be doing lots of it."

"I'm not tired."

They sat together outside the tent. Tommi asked her a bunch of questions about the raid that she didn't feel like answering, but she answered anyway. She got the feeling he was more impressed than he should be. He thought it had been some wild adventure, like he'd experience in a LiveDream.

Then he said, "Is it true you killed Dru? That's what they told me."

She hesitated. Here was something she definitely didn't want to discuss. She really, really, wanted to lie about it.

"Yeah, I did," she said. "And I had good reasons, but I don't want to talk about it, okay?"

He shrugged. "Okay," he said, and he was quiet for about a minute. Then he looked at her and said, "Markla, did he attack you? Was he trying to rape you or something?"

Her mind boiled over. "No, he was not trying to rape me! Don't be impressed by anything I do, Tommi. I'm not an action-adventure hero. I don't know what I am but don't be too impressed."

Her chest was heaving, and her head was pounding.

Now there was a longer moment of quiet. Tommi was looking into the darkness, and she felt hot all over. Somewhere nearby, there was the oblivious hooting of an owl. Finally, Tommi said, "Sorry. I just wanted to know. Don't be mad."

"I'm not mad at you. I'm mad at myself."

"Well, don't be mad at yourself, either—like you always are, ha. You've always done the best you could. I know because I was there."

That's true, she thought. *He knows more than anyone.*

"Tommi, maybe we should both get some sleep."

"Yeah," he said, and he headed into the tent. As he opened the flap, he turned to her. "You're my best friend, Markla."

He went inside and closed the flap, and she sat alone. She thought about everything he'd said—and she thought about Rune. Rune had never asked her too much about the violent things she'd done but he probably thought about it. She was sure he did.

She went into the tent where Tommi was curled up near the heating orb. She decided to lie down but didn't expect to sleep much.

***

Markla awoke before dawn as usual and slipped outside. She pulled the GoBug from the pocket of her jacket. It was early, and she wondered if Gort was awake and if someone might track her the instant she activated the device. Sparkla couldn't legally pursue her in Narna but she didn't trust the government of Sparkla one bit. Yet was there any news about Rune? She had to risk it.

She was just about to put the power crystal back into the device when she heard a noise, a murmur of voices, and her whole body stiffened—there were two silhouettes over by the ship. She swore and crouched behind an oak tree. She grabbed her vision magnifiers.

A man and a woman were rummaging around. The man was lanky with brown hair past his shoulders, while the woman was short like a stump with longer hair that was mostly gray. Markla couldn't hear anything they were saying, but they were looking across the clearing—and they were looking right where she was hiding. But they didn't seem to see her, and then her heart started beating fast as she thought about the tent. Maybe it wasn't far enough back in the woods. And who were these people, anyway?

There were people living in the woods of Narna, people known as *Basics*. Supposedly, the Basics shunned most technology and lived a primitive lifestyle like people from ancient times. It had been a common joke at school that Markla was a Basic because of the way she looked and acted, and because she didn't have a GoBug, and because kids were often mean and stupid. And now she almost laughed, remembering her recent school days—and how she'd considered those jokes to be a compliment.

But these people were not Basics. They were dressed in modern clothes, denim and leather, and the man held a rifle in his hand, and now he was pointing across the clearing, and he was walking across it with the woman by his side. Markla took a deep breath and got ready. They were coming right toward her.

She couldn't run because Tommy was still in the tent so she reached for the gun. She didn't want to use it, but it felt strong in her hand, and she realized this was the case with most weapons. Was she meant to be a soldier? Or was the weapon a tangible thing that made her feel less helpless? Yeah, that was it—that had always been it.

She shook her head. *Concentrate, Markla!*

She put down the vision magnifiers and watched the pair approach. When they were about fifty paces away the man called out.

"Markla!" he said. "Tommi! Can you hear me?"

At the sound of her name, Markla felt a shock. They called a few more times and she said nothing.

"Yeah, I can hear you," she finally said. "And I have a gun. So stop moving and put down your weapon. Then tell me who you are."

The woman glanced at the man, and the man dropped the rifle. They both put their hands in the air.

"We're friends," the woman said. "My name is Shala, and this is Jerome, and we're friends with Gort. He told us you'd be here, and that you'd probably need some help."

Markla studied the pair. They didn't look like 20 Eyes—certainly, the woman didn't. Most of the Eyes were younger, and most of them were male. Also, why would anyone in 20 Eyes know they were here, and that they knew Gort?

"How are you going to help me?" Markla said.

Shala smiled. "We're part of Free Sparkla. We've got relations there, and we've been part of the network for a long time. We hooked up with Gort on the streams but we don't talk to him that way. We use a speßcial kind of radio, and we're setting up some camps here in Narna to help with the fight. We know all about you, Markla."

"Is that a good thing?" Markla said.

"Yes," Shala said. "We need people like you. We have a place where you can stay and where you can monitor and send communications."

Markla hesitated. Now this was tempting. She lowered her weapon.

"All right," she said. "We'll come with you."

She didn't trust them, not really. But under the circumstances, she needed to trust someone—at least a bit.

She headed toward the tent to wake up Tommi. *We'll go with them but we'll stay on guard.* It was a hard habit to break.

Chapter 14

After his interrogation, Rune was loaded onto a hover-ship. Instantly, the good feelings he'd gotten from Stroll's incompetent questioning were put to a test—because where was he going? Probably some place farther from Markla, and this made his head swirl. As he was tossed into a bleak holding area in the back of the ship, he asked one of the officers about his destination.

The guy gave a snort. "A place you'll never escape from—no chance."

For a moment, Rune felt his heart sink. But the moment was brief. We'll see about that, he thought.

The holding pen in the ship had steel walls, a stiff bench to sit on, and no windows. There was a lighting strip along the low ceiling that cast a dim glow and helped create a hopeless atmosphere but it was no big deal. No situation was hopeless, and if they thought they were going to intimidate him they were wrong. While they flew, he tried to calculate the distance they covered based on the typical speed of a hover-ship and his estimation of the time that passed. He guessed it was well over an hour. As the ship was landing, Rune did the math and realized they were a long way from the capitol. Well, whatever. He would get to Narna somehow.

I'll find her, he thought. And then for an instant he was hit by a wave of sadness, and he blinked his watery eyes a few times, and he wondered how she was doing, and what she was seeing—and was anyone pursuing her?

He was planning to stay strong. As the doors swung open, he looked around fast and soaked up the images. It was important to absorb every detail, anything that might help him or Gort or Blog's friends. The information he gathered could be valuable when he escaped from this snake pit. And he would escape.

He studied the scene and sucked in his breath.

He was inside a fortress. But was it on a hill? In a forest? Near a river? The walls were so high that all he could see was open sky. He was standing on a landing field, and it was monstrous, and there were about a hundred hover-ships sitting around, looking like gigantic bugs. They were mostly gunships and transports, and they stretched out in every direction toward the great walls—and all along those walls were towers, rising like giant teeth. On the top of the towers were spiky antennas and the black barrels of guns.

Okay, Rune thought, this is a military installation—and wasn't he a great detective? But then he considered how there weren't a lot of fortresses in Sparkla and certainly not many this big. He recalled struggling to stay awake in history class with Mr. Kyle, and he remembered hearing his father, an ex-army officer, go on about this topic. The Sparklan military wasn't that large because the world didn't have that many people, and less people generally meant less reasons to fight. The world had been through a massive population explosion back in ancient times, and then a few disasters, and the small population of today was a key component of social policy, blah, blah, blah. But the bottom line was this—there were only so many places he could be, and it was limited.

One of the knobbers shoved him toward a low stone building, and as he walked he noticed another hover-ship nearby, and he guessed it had arrived from the capitol a bit earlier. People were unloading stuff, and it looked like electronic equipment, and then he saw two guys moving a console—it was MindCore.

He felt a chill go down his spine as he tried to block out the horrible possibilities. But he told himself to stay calm. MindCore was a terrifying possibility, but it depended upon who was operating it. Hopefully, it would be Diana. Diana was a friend, and luckily these idiots didn't know it.

He kept that positive thought in his head as he was led down a long hallway. He went past lots of closed doors, and then finally into a room that looked like a lounge. He was pushed down into a cushy chair with his hands still cuffed, and then someone else came in—and it was not Diana. It was Tanna Xantha.

Rune glared at her and felt a wave of rage rising. This was the girl who'd sent that message to Markla. This was the girl who'd made Markla cry. His first reaction was to lunge at her, despite the handcuffs—but he stopped himself.

Stay calm!

He took a deep breath. There was no point in being openly hostile. If he was going to get out of here, maybe it would be better to not be an idiot. That was usually the best plan.

He'd seen Tanna on mindstreams. In fact, she had her own stream where she bragged about herself and tried to sell lots of dumb health food products her father was always blabbing about. But mindstreams never showed the whole picture. Sure, they produced beautiful three-dimensional images that appeared to hang in front of a viewer's eyes in vivid color, but it wasn't quite the same as seeing someone in real life.

Tanna was dressed in black leggings with a matching shirt. She looked athletic, and she appeared to be ready for some kind of workout. As Rune studied her slinky shape, and her sensual face, and the snaky black ponytail hanging down her back, he couldn't deny that the mindstreams actually understated her appearance. This girl was really attractive. But she had a smug kind of smile.

"So you're Rune Roko," she said—and yeah, she sounded smug. "I guess you know who I am."

Rune cocked his head. "Yeah," he said. "You're an aerobics

instructor, right? I can't do aerobics with my hands cuffed. Maybe you should let me go."

She gave a short laugh. "Very funny. But I think you know my name. And I think you know why you're here."

Rune guessed she was waiting for a response but he said nothing.

This didn't seem to bother her. She smirked and said, "We want to know who smashed into the grid, and you're going to help me, and we can do this the hard way or the easy way. The easy way is you tell me what you know, and the hard way is we put you into MindCore and pull it out of your head." She paused. "The thing is, I'm not an expert at using that machine—not yet. I could overdo it and cause some kind of brain damage, right? So why don't you tell me what I want to know and save yourself a lot of trouble."

Rune didn't answer for a few seconds. Then he looked at her and said, "I never buy those supplements you sell, Tanna. They're a big scam."

She hesitated, and then she laughed again. "So you do know who I am," she said, and she seemed pleased. "Well, they're my father's supplements. But they probably do *something*—and I take them once in a while. But I think I'd still look good without them." Then she leaned toward him a bit. "What do you think?"

Rune scoffed. "I think arresting Markla's family shows that you don't care about justice. Because they had nothing to do with any of this."

"Maybe she should've thought about that before she murdered my uncle."

"Your uncle tortured her, and he said he was going to do it again." Then Rune sneered a bit and said, "Your uncle wasn't a very nice guy."

"Yeah, I know," she said. "But I still want to catch the person who killed him, and I still want to save the government, and you're going to help me do it, Rune. And when we do catch Markla, I'm going to make sure she pays for what she did."

"You'll never catch her. She's too smart for you."

Tanna narrowed her eyes. "Oh, really? If she's so smart, why did she live in such a dumpy little house, and why did she join a subversive group, and why is she running for her life?"

Rune shrugged. "Not everyone is born rich like you. Not everyone gets everything handed to them."

It was like he'd flipped a switch inside her.

"That's not true!" she snapped. "I work hard."

"I doubt it," Rune said. "You're just a snotty rich girl. And you're *mean*."

"I'm 'mean'?" she said, and she paused, like he'd punched her in the stomach. "I'm not mean. I just like to get things done, and sometimes people resent that."

"You mean the people who get passed over so the president's daughter can get whatever she wants? My father was the Centurion, Tanna, before he died fighting *your* father, and I know how the police force works. Why are you even talking to me? They have lots of people more qualified than you. But I guess they're not related to Gin Xantha, right?"

Tanna glared at Rune, and her dark eyes smoked with rage. But she took a breath, like she was telling herself to stay calm. And then she was calm.

"Markla's a murderer," she said. "You can say what you want about her, but that's what she is." Then she quipped, "And she's ugly, too."

Rune cocked his head. "She's beautiful. You're just jealous."

"Jealous?" Now Tanna gave a loud laugh. "Of that girl? You're as crazy as she is. Why would I be jealous of her?"

"I just told you why. Because she's better than you in every way."

Tanna rolled her eyes. "Okay, I can see we're not getting anywhere—not yet. But we will."

"I'm never getting anywhere with you, Tanna. Never."

"Right," she said—and now she really seemed annoyed, and Rune wanted to laugh because he didn't like her at all. "We'll see, Rune. We'll see." She turned to leave, but then she stopped and added, "By the way, we know Markla is in Narna, and it won't help her. We have a team tracking her down. They're real commandos, too—not lucky rich girls like me. She has no chance."

Once again, she started walking out of the room. But once again, she stopped and turned around.

"There's a lot you don't know about me, Rune—a lot."

Rune watched her leave. She had a sexy walk but there was nothing he wanted to know about her. Nothing at all.

Chapter 15

Markla kept Tommi close to her as the pair walked through the overgrown forest. They'd packed up the camp, and she and Tommi and Jerome were carrying everything. Markla was determined to stay alert concerning their new friends, and she was diligently watching and listening while saying very little.

Shala liked to talk. She had a bit of an accent, and Markla wondered if that was why she sounded a little dumb—or was it just the stuff that she said? Yeah, mostly that was it.

"Like I was saying, we don't know much," Shala said. "Just what Gort told us. He said your friend was captured, and that's all he knew at the time. And he told us to help you out. Well, I like to cook, and you look like you could use some food, honey. You're skinny as a piece of rope."

Markla gave a short laugh but said nothing. She hated when people told her she was "skinny."

Shala picked up a stiff branch and started using it like a walking stick. She seemed robust, like someone who didn't need much help doing things, and despite her big mouth, Markla more or less liked her. Maybe it's the hair, Markla thought. Shala's gray hair was brittle and untamed, like a much older version of Markla's style—or lack of it. Shala also smiled and laughed a lot, too. She was like a friendly grandmother from the wilderness. Meanwhile, Jerome didn't say too much, and Markla was more suspicious of him. He was tall and gangly and scuzzy-looking, like he was covered with a film of grease—and hey, maybe she shouldn't judge him purely by his appearance. But she'd spent a lot of time in the woods, and a snake pretty much always looks like a snake.

Supposedly, he was Shala's son, so maybe he was okay, but it wasn't just his appearance. Markla caught him looking at her a few times with those sideways glances, and those little smiles, and she didn't like it.

Shala said, "So you're really sixteen years old, Markla? You look younger. You're awfully young to be in so much trouble."

"Yeah, I have a real talent," Markla said.

"Markla's a warrior," Tommi said.

Shala smiled. "We need warriors—even small ones. You're really small, Markla. You're like a little mouse."

Markla held her tongue.

"She's no mouse," Tommi said with a grin. "Don't let her size fool you. She's a great fighter."

"Tommi, stop," Markla said because he was exaggerating. She was no great fighter, not at all. But then she laughed to herself—because her size did tend to fool people, and she liked it that way. She gave Tommi a glance that said "stop talking about me." He smiled at her, and he stopped talking.

They walked for about two hours. They slogged through the dense forest to a bubbling stream and then followed it for a while. All along the way, Markla noted their direction with her compass, and the time of their walk in each direction, and every landmark she could memorize. She wanted to make sure they could get back to the ship if necessary. There was nothing in the ship she wanted but in her mind it was the fastest way to Rune, even if she didn't know how to fly it.

They came to a cabin covered with leafy vines, and Jerome pointed and said, "This cabin's been abandoned for years. Our place is about ten minutes farther upstream."

Markla studied the abandoned house, and she smiled. It reminded her of the dilapidated house back in Sparkla where she'd gone to play as a kid, and where she'd stashed all her 20 Eyes supplies. She briefly recalled taking Rune there, and for a moment she felt happy—and then sad, so sad.

Before too long they reached another cabin. It was another battered old structure surrounded by low trees, and at first glance Markla thought it was a rustic version of her old home—which is to say that it was a bit run down or maybe semi-destroyed and had a great possibility to trigger terrifying flashbacks. In fact, there was a sudden feeling in her chest, like she was being crushed and couldn't breathe—but she fought it, and then it was gone, and luckily the inside of the cabin was totally different. As they walked through the front door, her eyes opened wide. The inside was airy and bright, and the wood floors were like polished glass, and the fireplace was made of handsome reddish stones. It was nothing like the cluttered house full of junk she'd grown up in.

Tommi seemed impressed. "This is amazing," he said. "I wish our house had been like this." Then he added, "I wonder how Mom's doing."

Mom—right. I forgot about Mom, Markla thought. In fact, she realized she'd given Sharli no thought at all since leaving her at the police station. Markla was worried about the four cats, and who would feed them, but she was totally unconcerned about who fed her mother. Sharli was easy to feed—just open the bottle and pour.

Tommi was staring at Markla like he could read her mind. And sometimes he could.

"You're worried about the cats, right?" he said.

"Yeah."

"They'll be okay. They'll go down to the Hanno's house. That old woman will feed them. That woman was crazy but she was a 'cat person' just like you."

Markla brightened a bit. It's true, Joya Hanno would take care of the cats. Between Markla and Joya, there had been lots of cat action on that street. That could've been my destiny, Markla thought. *If I'd killed less people and stayed out of prison, I could've been a 'crazy old cat lady.'* And she laughed because the idea actually appealed to her.

Sharla took them to a small bedroom in the back of the house and motioned toward an old dresser. "You can unpack your things," she said. "You can stay as long as you like. After we eat something we can try and contact Gort. We have a transmitter and a radio that uses something called 'short wave.' Jerome's the radio guy, not me… We can reach Gort, and they can't trace it."

"I'm not hungry," Markla said, even though she was starving. "Let's call him now."

"The radio's not in the cabin," Shala said. "The radio is out back by the power farm—well, that's what I call it, and I'll bet you didn't even notice the antenna, right? Because it's disguised, even though it's not that big. But it's out back, and Jerome can take you there later. I think it's best if you eat first, honey. You're so skinny and your brother looks hungry."

"I'm not skinny!" Markla snapped. "And Tommi's fine." Also, she didn't really want to go 'out back' with Jerome. But she regretted her anger. "I'm sorry, Shala," Markla said in a rush, and now her voice was soft. "I appreciate all the help you're giving us."

Shala smiled. Then she hugged Markla, and it caught Markla off guard, and for an instant she wanted to pull away—but she didn't. *Why does everyone want to hug me?* But it actually felt good.

"It's okay, honey," Shala said, and she ran her fingers through Markla's messy hair. "I know you've been through a lot, and I know you want to find your friend. Don't worry, we're going to help you. And by the way, it's okay to be thin. I wish I was as thin as you."

Tommi stood watching the scene, and he mumbled, "I'm pretty hungry."

"Yeah, me too," Markla said. "Maybe we should eat."

Chapter 16

Burno Blivi scowled. Twenty years in the Sparklan military, and this was how he was being treated? He scratched his cropped black beard and swore. There was a true rebellion going on, and there were all kinds of amazing targets out there, and all kinds of fantastic opportunities to do something really important—and here he was chasing a sixteen-year-old girl. How ridiculous.

He wasn't the pilot of the hover-ship, so he was free to stare with disgust through the cockpit window. They were flying low over the splashy treetops, and the setting sun was a blazing shade of tangerine, and the view was vivid if not downright spectacular. But to him it seemed like a wasteland. It was a gorgeous graveyard for his career.

He ran his fingers through his shaggy dark hair and glanced at his buddy Red Yobo who was piloting the craft.

Red grinned. "Come on, man, get over it," he said. "Look at it this way—this girl's a subversive, and a convicted murderer, and she escaped from prison, and she killed the president's brother, and she shot up a police station. So it's not like we're chasing some sweet little kitten. You're not respecting her. If a 25-year-old guy had committed the same crimes, you'd be totally impressed."

Burno laughed. Yeah, there was some truth there but he swore again and shook his head. "I'm hard to impress," he said. "Besides, even if you're right, who's going to know about it? We're not supposed to be in Narna, right? It's a secret mission, so how are we going to get any credit for doing it?"

"Well, we won't get on the news streams but the top brass will know. That's how it is with lots of missions, right? We're covert, brother. That's what we do."

"Maybe, but we're supposed to be an elite team—all of us." And he jerked a thumb toward the compartment adjacent to the cockpit, where three more commandos sat. "I still think we should be doing something more newsworthy."

"This girl is totally newsworthy! Plus she's armed, and she's got newsworthy friends. We can always say she put up a good fight, right? Either way, we'll get this done quick, and we'll be back to the real stuff."

"I hope so," Burno said. Then he snapped on his GoBug and once again examined an image of the target, and he frowned. Markla Flash was cute and crazy-looking, and he couldn't deny that she resembled his own daughter who was just a couple of years younger. He quickly turned off the GoBug and said, "How much longer?"

"We'll be at their last known location in about ten minutes. Once we find the ship it'll be easy. They can't be too far." Then Red paused and said, "What do you think about the orders to take her alive?"

Burno was checking his gun now, a wicked-looking black rifle. He snapped a new magazine into it, one that held twenty shells, and he shrugged. "We should be able to get her alive but the main thing is to keep it quiet. The president doesn't want any kind of international incident, even with a third-rate country like Narna. These stupid politicians, they want a war but they don't want any noise—which shows how little they know about war. So we've got to keep things very low profile."

"We'll need to track them through the woods. We've got the ground trackers, plus this new stuff—these 'rovers.' I tried them out and they work great."

Burno frowned again. "Yeah, I saw them."

The rovers were like flying eyes. Each one was made up of seven small spheres that flew together in a cluster. They blended images from their sophisticated camera lenses into one three dimensional image that the user would see through use of a

GoBug. They were controlled through a GoBug script, and they could instantly zoom in or dart away from their target. They could sense body heat, and they could see in the dark, and they could scan for a specific person's DNA—and it was difficult for someone on the ground to spot them. The only limitation they currently had was range. They needed to be recharged often.

"You don't like them?" Red said.

"I like them fine for what we're doing. But I'm not crazy about the implications. Every day it seems like there's some new spy machine out there, and it's all controlled by the people in power. Today we use it to catch a fugitive but what's it doing tomorrow? Looking in my kitchen window?"

"Well, what would it see in your kitchen?"

"Nothing. We don't cook much. But that's not the point."

"Right. The target is just ahead."

There was still a good amount of daylight left, and Burno could see the hover-ship on the ground just under the trees. In a few minutes, they were all loading their weapons and leaping out into the woods.

Chapter 17

Tanna stormed into Jorro's apartment and slammed the door behind her.

She'd just completed a LiveDream training session, a special combat dream. She'd fired a pistol, she'd used a knife, and she'd expected the session to relieve her fury. Yet she was still furious.

She hadn't told Jorro she was coming but she needed to talk to someone. She tossed her purse onto the living room chair and noticed a pair of shoes, a jacket, a portable EB, a few empty food containers, and some spilled rice—but no Jorro. Well, he was probably here somewhere. She wasn't really thinking about him, anyway. She was thinking about Rune.

Who did Rune Roko think he was? His father had been the Centurion of Sparkla, and Rune had grown up well-connected and hardly impoverished, so why was he pointing the golden finger at her? They actually had a lot in common.

What a hypocrite, she thought. Next time she'd tell him—and it would be soon. He wasn't going to get away with talking to her like that. And as for Markla Flash, what was the real story between those two? Rune was good-looking, to say the least, and Markla looked like a little savage. How had they possibly gotten together? That girl must be some kind of witch. Certainly, she had evil qualities.

"Jorro!" she called out. "Where are you?"

A scrawny guy with scraggily long hair meandered into the living room. He was Blint, one of Jorro's two roommates.

"Hi, Tanna," he said. "Jorro's in the back room. I think he's busy."

"Oh, yeah?" she said. "And I'm not?" Then she added, "So, what's new with you?"

She had no interest in actually knowing. But she wanted to be polite.

"Not much," he said, and that was a good answer. She walked fast down the hall to a bedroom and banged on the door.

"Jorro? Are you in there?"

She heard some fumbling around. She tried the door but it was locked, and she rattled the doorknob a few times, and then she heard him say something but couldn't make out the words. She pressed her ear to the door but still couldn't quite hear what was going on. But she could swear he was going to "call back later." Then he opened the door.

"Tanna," he said, and he was smiling—but it looked a little forced. "What are you doing here? I thought you were up at Fort Freedom."

"I'm back," she said. "I was bored. There's no kind of night life in a fort. And the daytime is pretty dull, too." She tried to peer around him and look into the room. "Why, are you worried? Do you have another girl in here?"

He laughed and stepped aside. "Yeah, she's in the closet—no, not really. You're the only girl who comes in here, Tanna."

She walked into the room and plopped down on the single bed. She noticed his portable EB was sitting on the nearby desk and his GoBug was sitting beside it. She glanced at the screen but it was blank. "Who were you talking to?" she said.

"Oh, I was just on a stream with some people, talking about the situation with the government."

"Ha. Well, I was just talking to Rune Roko."

"Really," he said, and he paused. "Hey, what's going on with that? How's he doing?"

"How's *he* doing? Why do you care about him? What about me? Why aren't you asking how I'm doing?"

"Oh. I'm sorry. Okay, how are you doing?"

"Terrible! It didn't go well at all."

He shrugged. "Well, what's the big deal? You have MindCore, right? So you can get anything you want from him."

She started to shout again—but stopped.

Yeah, that was true, and she'd told Rune that. But he hadn't seemed to care. He was only thinking about that horrible girl—Markla, Markla, Markla. It was infuriating. But in a way it was… what? Beautiful.

"Jorro, I have to ask you a question. And I want the truth."

She saw a flash of fear in his eyes. But he said, "Sure, Tanna. I always tell you the truth."

"No, for real, Jorro. This is serious."

He paused and then turned the desk chair to face her. He sat down and gave her an intense look.

"Okay," he said. "Go ahead."

Tanna sighed. "If I were running around in the woods with a bunch of people chasing me, would you care?"

He stopped looking scared. Now he looked more confused. "What?" he said. "Are you going into the woods for some reason? Who's after you?"

"No one's after me, you idiot! But we're sending a team of commandos after Markla Flash in Narna, and Rune is totally obsessed with her, and I was just wondering if anyone cares about me that much—I mean besides myself."

He hesitated. "How do you know Markla is in Narna?"

"Because we know! And is that all you have to say? I'm talking about me, and how self-absorbed I am." She threw up her hands. "You're supposed to be telling me I'm not that bad."

"Oh, right. I'm sorry." He rose from the chair and sat down beside her on the bed. He put his arm around her, and it felt nice. But she doubted his sincerity.

"Tanna, you're not that bad."

She turned her head and scowled. "I'm not that bad? Is that the best you can do?" He started to sputter a bit—and then she laughed. "I'm joking, Jorro. I *am* that bad." She looked away from his gaze. "I'm always thinking about me, me, me, and I always want to do some great thing, and I think it's because I want people to notice me—on mindstreams, or even in my own house where my parents never did—and now I'm whining about nothing like a spoiled little rich girl. And I think it makes me unlikable. And here's this guy, Rune, who's crazy about this totally murderous girl, and I was just wondering if anyone could care about me as much as he cares about her."

"I care about you, Tanna, and so do lots of other people. You've got lots of great qualities."

"Yeah, I know. But I have some bad qualities, too. And I'm thinking maybe I need to work on them." He squeezed her a bit, and this time it seemed more honest. Then she said, "I submitted your information, and you should be approved to start working on the team soon."

"Okay, thanks. That was a nice thing you did. So you're nice after all."

She shrugged. "I like you, Jorro. I think this will help me, too, since you can help me catch Markla. But I like the idea of helping you, too."

She noticed him looking at her now in a way he never had before. What was different?

"I appreciate it, Tanna," he said. "I do… But if I'm going to work on the team, what's all this talk about commandos? How would anyone know where Markla went?"

She smiled. "It's a secret but I'll tell you. Whoever helped them smash into the grid was pretty smart but not a total genius. A hover-ship took off right after the raid. It was parked right near there, and we didn't need a scanner for that because people saw it leave. But then it disappeared from the scanners because someone smashed into the system again and made it vanish. But here's the thing—we recovered the data, and we were able to track the flight of the ship into Narna. Technology gives, and technology takes away. That's how it works."

Jorro shifted a bit on the bed. "I see," he said. "I know Narna is a wild place but they do have a government, and Sparkla isn't supposed to be sending commandos there. Couldn't that cause some kind of problem?"

"Yeah, it could, and that's why it's the stupidest idea ever. But it wasn't my idea—it was my dad's. He's sending some kind of 'elite team' in there to get Markla, and they're supposed to keep things very quiet but I'm sure they'll screw it up. And even though I want to see her captured, I don't care if they screw it up because I told him it was a bad idea, and I'd love to say 'I told you so.' "

"Yeah… So, how many commandos are there?"

"I don't know. But like I said, don't tell anyone. They're supposed to get her alive but if she resists they have orders to kill her. So I guess we'll see what happens, and I guess we'll see how Rune reacts."

Jorro took a deep breath and rose from the bed. "Listen, I have a few things to do for school, okay? You didn't tell me you were coming over. Can you give me a few minutes?"

"Sure, I'll wait in the other room." She got up and smiled. "I'll be back."

***

The instant the door was closed, Jorro lunged toward the bottom drawer of his desk. That's where he kept the short wave radio.

In a way, the technology was ancient—but it was augmented by the best modern tech. The unit was larger than the hand-held radios used by 20 Eyes, but it was still something that would fit in his desk, and it packed a lot of power that could both send and receive. The collapsible antenna was small, too—he didn't need the massive antennas of yesteryear.

He was fumbling a bit, getting the antenna up, and punching in the frequency and sending an alert for someone on the other end to pick up. At the same time his head was spinning with Tanna's words. Not the stuff about herself—although he was a bit surprised to discover she was capable of such self-awareness, and did he actually feel a pang of guilt about betraying her? Maybe. But he'd deal with that later. Right now he had to think about how his digital disguise of the hover ship had been thwarted, and about what other things might be discovered about his situation.

He was sweating, no doubt about it. Then someone on the other end picked up.

Chapter 18

Markla looked at Tommi and said, "Don't unpack anything." They were in the bedroom after eating a dinner of vegetable stew. It had been an improvement over the insta-meals in the backpacks.

"But we could put our clothes in these drawers."

Markla shook her head. "No. We might need to move fast, and we don't want to be looking around for our stuff."

Tommi laughed. "Is this something you learned in 20 Eyes?"

"Some of it," she said. "Also, I'm paranoid, but I think it's the best way to be right now. Anyway, it's good to keep an 'escape bag' ready, and these backpacks are our bags. We can live out of them but don't unpack them, okay? And it's good to know where the exits are, too, in any building. Did you notice the back door is right there through the kitchen? And check the windows. Are they big enough? Do they work?" She went over to the window and opened it. "See, we can fit through this, and it opens and closes easily."

Tommi smiled. "Hey, you're really into this. But it's good. I'm ready to go anytime." Then he cocked his head and said, "I thought we came to Narna so no one would be after us. Is someone coming?"

She sighed. "I don't know, Tommi, but we can't be sure. We need to disappear and get new identities. Really, you should probably get away from me at some point."

"I'm not doing that. I'm staying with you and fighting the toads."

She stared at him, and she once again felt the guilt gnawing at her insides. This was exactly the kind of talk that had poisoned Tommi's mind, and it had all come from her. I ruined his life, she thought. And once again she wanted to cry but she didn't.

"Are you okay?" Tommi said. "Are you thinking about the cats again?"

"No."

"Are you thinking about me, and how you ruined my life?"

"Well, yeah."

Tommi threw up his hands. "My life wasn't that great, and you didn't ruin anything! I hated school, and you were right about the toads. Look at all the stuff the government's done. All the lies, and the things they did to mess up our minds. You were right about everything, so stop feeling guilty. I want to fight them, so let me do it, okay?"

Markla was quiet—and suddenly she felt a little better. After all, she'd wanted the same thing when she was his age, and there was some truth to his words, and she hadn't joined 20 Eyes only because her home life was a shambles of abuse and neglect. Sure, she'd been looking to belong to a new family, and Dru and Stono and 20 Eyes had betrayed her—but a lot of what they'd said had been true. And she'd wanted to fight.

"Why don't you play your flute?" Tommi said. "We could use a little music around here."

Markla gave a negative shake of her head. There was too much on her mind—but wait, maybe not. Suddenly, the idea of playing the flute appealed to her. She started to retrieve the instrument from her backpack but then she heard a beeping sound from somewhere in the house, and then Jerome was running into the room.

"We're getting a message," he said. "Out back in the radio shack. Why don't you two come and see what's happening?"

Markla and Tommi glanced at each other and ran after him, out of the house and into another building not far from the back door. It was a weather-worn shack of wood crammed with electronic equipment. Markla vaguely wondered how the equipment was powered. In fact, the cabin was in a shady area, and had no solar tiles on the roof.

"Power crystals," Jerome said, and he pointed upward. "They're in the trees—way at the top. There's a whole network of them, and you can see them in the daytime if you look. The trees kind of sparkle. But they gather the sunlight and store it in batteries. We have plenty of power."

Then he turned his attention back to the beeping sound, and he picked up a microphone.

"Gort!" he said. "This is Jerome. What's happening?"

"Jerome, did you find Markla and her brother?"

'Yeah, they're here with me now." Jerome smiled and offered the mic to Markla, who snatched it from his hand.

"Gort, what's going on with Rune?" she said. "What do you know?"

"Rune is fine, Markla, but I've got bad news. There are some people after you. The government sent a team of commandos into Narna."

"What?" Markla felt her heart start to pound. "I thought they couldn't track us! I thought they couldn't send people here."

"Yeah. Well, like you said, nothing ever goes perfectly—and you're right, they're not supposed to send people there. But the government of Sparkla does things they're not supposed to do, right? And isn't that why we're fighting them in the first place?"

"Where are they? How close?"

"I don't know. But they might be pretty close."

"So where are we supposed to go?"

It was difficult for her not to shout. But she was trying.

"Markla, stay calm and listen. Rune is in Fort Freedom, up in northern Sparkla. It's an isolated place but he's okay. No one's done him any harm."

"How do you know?" she snapped. "And yeah, maybe nothing's happened to him—yet. But what can we do? *What can I do?*"

"You can go south and find Stoke. You know him, right? He's commanding the fight for Free Sparkla, and he's set up a base in Sparkla, right across the river from Narna, and he might be able to help you. At the very least, he can get the commandos off your back."

Stoke—the name was familiar, and now she recalled meeting him right after the destruction of the Dream Center. He was the tall dark-skinned guy who'd offered her and Rune a ride, and she'd stupidly said no.

"Okay," she said, because she didn't have any better ideas. "Maybe we'll leave now."

"It's dark, and I doubt they'll start chasing you until morning. But listen—don't use the GoBug. There just aren't a lot of GoBugs in your area, and even if they don't know it's you on there, they can tell when there's one turned on, and they might guess it's you. So don't use it right now… Keep monitoring the radio, channel 8. The small radios you have might not be big enough to transmit to me, but you'll still be able to receive a signal, and I'll send you news if I can—but right now I've got to go. We'll talk again soon. Good luck to both of you. "

The transmission stopped.

Markla stared at the mic in her hand. She said, "Tommi, get ready to leave."

"Right," Tommi said. "I'll get everything together." He sounded excited, and then he ran back toward the house.

Jerome shook his head. "I agree with Gort, they won't find you tonight. It would be best if you stayed here."

Then he took a step toward her—and Markla felt her heart skip a beat. Because now she was alone in the shack with this dirty-looking guy, and he'd been giving her looks all day.

He stopped moving. "Markla, I want to give you something."

I'm sure you do, she thought, and she also thought about

the dagger strapped to her belt. She wanted to stop being so violent—but if he reached for her she was going to stab him. No threats, speeches, or hesitation. She was just going to do it because that's what worked best.

She moved her hand a bit closer to the weapon. But he didn't reach for her. Instead, he reached to his left, over to the wall where there were all kinds of tools hanging on hooks. On one rusty nail there was a string of beads, and he plucked the beads from the wall and handed them to her.

He smiled at her like he'd been smiling at her all day. "I have a daughter," he said. "And you remind me of her. She's about ten years older than you, and she's living up north with her boyfriend. But this necklace was hers, and she called it a good luck charm, and I've kept it here all these years. I want you to have it."

Markla narrowed her eyes. Was this really all he wanted? She got the instinctive feeling it was true. She reached out slowly and took it, and she saw they weren't actually beads but small stones—and even a few tiny seashells. It was totally her style.

"Thanks," she said. "I'll wear it."

"You're welcome. You're a nice girl but you and your brother are going to need some luck."

"Yeah, I know," she said, and now she laughed and thought about how paranoid she was becoming. "What's going to happen to you, Jerome, if they come here?"

He shrugged. "They have no jurisdiction here so they need to be careful. But you'll be gone before they get here, and we'll tell them we never saw you."

Markla's mind was racing. Suddenly, she had an idea.

"Maybe we won't leave yet," she said. "Do you have any explosives?"

Chapter 19

Rune was in another cell, and as usual it was dim and dismal with only a few necessities. He considered how maybe one day he'd start a mindstream where he reviewed different places of incarceration but so far they were all pretty much the same. People who designed prison cells had no imagination.

He thought about his father, and he wondered if spirits really existed, and if so, could Blog see what he was doing? What would Blog say to him? He'd tell me to be a warrior, Rune thought. *But am I that kind of person, like he was? And like Markla is now?*

Suddenly, the door clanged open, and two big goons entered. They chained his hands and feet and then led him to another room—and as soon as he walked through the door he felt a wave of panic.

He'd seen this kind of room before. There was a chair with restraints and a console for MindCore and he considered trying to run. But since his feet were chained, he wouldn't get far. He was pushed into the chair and strapped in place. Then the guards left, and his heart was pounding—and then Diana Drogo entered the room. Trailing behind her were two guys in lab coats.

Instantly, he felt a spark of hope. Diana had been a great friend to him and Markla at the Dream Center. But now she was just staring at him, and she wasn't speaking, and his mind started whirling. Maybe she was angry that Markla had killed Aldo. Maybe she was working with the government.

She turned to the two men behind her and said, "You can leave now."

"We're supposed to observe."

"I don't care what you're supposed to do. Get out and close the door. I don't need you here."

They shrugged, and they left, and Diana ran toward Rune.

"Rune, are you all right?" she said, and her voice cracked with emotion. "We don't have much time, and we need to talk."

Instantly, Rune felt a rush of relief. "There's no hurry," he said. "It doesn't look like I'm going anywhere. Where's Markla? Is she okay?"

"They haven't captured her," Diana said, and he saw a look of sympathy in her eyes. "Rune, I know you love that girl, but you need to prepare yourself for the worst. There are some pretty nasty people chasing her, and things might not go her way."

"They won't catch her. I know it."

Diana sighed. "I suppose it's good to have hope, but listen—Tanna wants to put you into MindCore this morning. She went to Liberta yesterday but she's coming back. She won't be here for a few hours, but when she gets here I'm supposed to show her how MindCore works. But we don't want it to work."

Rune gave a short laugh. "Yeah, you're right about that. Can you destroy it?"

"No. That would be too obvious, and besides, they'd just build another one. Gin put me in charge of all this stuff, and he asked me to go through Aldo's notes, and so I started thinking, what if MindCore had a weakness? What if there was a way to shield your mind and keep it from penetrating your memories?"

"Is there?"

"No, not at all. It can totally get into your memories no matter what you do."

"So that's not good. Can we fake it?"

She hesitated. "That's an interesting idea. How would we do that?"

Rune's mind was turning fast. "I don't know… How about if you tell Tanna...that the machine...has a problem when someone fills their mind with strong emotions. The emotions form a wall it can't penetrate! And then you write a script that makes it look like it happens. It would be a simple script, really… You just need to trigger it with a secret phrase—something like 'Tanna is a toad.' So when they connect me to MindCore, I'll think that phrase, and the script will switch on and show a blank screen."

Her eyes got bright, something Rune rarely saw from her. "That could work!" she said. "I can do that—and you're right, that's an easy script. But I'm using a different phrase. 'I'm in love'—that's the phrase. I like it better." Then she laughed, and then she frowned. "But how will I explain that you know about this flaw?"

"That's a good question," Rune said. "How about…you tell them I stole Aldo's notes about MindCore when I smashed into the dreambank and stole the camera footage of Markla's original crime—but I couldn't use those notes at the time because they were encrypted. Since then I got someone to smash through the encryption, and now I'm using this information to block the machine. Maybe you should add some fake information to the notes in his dreambank, too—and then encrypt them, just in case anyone checks the story. Say Aldo gave you the code to the encryption. Would he do that?"

"Yeah, maybe," she said. "He seemed to like me quite a bit." For an instant she looked sad again, but Rune smiled and quickly said, "This is going to be great, Diana. This is amazing."

She hesitated again. "Rune, while I was trying to find a weakness in MindCore, I saw some of the images in Aldo's dreambank, including some memories of you and Markla together." Then her face got red and she quickly added, "I also saw how she saved you from that 20 Eyes assassin. Seriously, that girl's a little scary—but she's brave, too. Anyway, I was just looking for something that could help. I'm sorry… I don't want you to feel like you've been violated."

"It's okay," he said. He was proud of his memories involving Markla.

"I also want you to know that no one else will be seeing those memories because I deleted them. Aldo's the only one who knew they were there, so I doubt anyone will notice they're gone. I also eliminated most of the ones he brought in from Markla—although not the ones in the LiveDream he created because they'd notice that. But the main thing is that we don't want any new ones coming in because then they'll know everything, right?"

Right, that's true, Rune thought. If they accessed his mind they'd see all his conversations with Markla—and they'd see his memory of Diana helping them to escape from the Dream Center. In fact, they'd see the very conversation they were having now. So Diana had good reason to help them. But he didn't think this was the reason she was doing it.

She likes me, he thought. *She might even like Markla, too.* Then he had another thought.

"Hey, where are we, Diana?"

"We're in Fort Freedom—way north of the capitol. I'm living here temporarily, and Tanna is also going to be getting a suite so she doesn't need to keep flying back and forth. Her father doesn't want her commuting so much due to the war… I'm sure her suite will be different than yours—and mine." Then Diana's eyebrows went up as a message came through on her GoBug. "Tanna will be here in a few hours," she said. "So I'll go write that script. Just remember—'I'm in love.' That's the phrase."

Rune grinned. He'd be ready.

Chapter 20

Markla glanced over at Tommi. He was lying on his stomach beside her, on top of the dry leaves, staring through a pair of vision magnifiers at the abandoned cabin they'd first seen while walking toward Shala and Jerome's place. It was a cute little cabin, and they were planning to destroy it.

The sun was rising, and he seemed excited. Markla understood his excitement but she also knew it was because he didn't know any better. And she hated that he was going to find out.

"When do you think they'll get here?" he said. His voice was charged with energy.

"Soon. But remember, we're not going to fight them. That's not the plan."

"Yeah, I know. But at least I can take a few shots." And he tapped the rifle by his side.

Jerome had given it to him. Markla had despised the idea, but then again she had a pistol with her, and it was loaded with exploding cartridges—and really, there was nothing wrong with Tommi protecting himself. But she suspected he wanted to do more.

She swore and said, "Tommi, did you hear me? If you get hurt I'll never forgive myself. So don't do anything unless I say, okay? Besides, do you even know how to shoot that thing?"

"I played sim games with Brude and Gianna. I'm a good shot."

"Yeah, well, this isn't a sim game in a LiveDream. People shoot back at you here—for real. Trust me, it changes everything."

He frowned and then looked at another device lying nearby. "Okay, I won't do anything. Is that thing really going to work? It's a thousand years old."

"It's not as old as it looks, and as long as they don't find the wire, we'll be fine."

She picked up the object of discussion, and she couldn't deny that she liked the weight of it. It was a real hunk of metal, unlike many electronic devices—but that was because it wasn't electronic. It was a relic from another time.

Most explosive devices were either detonated remotely by a signal sent to a receiver or by an electronic timer incorporated into the device. But this was Narna, and Jerome didn't have anything that fancy—he'd only had this old-style "blaster" and some sticks of dynamite. The dynamite would be detonated by a pin connected to a wire that ran to the blaster. She would twist the handle at the top, generating a charge that would cause all the damage.

Markla was no engineer but she understood the technology. She also understood damage.

"Will the whole cabin blow up?" Tommi said.

"Yeah, definitely. We used dynamite in 20 Eyes, and Jerome gave me seven sticks. That cabin is going to be gone."

"So, we're going to kill these guys?"

She hesitated. "*We* aren't doing anything. I'm going to do it, and you're going to watch—and they might not get killed. It depends."

"I don't care!" he blurted. "We're warriors, Markla. I was just wondering."

But she could tell that he did care, and she liked that about him. He's sweeter than me, she thought. She also realized that she actually cared, too, but she didn't say it. Instead, she said, "These people will kill us, or they'll capture us and torture us." And she recalled how she'd been tortured, and she pictured the same thing being done to Tommi, and now she didn't care what happened to these toads, and she wanted to destroy them.

Am a warrior? she thought. *And even if I am, does that make anything I do okay?* Maybe, maybe not—but she was still going to do it. It had to be done.

She squirmed a bit and tried to get more comfortable. "Are you ready with the camera? Because that might be more important than blowing up the cabin—but we still want to blow it up. At the very least, we need to slow these people down."

"Yeah, I've got it." He held up a shiny device in his hand that he'd gotten from Jerome. It had been one of Jerome's more modern pieces of equipment.

"Good. That's the only thing you'll be shooting with." Then she grabbed the vision magnifiers from Tommi's hand and returned her focus to the cabin.

Her main concern was the wire. The blaster needed a wire in order to send the charge, and luckily Jerome had lots of wire. Unfortunately, the wire needed to be hidden, and she'd spent a good part of the night carefully stapling it to the side of the cabin and threading it through a window and then into the cabin. The wire was brown, so it matched pretty well, but it still made her nervous.

Inside the cabin was just one room, and in the room was a table. Markla had pushed the table up against the wall, right under the window where the wire came in. Taped underneath the table was the dynamite. There was also a certain amount of junk in the cabin, and that was fine—it was nothing Jerome and Shala wanted, and it would help to distract from the bomb. Markla had found a box of toys in there, things for kids, including stuffed animals. She'd put a few stuffed animals on the table, and they seemed to be looking out the window. But they were really there to cover the wire. She'd laughed at the sight of a big stuffed toad. She'd enjoyed using that one.

Then she'd gone back outside to deal with the wire leading away from the cabin. She'd buried it under the soil, leaves, and pine needles, and now here she was lying in the woods. They weren't as far away as she'd like to be but she was far enough.

They were just inside the forest, on top of a small hill and across from a clearing around the building.

"Hey, Markla, what if they don't go into the cabin?"

"They'll go in," Markla said, and she took a deep breath—*because they better go in*. But she figured they'd have tracking devices, and she was pretty sure they'd be arriving from the same direction she'd originally approached from, and so this morning she'd backtracked a bit, and had re-followed that same path—except this time she'd gone into the cabin. She'd done this just as the sun was coming over the horizon, and her scent would be nice and fresh.

Her scent was on the ground and inside the cabin. It was all over the dynamite.

Using the magnifiers, Markla could almost make out the table through the window—but not quite.

She hadn't slept much, and she was nervous. But she didn't want to show Tommy how she felt. She needed to be strong. She needed to fake it.

Stay calm, she thought. *Record images of these Sparklans in Narna, blow them up, and run.* That was the plan.

Jerome and Shala had wanted to help but Markla had insisted they did not. No one else was getting hurt because of her. It was bad enough that Tommi was a fugitive and Rune had been captured, so she'd asked them to please, please, please, head north and stay away for a few days. These commandos weren't after them, and they weren't supposed to be in Narna at all—so if they came to their empty cabin Markla guessed they'd just pass by and continue their pursuit. There was no need for Jerome and Shala to risk themselves in a potential battle.

Suddenly, she saw movement in the vision magnifiers.

"Tommi, get ready. They're here."

Chapter 21

Rune kept his face blank as Tanna came striding into the room. She was wearing black tights and a loose gray top, and once again he couldn't deny this girl was sexy. He also noticed she glanced at her reflection in a dark window behind the MindCore console. Obviously, she had to look her best when she tortured someone.

She greeted Diana with a polite hello and then smiled at Rune. But it wasn't a warm smile. It was the same smug smile from their last meeting. He was guessing she'd been born with it.

"So, Rune, I have some bad news for you. Markla Flash is dead."

What? Rune felt the room spin. It couldn't be! He felt sick, like he wanted to vomit—and then Tanna laughed.

"I'm joking!" she said. Then she laughed a little more. "I was going to let you believe she was dead but I decided not to do it, okay?" Then she paused and added, "Because I'm not that mean. I'm really not."

Rune composed himself, trying to hide his anger, as well as his overwhelming sense of relief.

"Yeah, but that was a mean thing to do," he drawled. "And my mom always said, 'what you do is who you are'."

She hesitated. "It was a joke. And it only lasted a few seconds." She crossed her arms and glared a bit. "How about this: I promise I won't do it again until she's actually dead, okay? And that'll be soon. So prepare yourself."

Rune looked away and said nothing. Tanna was quiet, too, but then she spoke in a loud voice. "Diana, is MindCore ready to go?"

"Yes," Diana said. "But there might be an issue." Then she told Tanna the lie about Aldo's stolen notes and the potential weakness of the device. Tanna didn't seem concerned.

"I guess we'll see," Tanna said. "But if this doesn't work, don't worry. I have a backup plan."

A backup plan? Rune's heart skipped a beat at her words. Her confidence made him a bit uneasy—because he knew she was capable of something devious. But then again she seemed like someone who was always confident, even when falling off a cliff. Hopefully, she'd be falling soon.

Tanna placed a GoBug behind Rune's ear. "Remember these, Rune? I'm sure you had one before you started spending so much time as a fugitive."

"I'm a happy fugitive. We have a good cause. What do you have?"

"I have plenty."

"Yeah, and that's your problem, Tanna. You have too much."

She took a deep breath but didn't reply. Instead she returned to the console. "Okay, Diana, so how do I work this thing? It looks like a standard dream station." Then she glanced at Rune. "I studied dream writing in school, so this should be easy. I went to Kinly."

Kinly? Now it was Rune's turn to look smug. Kinly was known to be a school for people with big bank accounts and small imaginations—but he said nothing. He just smirked a bit.

"It's a good place!" she snapped.

"I didn't say anything," Rune said with a smile. "I'm sure you learned…something."

Her eyes flashed. "Rune, you have a lot of nerve. You keep acting like I'm some spoiled little girl. Your father was the Centurion of Sparkla. You had all the same stuff I had. You could've gone to Kinly, too."

"Yeah, but I didn't. My dad thought private schools would 'make me soft'. And maybe he was right."

"Do I seem soft?"

He laughed. "No. I'll admit, you're not soft. You're cold and hard like a block of ice. So maybe he just wanted to keep me away from the wrong kind of girls."

She paused like she'd been slapped. "You're joking, right? Have I ever stabbed anyone to death? Have I ever cut anyone's throat? I've never hurt anyone—ever! You keep acting like you're superior to me but you were a LiveDream writer and a GoBug fanatic with plenty of nice stuff in your house. You're nothing like Markla and her gang of lowlifes."

"Markla's not a lowlife. You don't know her at all. Go ahead and push the button."

"Fine! I will!" Then Tanna turned to Diana. "So, uh, what button do I push?"

Diana seemed amused by their conversation but she didn't comment. Instead she just touched something on the console. "It works like a standard dream station," she said. "First, you connect to the GoBug—like this. Accessing his memories will happen by simply switching this on."

Diana gave Rune a quick look, and Rune understood—and he also experienced that feeling he'd had before, like a spider was starting to crawl into his brain. He quickly thought of the secret phrase.

I'm in love, he thought. *I'm in love!*

He saw the two women staring at the screen, and he heard Tanna say, "What's this? It's just a red screen. Shouldn't we be seeing his memories here?"

Diana crinkled her forehead. "Yeah, we should be seeing memories but it looks like it's blocked. This is exactly what the notes described, and Aldo had no way to solve it. Rune seems to be preventing it from getting into his mind."

"How? By filling his mind with emotions?"

"Yes. Aldo said any kind of strong emotion seemed to be

capable of blocking MindCore. Hate, fear, rage—anything that the subject concentrates in his or her mind."

Tanna swore and looked at Rune. "You're filling your mind with hateful thoughts about me, aren't you?"

Rune laughed. "My mind is filled with good things, and none of it's about you. You're not someone I would think about."

He studied her reaction. She was angry, no doubt—but she didn't lash out. Instead, she cocked her head, almost like she was curious.

"What are you thinking about?" she said.

"I'm thinking about Markla, and how much I like her. I'm filling my mind with those feelings."

"Love? Are you kidding me? You're blocking MindCore with love?"

"Yeah, I guess. So love beats hate. It wouldn't be the first time."

Tanna was silent for quite a few seconds now, like she was pondering.

Finally, she turned to Diana. "Turn it off," she said. Then she looked back at Rune. "We need to know who smashed into the grid, Rune. My father has other people he can send to get the information from you—people you'd say are better qualified than me, and he *will* send them if I fail. Their methods won't be as accurate as a MindCore probe but they'll be a lot more painful. So think about that." She hesitated once again, and then said, "Hey, I don't really want to hurt you, okay? I don't even want to hurt Markla—even though she'd kill me in a second, right?"

She turned to Diana. "Thanks for your help. If you find out anything useful, just send me a message… Rune, get some sleep, and do some thinking. I'll see you tomorrow."

She turned and left the room.

Chapter 22

Markla felt that fear in the pit of her stomach—the kind she'd felt since she was six years old. Someone was coming to hurt her, and what could she do?

She took a few deep breaths and felt the cold metal blaster in her hand. Those days are over, she thought. *And I can do a lot.*

She glanced at Tommi, who seemed even more excited than before. She guessed he thought a massive firefight would be an adventure but she knew it would only be terrifying, and it was important that it didn't happen—because neither of them were trained for that kind of thing. This was strictly a 'hit and run' operation and maybe a little more, if her plan for the camera worked out. But that was only a possibility. The main thing they had to do was strike fast and run hard.

"What do you see?" Tommi whispered.

She squinted into the vision magnifiers. There they were—a group of five walking behind an H-dog tracker. The H-dog hovered in the air like an oversized black bug sprouting a bunch of hairy-looking antennas.

"They're coming," she said, and she pointed. "See? Get the camera."

"Right." He pointed the device and adjusted the zoom lens. They were in a good spot to film these Sparklan invaders.

The commando team was just coming out of the woods but then they stopped moving. They'd obviously spotted the cabin. The H-dog continued advancing as the team spread out with their weapons up and ready. They were sprinting around the cabin now, surrounding it. But they stayed back, near the trees. When the H-dog reached the door of the cabin it stopped. Someone barked a few orders but Markla couldn't hear what they were saying.

"They seem pretty serious," Markla whispered, and for an instant she considered abandoning the whole plan and running into the woods, and she imagined how relieved she would feel—but then what? These people would still be after her, and the fear would continue. It was best to settle this now.

There was the sound of a shot as the H-dog fired something at the door, and the door exploded from its hinges and fell. Then the H-dog went inside while the attack team positioned one person around each corner of the cabin. Markla assumed that one of them was using a GoBug to examine the camera images the H-dog was sending, and she held her breath. Would the H-dog find the dynamite? She knew it could scan for devices with a power supply—but the dynamite had no power. The blaster she had with her was really a tiny hand-cranked generator but until she turned the handle there was no electricity. It was just a chunk of metal.

"What's happening?" Tommi whispered.

"Shh!" she said. "Just wait. They're checking it out."

Two members of the team moved fast toward the front door and rushed inside. The other two were still outside, scanning the woods, and Markla figured they were wearing high-powered InfoGoggles.

"Stay down," she hissed at Tommi.

"Okay," he said. "But I need to capture this, right?" He was still recording with the camera, and now Markla looked at him and realized how shiny the camera was, and how the sunlight was reflecting from its surface.

"No!" she said. "Put it away!"

Suddenly, something was buzzing overhead. In the back of her mind, she recalled Rune mentioning "rovers." But now it was too late. Someone yelled and Markla reached for the blaster—but before she could turn the crank there was an explosion.

She was hurled backwards—and now she couldn't see! An exploding shell had struck nearby and thrown dirt and debris into her eyes. She heard Tommi scream and then he was shooting.

"No!" she said. "No!"

A salvo of shots ripped through the air. She groped around, searching for the blaster—*where was it?* She wiped her eyes and started crawling fast. She heard more yelling in the distance, and another shell burst in front of her, and now she heard gunfire coming from somewhere else. Someone was yanking her backwards and she saw it was Shala.

"Get back, Markla! Get back!"

"Where's Tommi?"

"I'm right here!"

He dropped to the ground beside her. They were just below the top of the hill while gunfire pummeled the ground on the other side.

"What about the blaster?" she said.

"The wire was hit! It's ripped in two."

Jerome was farther off to the left, back in the trees at the top of the hill, and he was firing at the cabin. Markla was blinking furiously. Her eyes were still teary but now she could see.

"The dynamite," she said. "We can still blow it up!"

She tossed Tommi her handgun and grabbed his rifle. Then she started running toward Jerome, away from the area being obliterated. She dove to the ground before reaching the trees and crawled forward just enough to poke her head over the hill. She aimed her vision magnifiers at the cabin and saw two commandos outside, crouched along the corners of the cabin. Another fighter was shooting from the window inside, and Markla swore—had they moved the table? Yeah, but hopefully not much. She was a lousy shot but that was her target. Then she checked the rifle and cursed again because there were only three exploding shells left in the magazine. How many shots had Tommi fired? And did he have more? She'd forgotten to ask and now there was no time. She took aim and started shooting.

The first shot wasn't too close but it burst when it hit the ground and gave her a good idea of how to adjust her aim. The second shot hit the side of the cabin and exploded, but it did minimal damage against the heavy logs. The third shot smashed through the window and sailed into the room.

There was a flash of fire and a deafening roar—and then pieces of wood were falling from the sky.

Markla instinctively covered her head as debris rained down. Luckily, she was a bit too far away to get hit by any of it. She looked around frantically for Tommi and didn't see him.

"Tommi! Where are you?"

"I'm okay!" he said, and then he was once again plopping down beside her. She sighed with relief. He seemed to be shaken but at least he wasn't hurt. He smiled and said, "Guess what? I recorded all of that." Then he turned the camera back on and continued recording.

"That's great," she said. "But we need to get out of here. We've got enough footage."

"Are they all dead?"

"I don't know," she said, and she squirmed a bit because the idea did make her uncomfortable. Then she scanned the air with jittery eyes to see if the rovers were still around. She didn't see them now but they were hard to spot. She guessed they were controlled through a GoBug, and hopefully whoever had been controlling them was out of commission.

She stared back at the smoke and fire below and wondered if anyone could've survived. As the smoke cleared a bit, she saw that a few pieces of the cabin walls were still standing. Apparently, the heavy logs had helped direct much of the energy from the explosion upward, and the roof had been blown off. Still, the walls and the inside of the cabin were mostly destroyed. She was sure the people who'd been inside were never coming out again, but what about the people outside?

She frowned just as Tommi pointed and said, "Look! Somebody's moving."

Her heart started pounding. It was a woman, and she was crawling on the ground, obviously injured. Then a guy was there, coming from the other side of the wreckage. He was limping a bit but he seemed more or less intact. He knelt down next to the injured woman, and Markla felt a little sick. Part of her wanted to start shooting again—and the other part wanted to help them.

Tommi was still using the camera but he glanced at Markla and spoke in a shaky voice.

"Shouldn't we be shooting at them, Markla?"

"No!" she said, and she was surprised by the sureness of her answer. "We probably couldn't hit them, anyway—and then they'd start shooting back. Hopefully, they'll just return to Sparkla. Especially after you give Jerome the camera."

"Yeah, that's true," Tommi said, and she could tell he was relieved at the idea of ending the fight. Then she looked up and saw Jerome. He was standing behind them, along with Shala.

"You need to get out of here quick," Jerome said. "Give me the camera and go. You've still got the small radio, right? I'll let you know what happens. But go find Stoke. He's the one you need. At the very least, he'll be able to protect you in case they send someone else—but I doubt they will, and I don't think you'll have much more trouble from this group. They need to evacuate the wounded, and that looks like all of them."

Markla stood up. She glanced at Tommi, who was quiet. She knew he was trying to be brave but he was pale and shaken up. She knew what she had to do. "I'm going alone," she said. "Shala, Jerome, can Tommi stay with you?"

"Of course!" Shala said. "In fact, that might be a good plan."

"What?" Tommi said. "No way!"

Jerome shook his head. "She's right, Tommi. They're really looking for Markla. She can go south and find Stoke. In time, you can meet up again."

Tommi's face turned red. "Markla, I'm coming with you. I can help."

"No," Markla said. "You almost got killed, and if you stay with me it's going to happen again. Besides, you can be more helpful here. You can use the radio, and you can get information, and we can talk. Don't worry, you're not running from a fight—this is a plan. Not every fight is about explosions and guns."

He hesitated. "I want to be a warrior like you."

"I'm not a warrior, Tommi. Do you know how I felt when the shooting started? Terrified. I'm scared and terrified more often than you know, and I don't want you to be that way, too."

He was about to respond but she didn't let him. Instead, she hugged him hard. "Sh!" she said. "Don't argue with me. I'll see you again. Help Jerome and Shala. You can fight the toads from here."

He looked stunned. "I'll miss you, Markla," he said.

She stepped back and smiled. "I'll miss you, too—but it won't be forever."

She said goodbye to Jerome and Shala, and then she went into the woods where they'd stashed their backpacks. She took out her compass and headed south.

Chapter 23

Rune smiled as Tanna exited the MindCore room. He often expected things to work out but today things had gone even better than expected. Totally stellar, in fact.

Diana didn't smile because she rarely did but there was a glint in her eye. Rune wanted to thank her—and to maybe help him work on an escape plan. But two big goons entered the room and he guessed it would be a bad idea to start discussing his exit strategy.

In a few minutes he was back in his stone cell, lying on a stiff metal bed and staring at the ceiling. He wasn't smiling now. There was only one thought running through his mind—where was Markla? *What's happening to her right now?* He didn't even have a window in this cell. He wanted to look up at the stars and know they were seeing the same sky. Corny? Yeah, but he still liked the idea.

He lost track of time. A small metal flap at the bottom of the cell door slid open and someone slipped a plate of cold rice and beans into the room. More time went by, and he found himself struggling not to fidget. He started banging on the mattress, like he was playing his drums back in the shed, and then he was thinking of Markla again and their moments together in the shed—and why had she never told him she played the flute? Someday they would play together—someday. And then he thought about his father, and what would Blog think of him now, and then he started doing pushups, and he felt like pounding on the door but he didn't. He sat back down on the bed and told himself to stay strong.

Tanna's words were still resonating in his head. It never occurred to him to cooperate—but even if he did, he didn't know Gort's identity. Maybe he'd just explain all that. But no, because he wasn't going to give them even a hint of cooperation—not after what they'd done to Markla and her family. No way.

Finally, there was a clanging noise and the door opened. Once again two big goons were standing there.

"Hi," Rune said, and he smiled. "So, are we going on a field trip? Why don't you give me my flyboard and I'll catch up with you later."

No reaction. Having a sense of humor was not a prerequisite for being a goon.

They took him back to the MindCore room. At the sight of the chair and the restraints he started to sweat. His eyes scanned the room for Diana—where was she? She wasn't here. But Tanna was sitting behind the console with a GoBug behind her ear, and now Rune felt a flash of fear. Had they discovered Diana's script? Had they arrested her, and was he about to have memories vacuumed from his mind?

Tanna smiled at him. "Hi, Rune. Have you thought about what I said? Are you ready to cooperate?"

"No. Where's Markla—and don't tell me she's dead."

Tanna gave a snort. "She's definitely not dead. But she's getting herself into more trouble, that's for sure."

What? Tanna knew something! Rune's ears perked up.

"What's happening?" he said. "Why is she in more trouble?"

Tanna gave him a look of obvious disgust. "I don't know what's going on with Markla, okay? You need to think about me, not her."

"You? Why should I think about you?"

"Because I just loaded a nightmare script into this dreambank," she said with a smirk. "And that's where you're going. Maybe you can block MindCore but you can't block a standard GoBug nightmare, right?" She looked extra smug now. "I wrote this nightmare myself—even though I only went to Kinly. So let me know what you think of it. And then let me know how willing you are to go through a lot more of them because we're going to give you nightmares until you start talking."

Rune gave her a hard stare. "Isn't that against the law?" he said. "This is exactly what Markla was fighting about—a government that lies to people and doesn't follow its own laws."

Tanna shook her head. "Rune, I am so tired of hearing about Markla Flash. I don't know what she was fighting for but I know she was part of a violent group that killed people, and I know that she murdered a few people herself, and I never did anything like that. Not even close."

"She had her reasons. You're just cruel."

"I am not cruel!"

Rune was a bit surprised at how upset she seemed. But he didn't care.

She turned to one of the goons and said, "Put him in the chair."

Rune tried to look unconcerned as he was strapped in place—but he felt his stomach quaking. Would Tanna's nightmare be any good? It didn't need to be sophisticated to cause serious agony.

Tanna came toward him. She put her hand on his shoulder as she placed the GoBug behind his ear. Rune recoiled a bit at her touch, and she frowned. She paused for a second to look at him, and her hand lingered longer than necessary. But then she quickly returned to the console.

"Are you ready?" she said.

"Sure. Go ahead."

Everything went black.

***

Rune rubbed his eyes and looked around. He was in a desert.

The sun was high in the sky, glaring down, and there wasn't a hint of a cloud. He could see to the horizon in every direction, and all he could see was sand. There were no hills or dunes—it was perfectly flat, and the flatness was disturbing. The endless open space was a thing he could feel.

He knew it wasn't real, but LiveDream nightmares looked and felt real, especially if the dream writer had some skill. And now he felt a blast of heat. It hit him like a wall, and it was smothering.

It was like he'd been tossed into an oven. It only took a few seconds for sweat to start dripping down his back and neck. In this dream he was wearing a light cotton shirt and a pair of khaki pants but the shirt had short sleeves and did little to protect him from the blazing sun. He once again scanned the desert, and now in the distance he saw a shimmering object. It looked like a palm tree.

Rune guessed if he started walking toward that tree he would never get any closer. But he started walking anyway to take his mind off the relentless temperature, and he wondered what else would happen. He started scanning the scene, expecting all kinds of monsters to rise up out of the sand. He imagined snakes with razor-sharp teeth and giant worms and starving vultures circling up above. Meanwhile, it kept getting hotter and hotter. The heat was unbearable, and sweat started dripping into his eyes. He tried to wipe it away but it was no use. His eyes started burning from the sweat, and his vision was getting blurry. What was the temperature? It felt like he was on fire.

The skin on his arms started turning red. He clapped his hands to his face, and he felt his flesh burning—and now he realized there were no monsters coming. This was the nightmare, a horrific dose of heat, and he had to admit the simplicity of it was impressive. It also felt totally real so maybe Tanna had learned a few things after all.

He could barely walk now. He was staggering. Everything was getting hazy, and he felt sick inside, and he realized he was being roasted alive. He looked at his arms, and he sucked in his breath. The skin was getting dark, like charred meat. But could he lapse into an unconscious state and be free of this? No, because the dream wasn't going to allow it. The LiveDream could take him to a point of extreme agony and leave him there indefinitely. In this way it was so much more effective than more primitive forms of torture.

He tumbled to the burning sand. He tried to shield his head from the fiery sun but there was no way. It was staring down like a furious eye. His breathing was labored now, and he knew he was beyond the point where a person would normally die. But he had no such luxury coming. Then he heard a voice. It was Tanna's.

Rune swore. So this was a guided dream.

There were two kinds of LiveDreams—guided and unguided. An unguided dream was simply a shell that was loaded into the dreamer's imagination without any contact from someone outside the dream. But in a guided dream, someone could make changes to the script as it happened, and someone could communicate with the dreamer.

"Rune, can you hear me?"

"No, Tanna. I don't hear a thing."

She gave a short laugh. "How do you like my nightmare?"

Rune hated her nightmare, and he didn't like her much, either. He wanted to say something that would annoy her as much as possible but he was in too much pain to think.

"You're just like your uncle," he said. "It's nothing to be proud of."

There was a long moment of silence, and Rune felt the heat increase. His stomach was churning with nausea, and he was gasping for air—his lungs were like cooked meat now, and they could hardly function. He'd never felt such agony. But he was still conscious. Would this never end?

Maybe I'll tell her something, he thought. *I'll lie to her.*

But his tongue felt thick. His mouth struggled to form words. And his mind flashed to something he remembered about Markla, how she'd been interrogated when she'd been arrested for murder—and how she'd said nothing. Not a word.

Rune grimaced with determination. I'm not saying anything, he thought. *Not even a lie!*

"You're a monster, Tanna," he whispered. "A monster."

There was no reply. But the heat continued, on and on, and it seemed like an eternity, and Rune gritted his teeth and thought about the moment it would stop—and suddenly it did.

The desert vanished.

It took an instant for his mind to process the change. But gradually, a wave of relief washed over him. For an instant he actually felt cold, but then a second later it felt like he'd stepped into paradise. He looked around, and his skin was no longer burned. He took a few deep breaths and his breathing was fine, and he was sitting on a beach with his toes in the cool sand. A warm breeze was blowing in from an ocean that was smooth like oil, and the water was a tranquil shade of blue that was just a bit darker than the endless sky. Also, Tanna was sitting beside him. He recoiled a bit but she showed no expression.

She wasn't right up against him. She was an arm length away, wearing her usual black leggings with a loose grayish top. Her ponytail was untied, and her black air was blowing in the breeze. She looked sexy in a viper-like way but Rune felt like punching her. But he didn't. This was only a dream.

Once again, she smiled at him. "I thought it would be nicer if we talked here, Rune, instead of in that boring room. So, do I know how to write a nightmare?"

Rune hesitated, and then he scoffed. "That wasn't a night-mare," he said. "A nightmare is more than just painful. It's scary. That was a torture script."

"Is that so?" she said, and her tone got sharp. "You think your nightmares are better than mine? Like the one you wrote for Markla? I watched it, and it was scary—but it was pretty painful, too. It was a 'torture script', so don't go lecturing me. You really hurt her."

"Once!" Rune said, and now it was his turn to be angry. "I only did it once! And I was trying to help her."

"Right, sure. You keep acting like you're so much better than me, Rune, but you're not. You're a lot like me."

"I'm nothing like you!"

She laughed. "Really? So why are you so mad? Because it's true."

"No, it isn't! I wrote one nightmare and I felt terrible about it. That's the difference between us. I hated making someone suffer."

"And you think I liked it just now?"

He stared into her eyes. "You seem pretty pleased with yourself. But then you always seem that way."

She turned away from his gaze and looked at the sea. "I didn't like watching you suffer," she said. "It bothered me."

"Is that so? Then why did you let it go on so long?"

"I need to get information. I told you that."

"So you're going to do it again, right?"

She shrugged. "If I don't, someone else will. Look, I'm doing you a favor. Even just talking to you like this—I'm trying to help you."

"You've never helped anyone in your life—except yourself."

"You don't know me!" she snapped. "You have a lot of nerve always judging me."

"I judge what I see."

"You haven't seen much! There's nothing I can do about your situation."

"Would you do something if you could?"

She hesitated. "Maybe," she said.

Her answer surprised Rune because it actually sounded sincere. She was fidgeting a bit now.

She sighed. "Rune, I didn't write that nightmare. I lied. I got it from a government dreambank. I've never written a nightmare in my life. I wasn't the worst dream writer at Kinly but I wasn't too good, either. I had no interest, and I never studied. I got decent grades because I paid someone else to write the LiveDreams for me."

"So you cheated?"

"Yeah, I cheated. Because I didn't want to fail, because my father always thought I was so smart and motivated, and I just couldn't let him think he was wrong."

"Why are you telling me this?"

"I don't know," she said, and then she was quiet. "Maybe I should end the dream."

Suddenly, she vanished. Then everything else vanished, and Rune was back in the MindCore room, strapped to the chair, and Tanna was sitting behind the console. He glanced around and saw they were alone. He stared at her, and she met his gaze but said nothing. Then two big goons came into the room and Tanna said, "We're done here."

She left without another word.

Chapter 24

Markla was tramping through the dense forest.

This was untamed land, and there were no paths. The ground was covered with rocks, leaves, broken branches, and fallen trees, and she wondered about the last time a person had walked in her footsteps. It might have been centuries. In a way, the thought appealed to her—but in another way, it was scary.

She glanced at her radio. Why were there no messages? Well, it had only been a few hours. Then she thought about wolves, and how she'd never seen one in Sparkla. But there might be some here.

She stopped for a moment and rummaged through her backpack for the third time. She had about twenty-five insta-meals, small packets of nutrient-loaded food. If she rationed them, they'd last her about a week. She was familiar with foraging, just enough to know that she wasn't very good at it. As far as meat was concerned, Markla wasn't a hunter, and she never ate meat. She loved animals, and that had been her main inspiration for becoming vegetarian—but it wasn't the only reason. Sharli had been a meat eater, and Markla loved to be different from Sharli.

And where is Sharli now? Marka thought. Was she supposed to care? She didn't, and she never would, and did this make her a horrible person? Well, if it did, she'd live with it. It was one more thing to toss onto her pile of infractions. All the kids at school had said she was crazy, and maybe they'd been right.

Still no messages on the radio. Didn't Tommi want to call her?

School—it had all been so recent, yet now it seemed like ancient history. What were those kids doing and thinking while this war was raging? She'd never had any kind of bond with them. Rune was the only one who'd actually seemed to like her. And look where it got him, she thought.

Look where it got him!

Still no messages! She stared at her compass. Okay, she had no idea where she was standing but she was definitely heading south, and that was the main thing. From what she knew, Narna had a minuscule population. But there were towns, and one larger town called Camarillo that almost passed for a city, although she was nowhere near that place. Narna also had a government, and they were members of the World Council, and what else? She'd never paid much attention in that stupid class. According to Jerome, Stoke had set up a base in Sparkla right near the border with Narna. She guessed Stoke had a sizable fighting force, and she hated the government of Sparkla because they were all such toads, but it wasn't the main thought on her mind. She just wanted to find Rune and set him free.

She picked up the radio again—and now it crackled to life. It was Tommi.

"Markla, are you there? Markla?"

"Yeah!" she said and realized she was shouting. "I'm here! What's happening? Are you all right?"

"I'm fine. Jerome said not to talk long. Are you okay? I miss you."

"I'm fine. I miss you, too!"

"Be careful. And come back soon. Here's Jerome—he wants to talk."

"Markla, are you okay?" Jerome said. "A hover-ship came and airlifted the commando team out of here but not all of them left."

"What?" Markla tried to keep her voice from shaking. "So what does that mean?"

"Hey, we might be able to help you."

"No! Do not come after me! I'll be okay."

"Markla, I'm thinking these people might leave soon. I'll be sending that recording to our friends, and there's a good chance the commandos will go. But in the meantime watch out for those 'rover things.' They had them at the cabin, and they might still have them now. They can use those to find you fast."

Rovers—right. Those little flying peas. Markla wondered how far they could travel from their launch point.

Tommi said, "I'm on the hill, looking down with the magnifiers. They collected their stuff. They don't have much, just a few big guns. The H-dog tracker was destroyed but they have those rovers in a box. I think they're charging them with some kind of portable generator."

"How many people?"

"Two guys. That woman was airlifted out, and I think the other two were dead." Tommi paused, and Markla felt a wave of guilt, but then Tommi continued in a quick voice. "The two guys are packing up everything now, and they're walking into the forest. And hey, they just put those rovers in the air."

"Are you sure?" Markla felt her pulse quicken.

"Yeah, I'm sure. They've got some kind of handheld tracker, and they have the rovers and a couple of guns, and a couple of big backpacks—and that's it. But they're on the move."

"Tommi, don't do anything stupid. I'm the one they're after so don't make yourself a target."

"He won't," Jerome said. "Don't worry."

"Okay. I'll see you soon. Don't risk calling me again unless it's an emergency."

They switched off the radio. Everything was quiet.

Markla took a deep breath and looked around. Now she heard birds chirping and leaves rustling but it still seemed quiet—and suddenly the feeling of isolation was overwhelming. She was filled with an urge to scream. She wanted someone to hear her.

She took another breath, and she thought about Rune, and how he had no idea where she was—and if she died, would he ever know what had happened to her? Well, he'd be the last person in her thoughts when she closed her eyes for the final time. Even if he'd never know it.

I've got to stay calm, she thought. She tightened the straps on her backpack and started walking again.

Chapter 25

Tanna stared at Jorro's chiseled face. He wasn't actually in front of her, of course. He was in his apartment while she was in the capitol building waiting to see her father. But Jorro's image was here on a GoBug call, and he had that gorgeous braided hair and a jawline strong like a piece of steel. Why wasn't she feeling it?

"Jorro, I'm going to a meeting with my father."

"Oh, yeah? Is it about all the stuff on the mindstreams? The commando fiasco?"

The mindstreams were filled with images of Sparklan commandos illegally "invading" Narna. It was a very secret mission that the whole world knew about.

"I guess," Tanna said. She forced herself to smile.

"You don't need to tell me about it—even though I'm on your team now."

"Yeah, that's true. But I keep wondering, Jorro, are you really on my team?"

He shook his head. "What are you talking about? Is this about the job, or is it about you being lost in the woods again?"

"No, I'm out of the woods," she said. Then she sighed. "I'm sorry. Maybe I just think too much."

"You do. You know I care about you. Why can't you trust me?"

"I said I was sorry."

But she wasn't. Despite his best efforts, he seemed distracted lately, and she liked to have a guy's full attention.

"Okay, fine," he said with a smile. "So, what's happening with Rune and Markla? I heard there's a problem with MindCore. What's going to happen with the commando team? Are they going after Markla again?"

"I don't know the new plan yet, but I'll let you know. I'll tell you all about Markla, Markla, Markla."

"Tanna, why do you keep talking like this? Are you still annoyed at me? I'm just asking."

"I'm not annoyed!" she snapped. Then she disconnected the call and thought about how annoyed she was—*Markla, Markla, Markla.* How had that little barbarian gotten Rune to love her so much? He seemed like a nice guy, and he was totally hot, and he'd handled that torture script like a real stud. He deserved better.

She strolled into her father's office. Immediately, she was struggling to not roll her eyes.

Strom was standing there, looking like a clown in his Centurion uniform and his dust-mop mustache. Gin was sitting behind his huge desk, wearing a short sleeve shirt that was obviously inappropriate for the cool weather—but of course he wanted to show off his bulging muscles, and Tanna knew he hated to see the end of summer. Well, it was fall now and winter was coming.

Gin grinned. "Here's my beautiful girl," he said.

Tanna gave him a dirty look. "I'm smart, too—not just beautiful."

"True," Gin said. Then he picked up a protein shake and took a sip. "I heard about the problem with MindCore. Does Diana think we can fix it? It could be a great tool to use on anyone we capture—not just Rune Roko. But it would be great to test it on him because he might know who smashed into the grid."

"Yeah, that's true," Tanna said. She also thought his mind was probably filled with images of him and Markla together, and why did that make her feel a little sick? "Diana can't fix it," Tanna said. "It's a design flaw. Uncle Aldo couldn't fix it, either."

"Are you serious? I'm sure it needs more development, that's all. I'll talk to Diana."

"I already talked to her."

"I know. But I think I need to talk to her."

"You don't think she'll listen to me?"

Gin put down his drink. "Tanna, you need to calm down. I'm letting you be part of this because you've got some good ideas. But you can't always have everything your way."

She frowned. "You're right, and I'm sorry. I'll keep working on Rune without MindCore. I think he'll start talking soon."

"Good. Now go to my private mindstream and we'll start the real meeting."

Tanna activated the GoBug behind her ear and selected the stream.

So who was this person in front of her? He had a beard, and she usually didn't like that on a guy but on this guy it looked pretty sharp. He was handsome in a rugged kind of way, and he seemed to be surrounded by trees. He was probably a member of that inept commando team, and so he was also an idiot. But at least he was a good-looking idiot.

Gin was scowling now which was rare. "Burno, do you realize we have an international incident here? I told you to keep things quiet, and is there anything less quiet than blowing up half the forest? All the mindstreams are filled with images of your raid! And the government of Narna has filed a protest with the World Council, saying that we're invading their country. Meanwhile, your elite team got wiped out by a sixteen-year-old girl! So what's the story?"

Burno shrugged. "She was lucky."

There was a moment of silence, and then Gin's face got red. "That's your excuse? She was lucky?"

"Yeah. It happens."

Burno seemed not the least bit apologetic, and Tanna couldn't deny she was impressed.

"Can you still get her?" Strom said.

Gin waved his hand in disgust. "What are you talking about?

We airlifted the injured and the dead out of there. Burno needs to come back. We need a new plan."

"Oh," Strom said. "I was just thinking we could say the mindstreams aren't real. We could say they're phony LiveDreams like the ones we always create."

Gin shook his head. "Maybe that could help," he said. "But the government of Narna is involved, and there was a hover-ship, and there are dead bodies, and this girl and her friends really beat us to the punch by distributing an actual recording. So other countries won't believe our phony LiveDreams because they already think this is real… Also, most of our streaming stations are still down. It's the private stations and underground ones that are still operating. We've destroyed some of them but there are too many. So we need to forget about this plan."

"Okay," Strom said with a shrug.

"No!" Burno said, and his voice boomed like a cannon. "Two people in my team are dead. I'm going after her."

Gin gave a snort. "Did you hear anything I just said?"

"Yeah, but I don't care. I'm staying and so is Red. In fact, we're after her right now, and no one will know we're here. We'll get it done."

Gin hesitated, and Tanna heard herself say, "Burno is right! Markla Flash killed Uncle Aldo. She has to die."

Had she just said that? Yes, she had, and she actually felt herself shaking a bit because she hadn't intended to say anything like that. But now it was done.

"Die?" Gin said. "I thought we wanted her alive so we could put her in MindCore."

"Why?" Tanna said. "She doesn't know any more than anyone else in 20 Eyes, and we have lots of other prisoners. Besides, people in the Free Sparkla group know who she is and all the mindstreams are turning her into some kind of hero. Getting rid of her would be a morale blow to them."

Well, I think so, Tanna thought. *Or maybe it will just make her a martyr—but whatever.* Either way, she would be out of the picture.

Gin mulled it over. "Okay," he said. "Burno, you can stay. But seriously, you need to do it quietly. No more explosions, and no more dead bodies—except for hers or maybe yours. Also, you're going to have minimal help from us and minimal contact. In fact, as of now you are officially a 'rogue solder,' do you understand? You're on your own."

Burno smiled. "That's all I ever wanted to be. Don't worry, we'll complete the mission."

He disconnected from the call. Gin dismissed Strom from the room and turned his attention to Tanna, who felt her body get tense. She knew he was going to ask something difficult.

"Tanna, why do you want Markla Flash dead?"

"What do you mean?" she sputtered. "I just told you why."

"Yeah, I know, and your reasons are solid, plus a few others you left out. But there are also good reasons to not kill her… She might know who smashed into the grid, right? And if she dies she might become a martyr."

Tanna squirmed a bit. "Right."

Once again he picked up his protein drink. "As a leader, clear thinking is important, so always consider all the possibilities and why you're doing them. Sure, you want revenge for Aldo, but don't let emotions cloud your judgement."

She gave a snort. "I've got no emotions for Uncle Aldo."

"You don't?" he said, and he raised his eyebrows. "Then why are you suddenly so fired-up about killing this girl? She never did anything to you."

Tanna's head was spinning, and she groped for some words. "Okay, maybe I do care about Uncle Aldo," she said. "Yeah, I guess I do."

"Okay," Gin said with a smile. "That makes perfect sense. But remember what I told you."

"Sure. I'll remember it."

She left her father's office. As she walked down the hall, her whole body felt jittery. But then Gin's words started fading away, and she felt better. She had to get back to Fort Freedom. She'd be talking to Rune soon.

Chapter 26

Markla had to watch where she was stepping. She kept looking down at the leaves and pine needles and broken branches. But she also found herself constantly looking up, scanning the sky.

Those rovers were a problem. She didn't know much about them—only what Rune had told her, and she thought about him now, and she felt that guilt in the pit of her stomach. But she also felt ecstatic thinking about him because she just did. Rune was great with technology, and if he were here he'd give these rovers some thought, and he'd guess how they worked and maybe come up with a plan. But he wasn't here, and she was alone. Well, she could do her own thinking.

She'd seen the rovers. They'd come right down in front of her face, and she recalled they made a buzzing sound when they were up close, like bees. So, how did they work? They were probably tiny flying cameras controlled by a GoBug script that functioned with thought commands. They travelled in clusters, maybe so they could blend different viewpoints and create some kind of panoramic "toad vision," and they probably could spot a target from the air and then zoom in close to make a positive identification. Maybe they could be controlled manually but she guessed they could also be configured to automatically search for certain things, and they were most likely zipping around the forest right now searching for her. She recalled Rune saying they could scan for DNA—and the toads had her DNA on file because they had everyone's DNA on file. If the rovers actually had that capability, they'd find her quick.

I need to destroy them, she thought. *Otherwise, they'll find me and keep finding me, and I'll have no chance.*

She stopped walking and ripped open her knapsack. She tore through it, looking for anything that might give her an idea—and she found an all-purpose *gathering bag*, and suddenly she had a plan. It was a long shot but she was used to long shots. They were all she ever had.

She took out the bag and unfolded it. It looked like a large brown paper bag, and it was, but it was coated with a special material. It was meant for gathering food but it was also water-proof, and it could be shaped to resemble a lightweight bucket and be used to collect rainwater. She had one at home, in her mom's broken-down house that now seemed so far away—but this one had come from the camping supplies Rune's mother had given them, and it was top quality. Obviously, Blog had been a guy who went for the good stuff.

I actually think he liked me, she thought. Maybe he'd just had a thing for crazy girls. She laughed. *Like father, like son.*

According to Tommy's information, the rovers were on their way—and that was the real trick, knowing when they were coming. She'd only been walking about three hours but her pursuers knew that, and they'd still launched the rovers, so they must have a decent range. Also, they must be fast. She had to hurry.

She started searching the area, looking for the perfect spot, and what about right here? It was one of many places where a tree had fallen, but this fallen tree was lying on top of another fallen tree, and there was some space between the top tree and the ground. She reached into her backpack again and found an extra pair of pants and a shirt, and she started stuffing them both with leaves. When she was done she had a crude-looking dummy, and she shoved it partly under the fallen tree. The dummy had no head, but it looked like the head was under the top tree while the body was sticking out.

Did it really look like she'd been crushed by a tree? No, not upon any real inspection—but it was something the toad machines might check out. They might get down close to it for further examination, and that's all she wanted.

Next she collected a pile of leaves, and she considered how her small size came in handy because she didn't need too many. She put the leaves right beside the dummy and then got down into the pile. She ended up lying on her back with her face fairly well covered except for her eyes. It was a little difficult to cover her head and still be able to see and hear, but she did the best she could. Meanwhile, the bag was in her hands, folded on top of her stomach.

For this to work, she needed several things to go her way. First, the rovers needed to actually have the capability to scan for DNA over a wide area—otherwise, they might not find her until she'd turned into fertilizer. Second, she needed the rovers to signal the operator when they had a DNA match, and the operator would need to zoom in for a closer look. But Markla thought it was human nature to do this; seeing is believing. If she were the operator, she would definitely zoom in.

She didn't necessarily need the dummy, but it would allow her to pounce on the rovers more easily if they were busy looking at something other than her face. After all, the dummy was right beside her DNA, and it looked more like a human than a pile of leaves.

Now she just had to wait and hope she was alert when they arrived. This is going to be some battle, she thought. *The world's greatest technology versus a crazy girl with a paper bag.*

How much time went by? Markla wasn't sure. She was tired, and she wondered if she'd fall asleep—but no, it was obvious she was going to be awake for a while. But she didn't have to wait long. Twenty minutes later she heard them. They were buzzing right above her.

Her heart started pounding, and now she saw them. They

were a bit larger than she'd remembered, and they hovered over her body, and then her head—and then they moved to her right, just out of sight. They were examining the dummy.

Markla pounced. They were right over the dummy's chest, and she sprung up out of the leaves, and she didn't hesitate—she saw them and slammed the bag down.

And she had them! They were buzzing inside the bag, and the bag was against the dummy's chest. She closed the bag and twisted it shut, but wait—she'd missed one! It was buzzing around her head like an angry bug. She shot out her hand and grabbed it, and now she felt it buzzing against her palm but she kept her hand closed tight. She carefully untwisted the bag and forced it inside. She closed the bag once again.

She searched the air with her eyes. Were there any more of them? She saw nothing and breathed a sigh of relief. Then she laughed. *Give that crazy girl a prize!*

She took the bag and ran to a large rock nearby that was wide and flat. Then she picked up another rock and smoothed out the bag. It wasn't hard to feel the little lumps inside, and she started smashing them while they were still in there, one at a time. They broke easily, and this didn't surprise her. When she was done, it was quiet. Nothing was buzzing now, and she laughed again. But then she leaped to her feet.

She might have destroyed the rovers but now they knew exactly where she was. She had to get moving.

Chapter 27

Rune was dreaming but it wasn't a LiveDream. It was a real dream.

He was indoors, stumbling around in the dark. Suddenly there was a bit of light, and then a few shapes and shadows appeared. He stretched out his hands and touched a wall. Then he bumped into a chair and a table, and he realized he was in the kitchen of his parent's house in Sparkla.

"Mom, are you here?"

No one answered.

"Mom, where are you?"

There was still no sound. And then someone grabbed him from behind.

Rune's heart jumped. A thick arm was wrapped around his throat, and someone had him in a chokehold. He clutched at the arm and tried to pry it loose, and he tried to twist and fight but it was useless. And then he was tossed to the floor.

He looked up, and a light appeared. The room was still dim but now a small dot was shining from the ceiling, and he saw his father standing there. He was wearing his Centurion uniform and staring down, and he looked tall as a tree.

"Dad," Rune said. "I thought you were dead."

Blog gave a grim laugh. "I am dead," he said. "But I'm still inside your head."

"Why did you attack me?"

"It was a test."

Rune frowned. "And I failed, right?"

"No. Not yet."

"Oh, good," Rune said, and he felt a wave of relief. "What do I need to do?"

"I can't tell you that, Rune. There are different ways."

Rune shook his head and stood up—and now he saw Markla sitting at the kitchen table. She was in the shadows but he could clearly see her face and her wild hair tumbling down.

"Markla!" he said. "Are you all right? I've been so worried about you."

She didn't smile. Instead, she touched something on the table, and Rune saw it was a 20 Eyes dagger. Why did she always have one of those with her? She tapped the bottom end, and it spun around.

"You don't need to worry about me," she said. "I'll be okay."

Rune looked at his father. "I don't know if I'm like you!" he blurted. Then he looked back at Markla and said, "I don't know if I'm like you, either."

Blog gave another laugh, and he vanished. Markla just stared at him with a blank expression. But she said nothing, and he could feel his heart beating. What was she thinking? More than anything, he wanted to know. And then he woke up.

He sat up fast and opened his eyes. He gripped the thin mattress and stared into the shadows. Then he took a deep breath as reality closed in around him. He was still in his cell. He sighed and plopped back down on the bed. But he couldn't get back to sleep.

Chapter 28

Jorro was sitting behind the desk in his cluttered bedroom, fumbling around with his portable EB. He was trying to use his GoBug to scan the streams for information but he was anxious and fidgeting a lot. He hadn't slept well but he still didn't feel like sleeping, and then Tanna was in the room.

She waltzed in, looking sexy as always—but also looking distracted. This was a new thing for her. She plopped down on the unmade bed. She not only seemed distracted but also dejected. This was another novelty.

"Hi," she said, and then she was quiet.

"Hi, Tanna. How come you never tell me when you're coming over?"

She shrugged. "I didn't know I was coming. I just ended up here."

"Well, that's fine. So, what's wrong? You seem unhappy."

"I'm not unhappy," she said with a scowl. "How's everything going with the project? Have you figured out how they smashed into the grid? I made that your job. I had them put another guy on something else so you could do it, and you haven't done anything."

He shifted a bit on his chair, and then he got up and sat beside her on the bed.

"I'm making progress," he said as he put his arm around her. "Things are moving along. But now I need a break." He kissed her on the neck, and she pulled away.

"I'm not in the mood."

Jorro hesitated. Now here was something really new because Tanna was always in the mood. In fact, it was usually her idea. Either way, he had to get her mind off the project he wasn't actually working on.

"Tanna, tell me what's wrong. Talk to me… How are things going with your interrogation of Rune?"

Now that got a reaction. She perked right up and started talking fast.

"MindCore still doesn't work so I've got this new idea to win him over and recruit him and I think it's a great plan—but it's hard to say what's happening." She paused for a moment and stared at the wall. "I can't tell what Rune's thinking."

"I see. Well, what about Markla? Is he thinking about her?"

"Yeah, exactly! He's always thinking about that little maniac—but there are still two commandos after her, and don't tell anyone! It's a secret. They're going to kill her."

"What? I thought they wanted her alive."

"No. My father changed the plan. They're going to kill her, and I think when she dies Rune will see she was always just a lot trouble, and maybe he'll decide to work with us. Not at first, I know, but eventually I think he'll come around. What do you think? That sounds like a good plan, doesn't it? It could happen, right?"

Jorro didn't think so. After the last fiasco with the commandos and all the stuff on the mindstreams it probably wasn't a brilliant strategy—and also, Rune was never going to go for Tanna.

Jorro wasn't blind, and he could see what was going on, and wasn't there a psychological term for a prisoner who falls in love with her captor? Of course this was the reverse but there was probably a name for that, too.

Jorro almost laughed, and was he a little insulted? Yeah, but not much because he wasn't in love with Tanna. She was nice to look at, and she was really fun sometimes, but so were lots of girls. Tanna was someone who would do anything to succeed, and she could be devious and heartless, too—and those things didn't appeal to him.

Tanna smiled. "I'm going back to the fort soon. Wish me luck."

He smiled back at her. "Good luck, Tanna."

He couldn't wait for her to leave. He really needed to send a message.

Chapter 29

Markla unzipped the SuperSeal sleeping bag and peered out. She saw spooky dark shapes and heard leaves rustling in the cool breeze. Naturally, she hadn't slept much, but she knew it was early morning. She was used to waking up early and guessed the first light would be in about half an hour. She didn't want to hike through the forest until there was some light but she could get up now, eat something, and be ready. Markla loved the early morning when the world seemed calm.

From her 20 Eyes training, she knew the Sparklan military used night vision goggles, and that meant her enemies could stay up later and start moving sooner. She'd had a three-hour head start on these people, and she was confident she was just as fast as they were, if not faster—but if they'd kept going an extra hour or so last night and started about an hour earlier this morning they would catch her soon enough. They no longer had the H-dog or the rovers but they probably still had some handheld trackers. So she had to get moving.

She'd camped near a stream, and now she purified some water, filled her canteen and washed herself. She brushed her hair, too, and tried to remove some of the knots and tangles. She didn't go crazy with the brush—she was just killing time until the sun came up. Fashion didn't matter much out here, and really, she didn't think it mattered anywhere else. Then she ate an insta-meal and started walking at a brisk pace. She quickly came to a spot where there was almost a path—not quite, but almost, and now the walking was easier. But this also made her suspicious, and she found herself glancing around with anxious eyes.

Were there people out here? She'd heard stories about the people who lived in the woods. The kids at school had often joked that she was one of them due to her clothes and messy hair, and she laughed at the thought because here she was in the woods, looking exactly like her unfashionable self. Maybe they'd been right.

They hadn't been right about much else. Janna, that toad queen, and Dimitri, that fool who liked Janna—they were all puppets of the toad government, even if they didn't know it. But where were they now? Probably sleeping in comfortable beds. She was still looking around, wondering about any local inhabitants—when she almost stepped in a hole.

Whoah! What was this?

It was right on the path in front of her. It was roughly square, about as wide as it was deep, and she guessed it was about three times her height to the bottom. She stopped right on the edge and looked down.

There was no way it had been made by nature. Someone had dug this hole for a reason. Was it meant to trap an animal—or maybe a human? It would definitely be hard to escape from this trap. She noticed a lot of branches nearby, but the hole was uncovered. If it was a trap, it didn't look like it had been used for a long time. It could be years old, she thought. Anyway, that's what she was hoping.

She shuddered and started paying even more attention to the ground. She found a solid branch and turned it into a walking stick. She could use it to prod the ground if she suspected any hidden traps. The morning light started filtering down through the leaves above, and it was a sunny day. She was glad about the lack of rain. Then she got a beep on her radio. Someone was broadcasting on the channel she was monitoring.

She yanked the radio from her belt. "Hello!" she blurted, and then she heard Jerome's voice.

"Markla! Can you hear me?" There was a lot of static.

"Yeah! I can hear."

"We just got a message a few minutes ago. Our man in the capitol smashed into a communication… It's not an official message—it's private. One of the guys chasing you is using a GoBug to communicate with someone at home, and it sounds like he thinks they're close to your location."

"What?" She caught her breath. "How close?"

"Not sure, but he said, 'We should be done real soon, and then we'll be heading home so have lunch ready.' So I'd say pretty close."

Stay calm, Markla thought. *Stay calm!*

"How are they tracking me?" she said. "Do you know?"

"No. We only have that one message. But I'm guessing they've got those handheld trackers. When they went into the woods, they didn't have anything big with them."

"Does Tommi know?"

"I haven't told him."

"Don't! I don't want him to worry. I have to go."

"Good luck, Markla."

"Thanks."

She swore, and her instincts told her to run, but could she really outrun them? Not forever. She needed a new strategy, and then she had one—but it was risky.

Situation normal.

She started scrambling, searching for branches. There were plenty around but she needed one big enough to span that hole, and she found plenty of them. Most of them were quite thin but she found a long heavy one and dragged it into place a bit to the right of the center. She created a crude frame of sorts and covered it up with leaves, and then she grabbed more leaves and scattered them around near the trap so it didn't look too obvious. She worked fast.

She leaped back a few steps and looked at her creation. Okay, it wasn't perfect. Someone might see this spot and get suspicious—or they might not happen to step on it at all. But what if they were chasing her? What if they were running fast right behind her and she ran over it first? Of course, that would be the risky part, along with avoiding gunfire from trained sharpshooters. But she couldn't outfight them, no way. Those trackers would tell them when they were close to her, so she couldn't ambush them, and she wasn't a good shot. So this was it.

She took a deep breath. Now for the second part of the plan. She had to let them find her but not shoot her.

I need to be as light as possible, she thought. So she stashed the backpack near a tree that wasn't too far from the hole. There was no point in carrying her survival gear because if this didn't work she'd be dead, anyway. But she still had her dagger and the walking stick, and she set off to find her pursuers.

She doubted it would be too difficult. If they were using trackers, they'd be following the exact path she'd taken to get here so she just needed to retrace her steps. But she needed the right spot to initiate things—and she found a spot that looked reasonable. It was at the top of an incline, and it wasn't too far from the hole, and there was an unusually nice line of sight through the trees so she'd see them coming before they saw her. She got down behind a wide oak.

She tried to control all the raging thoughts in her head. But she was sweating even though it was a cool morning, and the thoughts were coming like a storm.

If they had time to get a clear shot, they'd probably kill her. They needed to start chasing her, and they needed to be following right behind. But they couldn't get so close that they'd catch her, and they were probably fast, so she had to get to the hole quick—and hey, maybe this spot was too far away. Yeah, I need to move, she thought. But then she heard some sounds, like footsteps in a forest. She peered out from behind the tree and saw them.

Her heart skipped a beat. They weren't too far away, not really, and there were two of them, dressed mostly in black with light body armor and stylish combat boots. Of course, their fashion sense didn't matter—it was their equipment that interested her. What did they have? Definitely a handheld tracker that was probably scanning her scent. Unlike the H-dog, the handheld devices couldn't move on their own and fire darts and bullets but they were still pretty accurate. Now they were stopping—and now they were pointing right at her.

She swore and leaped to her feet and started running.

As she raced down the incline, she knew they couldn't see her, and that meant they couldn't shoot her. But they were running hard, and she looked back and saw they were behind her now and gaining. She weaved through the trees and headed for the path. She heard a shot—one of them was firing a pistol. This was bad because he'd probably stopped in order to do that, and she needed them to stay together. Well, at least he'd missed.

What a stupid plan, she thought. *I'm not going to make it! They're going to kill me before I reach the trap.*

But here it was, and she was going to run right over it. That big branch was just off center, and she was small, and she'd only need one step. She heard it crack as her foot landed, and the branch bent a bit—but she hit the ground on the other side of the hole, and then she raced for the trees, and there was another shot, and she stumbled and fell.

For an instant, it felt like she couldn't breathe. *Am I hit? Am I dead?*

No, she wasn't. She scrambled to her feet and looked back, and they were about thirty paces away, running hard. The one guy was holding a pistol, and the other guy had a rifle in his hands, and they were staring right at her and grinning. Then there was a snapping sound, like a branch breaking, followed by a crashing noise and some shouting—and they were down in the hole.

They shouted again and one of them swore. Markla's heart leaped and she pumped her fist in the air.

"Yes!" she thought. But then she told herself to stay cool. *Don't get cocky!*

She raced to her backpack and grabbed the gun. Then she took a moment to gather her thoughts.

She didn't get too close to the hole because she knew they could shoot her from down there. But she moved near enough to the lip and stood on her tiptoes. She held the gun up at a high angle and fired a few shots. She hit the top inside wall of the hole but that was fine. She heard them curse and dive for the ground. That was okay, too. She just wanted them to know she was armed, and that they couldn't get out of the hole without getting killed. She dropped down on her stomach and started shouting.

"Hey, you in the hole! Can you hear me?"

There was a moment of silence. Then there was more swearing and someone said, "Yeah, we hear you." It wasn't a happy voice but most people aren't happy when they're down in a hole.

"Good," she said. "I have a gun, and I have three grenades. Now you're going to do what I say or I toss a grenade in there, do you understand? I've set the timer for two seconds. Answer me or I'm throwing it in!"

"Yes! We hear you!"

"Good! If I wanted to kill you, you'd already be dead. I just want you to stop following me. Now throw the rifles up out of the hole. Toss them far because I'm not coming too close. If you don't toss them far enough I'm throwing a grenade."

She heard even more swearing and then some arguing.

"You had your chance!" she said.

"Wait! Wait!"

Two rifles came flying up out of the hole. They didn't land too far from the edge because it wasn't really possible, but they were far enough.

"Good. Now the pistols! You've each got one. Also, the extra ammunition—you've got two seconds!"

"Listen, honey—"

"Do I sound like your honey?" She was shrieking now—deliberately. She wanted them to think she was crazy. *"Forget it! It was nice knowing you!"*

"No!" they shouted. "Wait!"

Two pistols landed near the rifles.

"Good," she said, and took a deep breath. "Now the night vision goggles—two pairs. And the two trackers. I know you each have one."

The goggles and trackers landed near the other stuff.

Markla smiled a bit. This was going better than expected—but then again, there was no way they could just leap out of that hole, and if she tossed a grenade in there they were definitely dead. Of course, she didn't have a grenade, but how could they know that? It was quite possible she had one, and wasn't she the sort of person who'd use it? She'd blown up a cabin, and she'd murdered Aldo as well as two others. Her sociopathic reputation was coming in handy this morning.

What else? she thought.

"Your GoBugs," she said. "Throw them up!"

"What? How will we get back home?"

"How many times do I have to tell you not to talk? I've been nice so far, but I've had it!"

"Wait! No!"

Two GoBugs came up out of the hole.

"Great. Now toss up your grenades."

There was a pause. "We don't have any grenades," someone said.

"I know you do! I saw them!"

This was a lie. There was no reason for them to have grenades while chasing a girl through the woods. But she knew these commando types were deeply in love with their weapons, so it didn't hurt to ask—and what do you know? They tossed up a belt with five grenades.

Now Markla laughed out loud. How hilarious was this?

She put down the gun and picked up her walking stick. She stayed on her stomach and used the stick to sweep all the booty together into a pile. She was still careful because who knew what else they had? These kind of guys were always armed to the teeth; they were always pounding on their chests like a bunch of apes. Well, the apes were losing, at least today.

The first thing she picked up was the grenade belt. She studied it for a few quick seconds and made sure none of the timers were set, and they weren't. Should she toss one into the hole? No, she wasn't going to do it. But she needed to make sure they wouldn't follow her. That was the main thing.

"Your clothes," she said. "Take them off and toss them up."

"What? Are you kidding me?"

They sounded incredulous, and it amazed her that they were still talking back. They really have no respect for me, she thought, but she laughed again. She didn't care.

"Not everything," she said. "Just your boots, your shirts, and your pants—and the body armor. Hey, you wanted to put a bullet in my head, and now you're getting mad when I ask for a pair of boots? You were grinning about it, too—grinning! You should be kissing my feet, you stupid toads! You know what? I'm tired of your back talk. I'm going to kill you with your own bombs."

"No! Please! I have a wife and a daughter!"

"Really?" she said. "And how many people have you murdered, and how many of them had a wife and a daughter? Did you ever think about that? You're mean and you're cruel, and I'd be doing the world a favor."

"No!" they both shouted. "Look, we'll go back to Sparkla!" Then the family guy said, "I promise! Please, don't do it. Please."

She laughed again, and then she hesitated. Let them sweat, she thought. She picked up a grenade and set the timer for two seconds. *Let them think I'm pushing the button on top of this bomb.* And her thumb hovered over the button—and she almost pressed it. She almost threw it into the hole. It made perfect sense to do it. But was it necessary? No, not really—and most of all, when she told Rune this story someday, she didn't want that kind of ending. Not this time.

"Well, what's happening?" she said. "I don't see any clothes up here. I'm giving you one last chance."

The clothes came flying up out of the hole—boots, pants, shirts, and the body armor.

Once again, she used the stick to sweep them closer to her, and then she stared at the pile. How was she going to carry all this stuff? She really needed to rent a trailer.

She slung the rifles over her back, and she put the pistols, ammo, GoBugs, goggles, and trackers into her backpack and her gathering bag. The clothes she stacked on top of the other stuff in the bag; she would carry it in her arms. It was way too much stuff but she wasn't planning to carry it for long.

She looked back at the hole, and she smiled. Wait until I tell Rune about this, she thought. *And I will get to tell him—I will.* Then she walked away without saying another word.

Chapter 30

Diana shifted a bit in her chair and tried to control her anxiety. She was sitting in her new office in Fort Freedom, and Tanna was coming to see her, and it was probably about fixing MindCore. My days are numbered, Diana thought. *I should pack my things and go.* But then what would happen to Rune?

No. She was staying until the end. In a bottom drawer, she had a gun that she'd never fired but she was ready to use it. She'd only need one shot—right through her own head. She also had a stash of things her son Kala had left at her house—a high-powered rifle, another pistol, and some 20 Eyes "survival gear." Why had she brought all this stuff with her to the fort? It reminded her of Kalo. It was all she had left of him.

She looked up as Tanna came striding into the room. Tanna was smiling.

Diana tried to keep her expression neutral but this girl was annoying. Also, she seemed kind of evil. Not all the time but definitely some of the time.

"I don't know what's wrong with MindCore," Diana said, and now she realized that she wasn't afraid of Tanna—or her father, either. She was merely disgusted by them. She didn't care anymore, and it felt liberating, and she had that gun in the bottom drawer.

"Don't worry about it," Tanna said. "I don't care about MindCore because I have a new plan. We don't need to invade Rune's mind."

"Oh, really?"

"Yeah. I'm going to use regular nightmares to turn Rune against Markla. Then he'll tell us everything we want to know."

Diana didn't laugh out loud too often. But she did it now.

Tanna frowned. "What's so funny?"

Diana laughed again. "You're never going to turn Rune against Markla—not a chance. He'd do anything for that girl."

Tanna scowled at her. "Yeah, so far. But wait and see. Wait and see."

"Okay, I'll wait. I'll see."

Diana knew she was aggravating Tanna, and it felt good.

Tanna seemed undeterred. She said, "I've also got a special LiveDream we can use if we ever get MindCore working, and if we ever capture Markla. It's called 'Arena.' It could be really useful. Check it out."

"I'll look at it."

"Okay, thanks."

"Don't mention it."

Tanna seemed pleased with herself as she left. Diana sipped a cup of tea and opened up the LiveDream.

She was a bit surprised. As she went through the potential scenes, she saw that it was not the horror-script she'd been expecting from that slippery witch. Well, Tanna was always up to something. But Diana had access to all LiveDream scripts here at the fortress. There were a lot of potential variables in the script, and it was hard to predict how things would go, especially if someone was guiding the dream.

She smiled and connected her GoBug to the script editing feature. It wouldn't hurt to make a few changes.

Chapter 31

Once again, they took Rune to the nightmare room. As the goons led him down the hall, he felt the blood pounding in his ears. He knew he needed to stay strong—but at the sight of the nightmare chair he felt his stomach start to churn. And then he thought about his father, and how he'd been tough as a block of granite.

Rune stared at the chair again, and now his look was hard like stone. He was ready.

Tanna came striding into the room, wearing her usual black leggings with a colorful pink top. Her hair was once again tied in a ponytail that swung down her back like a viper. She was smiling, and when she spoke her tone was less smug than usual. In fact, she seemed friendly.

"Hi, Rune," she said. "It's good to see you."

What? Was she kidding? Rune gave her a quizzical look and didn't respond.

She sighed. "I know you don't like me, Rune, but I'm just doing my job. And I've decided to do it a little differently today."

He still said nothing. He was sure whatever she had in mind was devious.

The goon strapped him into the chair. Tanna came toward him again and attached the GoBug behind his ear. Like before, she touched his shoulder with her other hand as she did this—but this time she gave it a little squeeze.

"This will be interesting, Rune," she said. "You'll probably still hate me but maybe not as much."

"My feelings for you are etched in stone, Tanna."

"You don't know me," she said, and she walked to the console.

Why did she keep saying that? He had no intention of knowing her.

She waved her hand over a control, and the room vanished.

***

He opened his eyes, and he was in a pub. The pub was filled with smiling people, and most of them were his age or maybe a little older. They were all holding heavy mugs of ale, and the air was filled with the sounds of laughter and clinking glasses—and he could smell *crispila,* a popular Sparklan food made from fried dough and powdered sugar.

Rune winced and kept himself on alert. He never went to pubs. There was no minimum age requirement for being in a Sparklan pub but he just never bothered. He'd always been more interested in his GoBug, his flyboard, and his drums.

This particular pub was cozy, with walls of grainy natural wood and knotted oak beams that stretched across the ceiling. There was a band in the corner with a long-haired guy playing bass, and a pixie-like girl playing synth and singing, and another guy playing bubbly percussion—exactly the kind of stuff he played. How had she known this? Maybe she'd seen pictures of his drum-filled shed back home, and he realized that the pub was in many ways a larger version of his shed, and he felt comfortable here.

So Tanna had done some research. She was mean but she wasn't lazy.

Lots of people were sitting on stools at the bar, and as Rune studied the scene he recognized one of them—Aldo Xantha.

Aldo, who had tortured Rune and Markla with LiveDream nightmares. Aldo, who Markla had killed.

Aldo was wearing his InfoLenses and his typical white lab coat, and he looked very bug-like. Rune braced himself as Aldo approached.

Aldo spoke in a smooth voice. "Hello, Rune. How are you?"

"I'm fine," Rune said, determined to sound calm. "I'm in a LiveDream, and you aren't real, and it's better that way."

"Yes, but I can tell that your heart rate is elevated. I can see the numbers in front of my eyes… And obviously this isn't real, since I'm dead. In fact, I was murdered quite brutally."

Rune hesitated. Since this was just a LiveDream, why respond? This was Tanna talking through a character—but he wanted to respond to her.

"You tortured me," Rune said. "You tortured Markla, and you made me hurt her. You were a monster."

"Oh, I know," Aldo said. "I was never the nicest person in the world. But it was still just a dream."

"It seemed real. The pain felt real, and it seemed like I was turning against her. You were trying to plant that idea in her head."

"But did it work? Here you are, still in love with her—even though she did this."

He spun around, and Rune saw the dagger sticking out of his back.

There was a lot of blood, and it was a harsh image. Then he turned back toward Rune and said, "That was real, Rune— murder. That's what happened to me. And why? Because I created a dream. Don't you think that was a bit extreme?"

Well, maybe it had been extreme—because Markla was an extreme person. But Rune wasn't going to discuss it with Aldo or Tanna.

"I don't want to talk about it," he said.

"I'm sure you don't," Aldo said with a smirk. "But if you believe in 'an eye for an eye' it's not the same thing because she took more than an eye. She took everything. And how long until you're the one who ends up like me? It could happen."

Rune laughed. "I don't think so."

"Are you sure? Could you ever do the kind of thing she did? Think about it. Markla is violent. She's a proven killer with unstable tendencies."

Tanna's trying to play with my mind, Rune thought. And he preferred this to being cooked in a desert. But it was also more insidious.

"I like her the way she is."

"Murderous and insane?"

"You don't know her, Aldo—and neither does Tanna."

"Maybe you're the one who doesn't know her," Aldo said, and he turned around again, showing the dagger once more as he walked away. Rune watched him go, and then he scanned the room because what would happen next? It only took a moment to find out.

The bar vanished, and he was back in the Dream Prison.

He was in Aldo's bunker, where Aldo had been killed—and Markla was there. It was the exact scene Rune remembered, and Markla was stabbing Aldo in the back. But the scene was repeating, over and over and over. Aldo was gasping, and Markla was stabbing him again and again.

Rune caught his breath. He'd wondered if the events in that room had been recorded, and now it was obvious they had been. He couldn't deny it was disturbing to watch, and then it got worse.

The scene speeded up. The action got faster and faster until Markla seemed to be in a frenzy. She was flailing away at Aldo with the dagger, puncturing his back a dozen times at rapid speed. Aldo's gasps blended together, and it sounded like he was hyperventilating—and then the scene froze. Rune saw the shock in Aldo's eyes, and he saw the expression on Markla's face, a look of cold rage. Had Tanna enhanced these images a bit? It was hard to say.

Rune turned away. But he felt his chest heaving, and suddenly it was quiet.

He turned back around and saw Aldo's body on the floor. He noticed the dagger was no longer in Aldo's back. Rune stared at Markla and saw that she was still holding the bloody weapon—and she stared right back at him and smiled, and with one quick move she stabbed him in the stomach.

Rune grunted. She pulled the blade out and stabbed him again.

This isn't real, he thought. But it felt real.

He took a few heavy breaths, and now he felt a burning pain, and it was hard to move. He staggered backward and put his hand on the desk. Meanwhile, Markla was staring at him again. Her face was blank like a wall. She still had the weapon in her hand, and she was coming toward him once more. With a quick motion she stabbed him again—but this time he fought through the pain, and he reached out and grabbed her, and he wrapped her in his arms. Then he kissed her on the lips.

For one ridiculous moment it felt good. For one instant, it was like she was here with him again—and then it was over, and he fell to the ground.

"I love you Markla," he said. "No matter what they make you do."

He closed his eyes. When he opened them he was back in the nightmare room.

He was strapped in his chair, and Tanna was behind the console. She was staring at him, and she looked like she'd just had the wind knocked out of her. Rune took a few breaths, trying to calm down, and he waited for some smug words from this snaky girl. But she didn't say anything. She didn't smile, and she didn't frown. She looked into his eyes for a few seconds and then left the room.

Chapter 32

Burno couldn't believe how hard it had been to escape that hole. Red had a badly sprained ankle, and Burno had boosted him up, and Red had grabbed the lip and managed to claw his way out. But they had no kind of rope, so Burno had to dig footholds into the side of the hole and use them to climb out. It had taken several attempts.

Now they were sitting on the ground in their underwear exchanging glances of disgust.

"So, what now?" Red said. "I can't walk. We've got to call for extraction."

Both commandos had micro transponders implanted in their forearms. These were for emergency situations, and when they pressed the transponder three times it would send a signal and a hover-ship would come to "extract" them. Unfortunately, without the GoBugs, they couldn't communicate in any other way. They could send the signal but they couldn't elaborate about their situation.

Burno swore for the thousandth time. "I guess we don't have many options," he said. "But how are we going to explain this? We look like complete idiots! This is embarrassing."

Red laughed. "I know. I almost wished she'd killed us… But hey, at least we've got the transponders. I'm surprised she didn't tell us to cut off our arms and toss them up, too. Are we chasing the smartest girl in the world, or are we just a couple of morons?"

"We could've done better."

"That's an understatement. But you also didn't respect her, and we got sloppy."

"So it's my fault?"

"I told you to look at her record—not at her size, or her age, or the fact that she's a girl. I told you that."

"All right, all right. I'll admit, I underestimated her. That girl is clever."

"Yeah, she is. She's crafty. I mean, I wish she was on our side… So, what now?"

"Hit the button. When they get here you can go. But I'm still going after her."

Red laughed again and rolled his eyes. "With what? The extraction ship isn't bringing us any new gear. They're not even going to bring you a pair of pants. Are you gonna run through the woods barefoot in a loincloth?"

Burno scowled. "I'll figure something out. Have you forgotten about the two dead people in our team?"

"No," Red said, and he shook his head. "I haven't forgotten. But we've killed our share, Burno. It's the nature of the job, and I think this job might be over, at least for now. You know they're going to chew us out."

"Yeah," Burno said, and now his tone was sharp. "That's how it always is—forget about the million things we did right over the years. Forget about all of that stuff, and all the times they took credit for it. It's always about the one thing that goes wrong. I should quit and go into the restaurant business with my brother. He's got a place in Turnaround, and it does pretty well."

"I thought you said you didn't cook much."

"I don't," Burno said with a laugh. "And maybe that's why I'm not going anywhere. Not until I complete this mission."

Chapter 33

Markla didn't carry the commando's stuff very far. As soon as the hole was out of sight she started getting rid of it. The first thing she did was remove the power crystals from the GoBugs because the toads could track those in an instant. Then she smashed the GoBugs with a rock because smashing GoBugs felt like a form of therapy.

The night goggles seemed like a useful thing to have—but they weren't because when they were activated they automatically connected to military mindstreams. The trackers were the same way. Every electronic device could tell someone where the operator was located, and it's one of the things she hated about all this stuff. So she removed the power crystals from those devices and smashed them as well. Then she dumped the mangled pieces into a hollow tree. Markla frowned as she did this because she hated to pollute the forest with all this toad gear, but there weren't a lot of options.

Next she examined the rifles. Each was a fully automatic ST-25 standard army issue weapon. She'd never used one in real life but she'd had the 20 Eyes training in a LiveDream, and she felt like she'd fired this weapon many times. It wasn't that big as far as rifles went but it was a bit heavy. She almost kept it, but no—she liked to travel as light as possible.

She hurried toward the stream she'd been following south. The stream was deep in some places, and it served as a watery grave for the rifles, the body armor, and the boots. The clothes she stuffed inside another tree. One of the pistols went into the water—but these pistols were extremely light, and she kept the other one along with all the ammunition. The ammunition fit the gun she already had, and there was even a magazine of exploding shells. Of course, she kept the grenades.

I'm a killing machine, she thought. *If I roll over in my sleep I'll blow up half the country.*

She took a deep breath and started walking south again. She wondered about Rune, and if his adventure was anything like hers. It was unlikely—she knew his was worse. Sure, she was out in the woods fighting for her life but at least she was free. She'd been to prison, and there was nothing better than being free.

He'll be free again, she thought. *I'm going to make that happen.*

After nine hours of walking through the woods she was breathing hard and looking for a place to rest. This meant she was looking to plop down under a tree, and there were plenty of them around. She wondered about wolves, and if she might get eaten by one—but at the moment, she didn't care. She picked out a tall tree, sank to the ground, and closed her eyes. She could fall asleep right now, and it would feel amazing, but that would be a bad plan. There was still some daylight left, and she needed to make the most of it because she wouldn't be going anywhere at night. This forest was impossible to navigate in the dark, not to mention spooky. In fact, it was spooky right now.

She almost nodded off to sleep—but then she heard a noise and jerked herself awake. Was someone there? She scanned the woods with wide eyes but saw no one. Could it be those commandos? Were they still following? No, that was impossible. I need to get a grip, she thought. She got to her feet, looked at her compass, and continued moving.

Once again, she heard a sound like someone crunching a branch.

She whirled around. "Who's there?" she said. Her voice echoed in the wilderness and died.

She wasn't imagining it, no way. Someone else was out here. But now there was only silence.

She thought about 20 Eyes and the thought made her sweat.

They had spies in the government, and they might know exactly where the commando team had been sent, and they could send people—but wait, how would they find her in this exact spot? No, it was unlikely. But then what about the government of Sparkla? Maybe they'd dropped another team of commandos nearby. Would they really do that? Was she that hated? Maybe, but they wouldn't just be sneaking around. They would have shot her by now, so it wasn't them. She needed to stop with this.

I really am going crazy, she thought. But why now, after all these years? She gave a short laugh. Maybe it was just an animal—but if it was a person, that person was behind a tree.

She started walking again as quietly as possible, straining her ears and scanning the trees. She heard no other sound now but she was on high alert. If someone was out here she wanted to find out before it got dark. She was a light sleeper but she was also exhausted, and she didn't want someone sneaking up on her while she was inside the SuperSeal bag. She imagined a few scenarios, and they were all terrifying.

Run! she thought. *Just run!* Suddenly, she started to do it—but she stumbled on a fallen branch, and she swore and fell to the ground. For a moment she didn't move, but then she rolled over onto her back, and for one instant it felt nice. She stared at the sky, and she felt a chill run through her body. It was starting to get dark, and it was starting to get cold. And she heard another sound. She banged her fist on the ground. She stood up and reached for her pistol. It was loaded with standard cartridges.

She was tired of walking, and tired of fighting, and she didn't want to hurt anyone. She really just wanted to give up and go home—but where was that? She had no home.

When I'm with Rune again, I'll feel like I'm home.

She studied the collection of trees. They were like obstacles now, pylons rising out of the ground that hid a tormentor. Maybe.

But now she heard nothing. Stay calm, she thought. She took a step—and she saw someone. It was from the corner of her eye, a person about thirty paces away, slipping between two trees. Her heart skipped a beat.

Once again she wanted to run, and she almost did. But she stopped herself because she was in no state to outrun someone, and besides, there was nowhere to go. She was going to have to deal with this.

She took a few steps in the direction of the intruder. "Who are you?" she said. "What do you want?"

A tall and wiry man stepped out from behind a tree, and Markla caught her breath. He had a shaggy beard, and he wore strange clothes. His pants looked like denim, but his shirt and jacket were obviously made from animal skins. He looked like something from a horror LiveDream. As she stared at him another similar-looking person appeared to the stranger's left. And then another, and another.

She spun around in a circle. There seemed to be a few more of them in the trees, and they were not all in front of her—some were behind her. They were scattered around, and she was surrounded.

"Who are you?" she said again.

The man spoke in a deep voice. "We live here," he said. "And we have some questions."

Chapter 34

Tanna stared out the window of the hover-ship as it flew from Fort Freedom to Liberta, and she tried to lose herself in the leafy fall scenery. But it was impossible. She could not believe what she'd seen. That LiveDream had been meant to make an impression on Rune—but instead, it had made an impression on her.

Who was this guy? How could he possibly be so committed to that horrible girl? It had only been a LiveDream, yet Tanna had felt the power of his feelings. It had been amazing, really—and now she needed a new plan. But first she had to take care of this situation with her father.

She was here to meet with him. She could've used a mind-stream but she knew that she was more persuasive in real life. And she had a feeling she'd need to be persuasive.

Soon she was back in Gin's office, and all the usual idiots were there. Her dad was behind his decadently oversized desk, and the Centurion, "Strom the Stupid," was sitting in a nearby chair, and the two commandos were communicating on a secure mindstream via GoBug—but apparently it wasn't one of their GoBugs because somehow they'd lost their GoBugs, and they were using a GoBug borrowed from the pilot of a small extraction ship that was still sitting in Narna but needed to leave quick before it showed up on all the propaganda mindstreams.

Also, the commandos were in their underwear. What was that about? Obviously, the "rogue soldier plan" wasn't going too well. Gin was frowning and talking to Burno and the other commando, Red.

"Let me understand this," Gin said. "You lost all of your weapons and all of your clothes?"

"Not all our clothes," Red said. "Just the pants and shirts. And the boots. And the armor."

Burno flashed Red a look that clearly meant he should stop talking. Then Burno said, "Things didn't go our way, sir. That's all I can say."

"Where is Markla Flash?"

"I don't know."

"Did you find her?"

"Yes, sir."

"But you didn't complete the mission?"

"No, sir. She escaped."

Gin shook his head. "What are you saying? Is she with the Free Sparkla people? How many of them are over there? Or does she have someone else helping her now, someone we should know about?"

Burno hesitated. "No. She seems to be alone."

"Alone? And she got away from you?"

"She's very resourceful, sir."

"Crafty!" Red said. "She's a crafty girl. She blew up our team, and destroyed our rovers, and trapped us in a hole and took all our stuff. If we had ten like her we'd win this war in a week."

Burno flashed Red another fierce look, and Gin threw up his hands.

Meanwhile, Tanna felt like her head would explode. She was so tired of hearing about Markla Flash.

Gin said, "All right, get back here. The mission is over." Strom nodded.

Burno said, "No, sir. I'm staying. I can still get her."

"What?" Gin said. "You had your chance, and then you had another chance, and how much humiliation are we going to take? Forget it. You're a failure."

"I'm not a failure!" Burno said, and his respectful tone vanished. "Listen, Gin, you sit there in your cushy chair all day, showing off your big arms, but as soon as things get tough you want to run like a scared rabbit. You guys in Liberta make me sick, all of you, and Red's right—I'd take that girl into battle with me over every sleazy politician in Sparkla. Not even close." He stopped and took a breath. "But she killed two people in my team, and I can't let that go. I'm staying."

Gin seemed stunned by the outburst, and Strom's face was turning red like a tomato. Tanna could see an explosion was imminent.

"Wait a second!" she said. "Dad—wait!"

She flew through a series of thought commands and now everyone on the mindstream was seeing information from a different stream. It was a biography page from the Sparklan military—a bio of Burno Blivin.

"Read this," Tanna said. "Look at all the things Burno's done for Sparkla. He's a great soldier! You shouldn't be judging him because of this one incident—an incident that he can still fix. I think you should give him another chance. We can't let Markla go. We just can't."

Gin hesitated. "Tanna, we can't afford any more embarrassment. Besides, we have bigger things to worry about."

"Do we? They're talking about her on all the mindstreams. How embarrassing is it going to be if we quit?"

Burno was nodding his head. Gin leaned back in his chair and stared at his daughter.

Tanna said nothing else. She could tell he was going to decide in her favor—and when things were going her way, she knew enough to stop talking.

Gin looked at Burno. "So we need to resupply you?"

"No," Burno said. "I can work that out with the pilot here. They brought some standard supplies, and you won't need any more extraction ships—except for when I'm finished. I'll take care of everything."

Gin sighed. "All right. But don't call for help again. I don't want to hear from you until this is done. Even then, I barely want to hear from you."

Burno smiled. "You'll only hear the last shot," he said, and he ended the connection.

Gin turned to Strom. "So, how are we doing with the plan to destroy all the enemy broadcast stations? Because I see there's a lot of them still out there."

Strom's fat mustache twitched a bit. "It's very easy for anyone to broadcast to a mindstream. We've taken out the big broadcasters but there are a lot of people out there. We're trying to track them down."

"Jorro is helping with that!" Tanna said—although really, he hadn't helped much at all. In fact, he'd been surprisingly useless but she felt obligated to put in a good word for him.

Gin shook his head. "All right. Give me a report tomorrow. But before that happens, try to do something right."

Strom left and Tanna was alone with her father. She braced herself. Questions were coming.

"Tanna, are you making any progress with Rune? Because whoever smashed into our grid and connected to the police station is still out there, and I'm sure that person is connected to a lot of others, and those are the people we need to find and eliminate. I have other people who can interrogate him."

"That's not necessary," she said. "I think he'll give me information soon."

"But he hasn't told you a single thing."

"He's a tough case."

"How do you know? He's the only case you've ever had. Maybe you need some help."

"No! I have a plan," she said, and she looked at him with her best puppy dog eyes. "Please Dad, give me a little more time. I can do this."

He hesitated. "All right. I'll give you a few more days. But we need to see some progress."

"You will," she said. "I promise."

Tanna left the office and hurried down the hall. Along the way, she breathed a sigh of relief. She had to get on a hover-ship now. She had to get back to Rune.

Chapter 35

Markla felt like there was a knot in her stomach. These people were Basics. She was sure of it.

Basics were people who rejected modern technology and lived in the wilderness like primitive people from ancient times. There were some in Sparkla but she'd never seen them. There were supposedly a lot more in Narna although Jerome and Shala hadn't mentioned it. But she was a long way from Jerome and Shala now.

Markla noticed they wore a mix of self-made clothing and mass-produced stuff, and many of them were holding rifles—so they didn't reject *all* technology.

"I'm just passing through," Markla said. She tried to keep her voice from shaking.

The man pointed at the pistol in her hand. "You have a weapon."

"It's just a precaution. I didn't know who you were."

She had no intention of using it. She could never kill them all, and she didn't want to hurt them, anyway. She just had to get past them.

Now a woman appeared beside the man, and Markla felt a new flash of fear—she looked even more alarming than the guy. She had stringy black hair streaked with gray and a mostly black dress made from the skin of some dead creature. When she spoke, her voice was like a harsh half whisper. "Is someone chasing you?" she said. "Are you bringing something evil here?"

"I'm not bringing anything. I'll be gone soon."

The woman narrowed her eyes and studied Markla. "You're just a little girl," she said. "How old are you?"

"Sixteen."

"You look younger."

Markla shrugged. "I'm not big."

"Did someone hurt you?"

Markla hesitated. It was an interesting question. Lots of people had hurt her.

"Not today," she said. "I'm just heading south, looking for a friend."

The woman shook her head. "You did something terrible, and now you're running away."

The words caught Markla off guard—because weren't they true?

"No!" she blurted. "I didn't do anything, and I don't want anything."

The woman looked out among the trees at the other people, and she nodded her head. The others began moving toward Markla, and now she was filled with panic. But she didn't raise the pistol—not yet.

"What are you doing?" she said.

There were at least twenty of them. They were all lean and lanky, men and women young and old, and even a few children who were grinning. Some of them were carrying guns but many held knives or clubs. They were all staring at her as they walked, and the circle was closing.

"Stop!" she said. "Don't come any closer!"

The woman smiled but it was not a friendly smile. "Are you going to try and shoot us?" she said. "It would be a mistake."

Markla's heart was racing. This was just too strange but she had to do something. She turned toward the direction she wanted to go. There were a few people advancing and she fired two shots near their feet. She expected them to dive out of the way—but they didn't. They grimaced and stopped moving for an instant but then they stepped aside like they were clearing a path for her. Well, that was fine. She started running.

She ran right past them, and at first they did nothing. Then someone let out a whoop and they were right behind her.

She leaped over a broken branch and crashed through the foliage. Then she stumbled a bit as she waded through some leaves. From the corner of her eye, she could see they were following on either side of her. She heard them plowing through the forest but they weren't coming at her—they were shadowing her. Now someone was getting closer, and she swerved, changing direction. Then another man was standing there, and she swerved again. She realized they were controlling her direction. They were herding her like an animal—right into a pit.

She shouted as she fell into it. It was a hole covered with branches and leaves.

She swore as she hit the ground. But it wasn't deep, only about the height of her head. She saw the people around her now, still coming toward her. She grabbed the soil around the pit and tried to scramble out but then she felt a sharp sting on her neck. She'd been hit by some kind of dart! She swore and pulled it out. They were still coming toward her—and suddenly she couldn't move.

What? She felt only terror now. The pistol fell from her hand, and she realized she was paralyzed.

She let out another shout and collapsed against the side of the hole. She gave a desperate wail but she was frozen like stone. She felt herself sliding down to the bottom of the pit, and for an instant she thought about Rune and Tommi and how she'd failed them. Then she tried to turn her head to look around but she couldn't do it, and all she could see was a wall of earth in front of her eyes. But she could tell they were standing over her, and then two of the men were in the pit, grabbing her, and she was trying to fight them as a million horrible thoughts raced through her mind—but she still couldn't move, and they were pulling her up out of the hole and dumping her on the ground.

When she tried to speak her words were slurred. "Letmegoooo!" she said. "I didn'tdooooanythingtoooyou!"

They were ripping off her backpack. They were taking her things. Now her mind flashed to a scene with her mother—a moment when she'd felt helpless to stop what was coming, and her whole body shook with rage. Now she was ready to kill but she could not. She tried to scream again but the sound died in her throat. Then the woman reached down and took her dagger.

The woman held the dagger in front of Markla's eyes and said, "You've hurt people with this, haven't you? And you might do it again. But maybe not—we'll see."

Markla tried to speak, and she tried to shake her head, but it was useless.

The woman smiled again. "Don't worry, you'll get what you deserve. Everyone does."

Markla found herself struggling to breathe. Everything went dark.

Chapter 36

Rune was no longer in his drab prison cell. The goons had moved him, and obviously something new was going on. But what?

His new location had three spacious rooms painted in a watery shade of turquoise. There were no windows but there was a bathroom with baby blue tiles, and a little dish filled with different-colored pieces of soap, and a shower. There was a bedroom with a fluffy bed big enough for three, and another room with a fat cushy sofa—and there was a bola drum. Yes, someone had actually given him a drum to play, like the kind he'd played back in his shed at home. But he didn't want any gifts from these people. He didn't need a sofa or multiple shades of soap—and he'd play the drums again when he was free from this place and Markla was back in his life. Tanna might be changing her tactics but Rune laughed because nothing she tried was going to work.

No doubt Tanna had thought the scene with Aldo would be disturbing to watch. No doubt Tanna was trying to rattle his resolve and his feelings toward Markla. Yet she had totally failed and would continue to fail—because Rune knew something Tanna would never know. He knew why Markla's mind was filled with rage and turmoil, and he knew that in her heart, beneath the storms and chaos, she was really very sweet.

Rune flopped down on the bed and stared at the ceiling. *Where was Markla now?*

Tanna had mentioned some commandos, and the thought of Markla being hunted and killed in the woods by a group of trained assassins made him feel sick. He had to be there with her. He had to get out of here but there was no way out. He mulled things over for a while, and finally he lost track of time and fell asleep. When he woke up, he was taken to the nightmare room.

As they pushed him into the usual chair, his stomach filled with butterflies because there was no guarantee this wouldn't be a session of suffering. Tanna could mix things up. Also, she'd mentioned that if she didn't get what they wanted her father would send someone else to do it. Well, she hadn't gotten anything so far, so Rune really didn't know what was coming.

One thing he could count on was that Tanna would be wearing black leggings—and she was. For someone so wealthy, she didn't have much of a wardrobe. She also wore a loose pink shirt and her typical ponytail.

"Hi Rune," she said with a smile. "Did you get any sleep?"

"Where's Markla?"

"I don't know. Maybe she's busy cutting somebody's throat."

"She's a warrior. She's trying to survive."

Tanna started to respond—and stopped herself. Then she said, "Strap him in the chair."

Rune waited for Tanna to put the GoBug behind his ear but this time she had one of the goons do it, and for some reason this made Rune uneasy. Then Tanna touched something on her console and everything went black.

***

When Rune blinked he was surrounded by sunshine. Also, there were a lot of people around. He was in a field of green grass on the outskirts of a forest, and everywhere he looked there were happy faces and tables filled with pastries, pies, and other things to eat. It was a festival of some kind, and he saw colorful booths decorated with ribbons and banners, and primitive games, and long wooden tables where people were eating, talking, and laughing. There was a band playing on a small stage, and the music was loud and bouncy, and the vibe was similar to the one he'd initially felt in the pub.

As the memories of that LiveDream flooded his mind, he tried to keep his anxiety in check. He scanned the rollicking crowd. Was Aldo here? Was Markla walking around with an axe in her hand? His mind raced with possibilities. There were so many horrible things that could happen in a LiveDream nightmare. What kind of terror was coming to ruin the party?

Okay, he saw nothing obvious, so he braced himself and started wandering around. Then he smelled the food cooking, and he decided to get some fried potatoes because he liked fried potatoes. But he had no way to pay for them, or did he? He found some coins in his pocket, even though coins of this type hadn't been used for centuries. He recalled a nightmare script where a piece of food expanded in the victim's mouth, bigger and bigger until it was stuck, and the victim clawed at his face, desperate to remove it—but it was no use, and the person's jawbone cracked, and the food worked its way into the windpipe, and the victim's eyes bulged as he tumbled to the ground and choked and gagged to death. While these thoughts whirled through Rune's mind a cute green-eyed girl behind a counter smiled and handed him his food. He peered at her with suspicion, but he didn't recognize her, and now he wasn't sure if he still wanted to eat. Then he turned around—and there was someone he recognized. It was Tanna.

She bumped into him and laughed. "Hi, Rune," she said. "How do you like my LiveDream?"

He scowled a bit. "What are you doing in here?"

"It's a guided dream. I can be here. You know that."

It was true. As the dream guider, she could be in the LiveDream as a character, and she could manipulate her character and communicate through it—but she would not actually feel anything that happened. She would be observing the action through her GoBug as it interfaced with the dreambank and console. MindCore, on the other hand, could put them in the same dream together, and they would both feel everything, and that's what made it so special. But as far as Tanna knew, MindCore wasn't working.

Tanna still seemed awfully happy.

"Can I have a potato?" she said.

She was wearing different clothes in the dream. Instead of black leggings she had a tight black skirt that stopped just above her knee. Her legs were bare, and Rune noticed she had lighter skin than most people in Sparkla. They were nice legs but it was a LiveDream, and she could make them look anyway she wanted, although Rune had a feeling the images were accurate. Her top was a simple pink shirt, clingier than usual to show off her shape—and her shape was sexy. But Rune had never thought her looks were a problem. It was everything else.

"It's a dream, Tanna," he said. "You won't taste them, so why bother? Only I can do that—because I'm strapped into a chair with a dreamshell loaded into my brain. Your uncle and your father killed my dad. Do you really think you can change that with a few potatoes?"

"I'm not my uncle or my father!" she snapped. Then she gestured with her hands at the boisterous surroundings. "Doesn't this look nice?"

"I'm guessing it will change."

"You're guessing wrong. Maybe I just want to show you a few things." She paused and added, "I wrote this LiveDream by myself. Nobody helped me, and there's nothing scary here."

Rune narrowed his eyes a bit. This LiveDream wasn't badly written. It felt *immersive* and real but what was her game? Maybe he'd play along.

He shrugged. "You told me you weren't a good writer. This dream is pretty good."

"I wasn't a great dream writer. This is the best one I ever did but there's not much to it. It's just about having fun."

"Well, that's something most people want."

"Yeah, but I have no interesting characters or story. It's just a lot of background. I never finished it. I didn't know what else I wanted to do."

Rune ate a piece of fried potato. It was crispy and chock full of flavor, and he didn't choke—and while he was eating he kept looking around. It was a scene filled with bright colors and carefree people. No one seemed to have a serious thought in their minds.

"Tanna, did you really write all this? It seems so bright and cheery."

"I'm not bright and cheery?"

He hesitated, and he thought about how Tanna had roasted him alive in a desert, and how she'd had Markla's family arrested for a crime they didn't do—and how she often had a smug demeanor. But he decided not to mention those things. The potatoes tasted fine, so why agitate her?

"You seem more serious than this," he said. "You're very… focused and businesslike."

"That's what everyone thinks! But I'm not like that all the time. I have this whole other side to me—look! There are some games. Do you want to try one?"

She pointed to a line of booths that held all kinds of primitive games. In these festivals, the games were usually simple—no GoBugs or technology required. It was uncomplicated stuff like throwing a ball through a hole or whatever. She grabbed his hand and pulled him a bit.

"Come on," she said. "Just try this one."

Rune didn't move at first but then he followed her to a booth nearby.

He was on high alert now. Something was going to happen, and how much pain and humiliation would be involved? She's trying to catch me off guard, he thought. *She's going to spring some horrible surprise and laugh while I suffer.*

He mentally prepared himself. He was ready.

The booth was painted like a rainbow and made of wood, and it was manned by an old guy with a gray beard and a wide-brimmed hat made of purple felt. The object of the game was clear enough. There was a transparent gun loaded with harmless looking balls, and there was a moving belt maybe five paces away that had two-dimensional shapes that resembled animals. The object was to fire the gun and knock down the shapes. Every time the shooter was successful, a bell would ring and a nearby screen would show a score.

"Go ahead," Tanna said. "Give it a try. It's kind of pointless for me to do it."

This was true. Since she was guiding the dream, she could give herself any level of proficiency.

Rune picked up the gun. "Yeah, I'm sure you'd never miss."

"It's not a hard game even in real life."

"Would you miss any in real life?"

"I'd miss a few."

For a moment, they locked eyes. What did he see there? Anxiety, maybe—but it was hard to say.

He turned toward the targets and started shooting, and he only missed once. He put the gun down and waited. It was time.

He turned to her. "I'm out of ammo," he said. "So, what happens now?"

She shrugged. "I don't know. I didn't really plan this. I just wanted to show you my half-finished dream and see what you thought of it."

He cocked his head and stared at her. Was this the surprise?

It was working. But then again it was a guided dream, and she could still toss him into a tar pit.

But she didn't. Instead, she moved a little closer to him. She didn't actually touch him—but it seemed like she wanted to. Then she started speaking fast.

"Rune, I know you don't like me, and I know you have good reasons, but I don't dislike you, okay? And I don't want to torture you. So maybe if you tell me a few things that my father wants to know, we can make these LiveDream sessions happy instead of horrible—and then who knows?"

Now she touched him, just for an instant. She took his hand and gave it a quick squeeze. Then she looked up at him with her big brown eyes, and time seemed to stop, and he got a very distinct feeling that if he kissed her she would like it.

This was crazy.

He did not kiss her. But he did not recoil from her in disgust, either—because he thought about that tar pit. Also, she seemed a little nicer than usual, and maybe a little stranger, too. Rune couldn't deny he'd always been fascinated by strange girls. Even if they'd done something horrible—like tortured someone. Or killed someone.

I have to get out of this prison, he thought. *I need a way out.*

He took a small step back but he also gave her a quick little smile.

"I'd have to think about that," he said. "Maybe you should end this dream. At least for now."

Chapter 37

Markla opened her eyes. Where was she? She could only see shadows. Then it all came flooding back to her, and in her stomach she once again felt a knot of terror.

She was lying on a dusty wooden floor in a darkened room. There was a tight cloth gag in her mouth, and her hands were bound behind her back with a piece of rope, and her legs were tied at the ankles. She was seized by panic—and then rage. In her mind, she flashed back to her mother's house, and she was being beaten with a belt, and she was confined in a closet, and she was crying and screaming. With all her strength, she twisted and turned and pulled against her bonds. She tried to scream—and then she stopped.

Stay calm, she thought. *I've got to stay calm!*

But her pulse was pounding, and she couldn't keep from going through the entire episode again—the pulling and the straining and the twisting until she was exhausted. Finally, she stopped and caught her breath.

She was still now, panting hard, and trying to think. Then she heard footsteps on the creaky floorboards. Someone had entered the room.

From her position on the floor she could only see a silhouette. Then someone opened a window, and a stream of light shined down, and Markla saw a guy about her age. He was average height with long black hair, and he was wearing denim pants and a shirt and jacket made from animal skins. He was studying her, and she braced herself for an assault because she guessed that's why he was here.

He's going to rape and kill me, she thought. *But I'm not going down without a fight.* Her mind raced through a list of targets—the eyes, the testicles, the jugular vein. Yeah, if he got on top of her, she could bite through that vein in two seconds. She knew exactly where it was. She was ready.

He bent down and looked into her eyes. Did he see the rage there? She did nothing to hide it. He had smooth coppery skin and a handsome face. He smiled and removed her gag.

"Hello," he said. "What's your name?"

Markla hesitated. "My name?" she spat. "Why, do you need to fill out a form or something? Just do what you're going to do."

"I'm not going to hurt you," he said. "I just want to know your name."

"My name is Markla Flash."

Now he grinned. "I knew it!" he said. "That's what I told my mother."

"You told her…what?"

"That you're Markla Flash—the girl being chased by the government of Sparkla."

This was too weird. "You know about that?"

"Yeah, of course. We monitor the news and communications. You're in a lot of it."

"Oh, yeah? I thought you didn't use technology."

He laughed. "That's an exaggeration. We aren't *enslaved* to technology—but we use some of it because, well, it's useful."

As he spoke, he untied her wrists and ankles, and now she was free, and her first inclination was to clobber him, and then to run—but she didn't. Her instincts told her it was no longer the best plan. Instead, she rubbed her wrists and sat up on the floor and stared at this guy in front of her. She was still furious.

"Why did you attack me out there?" she said. "Why did you tie me up like that?"

He sighed. "That was my mom's idea. She's a little stuck on the old ways. But don't worry, now that we know who you are, you won't have any more trouble."

"Your mother is a 'little stuck'? I thought she was going to build a bonfire and burn me alive."

"Yeah. She has some issues with that… But we have this tradition of defending the land against certain people—people with weapons like that pistol you were carrying."

"Well, I want it back."

"Sure. I'll get it for you."

"And all my other stuff, too."

"That's not a problem."

"The food—make sure none of it's missing."

He laughed. "You're so demanding."

Markla scowled at him, and then she shook her head. Maybe I'll just go with the flow, she thought, and she sighed.

"So, what's your name?"

"Ronelo," he said, and he smiled again. "Are you sure you want to leave so soon?"

"Yeah, I need to get going. And I'd like to do it without seeing your mother again."

"She'll be fine now, trust me."

"She's creepy, and I don't trust you at all."

"You don't hold back much, do you?"

She glared at him.

"Hey, I know how my mom is," he said. "But stay for dinner. We can help you."

"Thanks, but I don't want any help."

Ronelo reached out and grasped her hand. "Markla, I'm sorry for the way we treated you—but stay a bit. You'll see. Things will be great. Just for a few hours."

"What happens in a few hours? You turn me into a human sacrifice to help the crops grow?"

He laughed. "No. We're not like that—I swear. We only

sacrifice animals for that kind of thing—that was a joke! No one will hurt you. I promise."

He was looking at her face now, and he had deep brown eyes and teeth like bright stones, and he seemed sincere. But Markla was skittish and skeptical by nature, and did he really think that after herding her into a pit and tying her up he was going to win her over with some primitive pretty-boy charm?

No, he was not. But then again, she couldn't really outrun these people, and she had no idea how many of them were out there or what kind of weapons they had, and maybe it was best to play along and leave on good terms. Besides, what if they could help her? Crazier things had happened.

"All right," she said. "But first bring me my stuff. All of it."

He hesitated. "All of it? I don't know if I can get all of it right now."

"You want me to trust you but you stole all my things. I want everything back—including the dagger and the gun."

He grinned and shook his head. "You drive a hard bargain, Markla. But I'll get it, okay?"

"Sure. I'll wait here."

"Will you really?"

"Maybe."

He stood up. "I'll be right back. Give me five minutes."

He raced out the door, and she leaped to her feet. She could go—she could run. But she had nothing with her.

I'll wait, she thought. She didn't like the plan but she didn't see any option.

Chapter 38

Rune was lying on the bed in his new prison suite, trying to think. It was harder to break out of this place than he'd expected. They kept the door locked all the time.

What would my dad do? He'd tell me to 'act like a man'. What would Markla do? She'd find a way, of course. But here he was going nowhere and doing nothing. He needed to make something happen, but what?

His mind turned to Tanna. She was suddenly being a lot nicer, and her new strategy was definitely more comfortable than torture—but what would happen when he still didn't give her any information? She'd put him right back in the nightmare room and burn his flesh a thousand times. She'd be putting on lipstick while his skin fried.

But she squeezed my hand, he thought. *She looked at me with those beautiful brown eyes.* Had she been coming on to him? Would she really do that just to get information? Yeah, she might, and he couldn't deny that she was pretty, very pretty. She was the most gorgeous viper in the jungle.

There was a knock at the door, and he sat up.

He had a queasy feeling in his stomach like something was about to happen. He was a prisoner, and he couldn't open the door, and wasn't that obvious? But then someone knocked again and said, "Rune, I'm coming in there."

The door opened, and there was Tanna. Right behind her was a big goon.

She was wearing her usual black leggings along with a white shirt, but her hair was not tied in a ponytail. It was hanging down, loose and filled with luster. She had all the best products, of course. Also, she was wearing almost no makeup. She'd never worn much anyway, but today she wore even less—just a touch, and she was skilled with it. She looked wild and natural.

Okay, she looked amazing. So what? He was actually glad she'd brought the guard because it meant she probably wasn't going to try and seduce him, and that was fortunate because he knew it would be a bad scene when he refused her. And he would refuse her, no matter how stunning she looked.

He also noticed she had a GoBug behind her ear. He noticed the guard had one, too. *I really miss those things,* Rune thought. And then he thought about Markla, and what she would say about GoBugs if she were here. "Toad machines," naturally. He laughed to himself.

"Is this room service?" Rune said. "I didn't order anything."

He wasn't going to be hostile—not yet, anyway.

"I wanted to talk to you," she said.

He smiled. "Well, I'm always around. But I usually only see you in the torture room."

Tanna ignored his comment and turned toward the guard. "Stillo, you can wait outside. But stay alert."

Rune raised his eyebrows. "Is that a good idea? I'm a dangerous prisoner, remember?"

"Yeah, but I don't think you'll try anything stupid. You're not like that. Besides, I can take care of myself."

"Oh, really? Are you some kind of martial arts guru?"

"No," she said with a smile. "But I've had lots of hand-to-hand combat training." Then she shrugged. "It was mostly in LiveDreams, and I treat it like an exercise—but I've learned a lot, too. And I'm very into working out."

Rune had seen her personal mindstream a few times, and of course she was bragging, but he also knew it was true. She was quite fit.

"Okay," he said. "I guess I'll be careful."

"Do you want to see a take-down?"

"What?"

She quickly moved her right leg behind his right leg, grabbed his shoulders and pushed—and he started to fall. But she grabbed him and prevented him from going down. She was holding him tight, and she was strong for her size.

"What do you think?" she said.

Her face was so close to his. Her lips were right there, and their bodies were touching, and her leg was pressed against his, and he said nothing—but he once again had the feeling that if he made a move on her she'd go for it. But this was no LiveDream. This was real, and she felt warm and alive—and she was pretty, very pretty.

He regained his balance and stepped out of her grip.

"I think that could work," he said.

"Right," she said. "It works really well." She looked away from his gaze, and did she seem a bit flustered? Maybe he was imagining it. Maybe it was all part of her scheme.

She turned back toward him and sighed. "Rune, here's the situation: My dad's not happy with my lack of progress, and if you don't give me some information about who smashed into the grid, he's going to send someone else. I know you think I'm a monster but it's not true. I really don't want to see you get hurt. So maybe you should start talking. Just tell me *something*."

She was almost pleading now, and it sounded a little strange.

Rune shrugged. "I don't think you're a monster. You're just not the nicest person I've ever met."

"You don't know me."

"You keep saying that."

"Because it's true. You'd be surprised how nice I can be. My father wanted to kill your girlfriend—but I stopped him. So that was nice of me, right?"

Rune felt the room spin. "What? Did they capture Markla?"

"No, she's not captured—not yet. But she's being hunted by

a team of commandos in Narna, and my dad wanted them to kill her because she killed his brother, and I talked him out of it—at least for now."

Rune was speechless, and his mind filled with images of Markla running for her life from a bunch of bloodthirsty toads. *What if I never see her again?* He couldn't comprehend it. It would leave a hole in his heart that would never heal.

"Rune? Are you listening?"

"What? Yeah, I hear you."

"Good. I told him she was worth more to us alive. I did that for you."

"You did?"

"Yeah. It's not because I care about her. I'd be lying if I said that. But I think you could do a lot better, and I don't know what you see in her… I thought if I helped her a bit, maybe you'd help me."

"Oh, I see. And if I don't help you?"

She shrugged. "Nothing changes. She killed my uncle but I can be forgiving—more than she'd ever be. I'm not the person you think I am."

She took a step toward him. She better not kiss me, he thought. But despite her often confident demeanor, he got the feeling she wasn't going to do it. He could see her hesitation, and why was that?

Fear of rejection. Maybe she was a little scared, and he wondered if this was something new for her.

She was staring at him now with those eyes. "Just think about what I said, okay?"

"Okay," he said. But he was done thinking. Then she opened the door, and the guard was there.

Tanna hesitated and said, "Hey, Rune, do you want to learn that move I showed you?"

"You mean your takedown move? I don't know. Maybe."

"I'll show it to you again. Stillo, do you mind if I try something?"

The guard grinned. "Sure, go ahead. But don't tell your father. I don't want him getting the wrong idea."

She moved fast, putting her leg behind his and pushing him hard—and he went down and hit the floor.

Tanna looked at Rune with a big smile. "He's a lot heavier than me, right? But there he is on the floor. Do you want me to teach it to you?"

"Sure," Rune said, and her whole face lit up.

"You can try it on Stillo… I'll show you what to do."

Stillo didn't seem to like this idea, but he did seem to like Tanna. He grinned at her and said, "Okay, one time." Rune guessed Stillo was about her age.

Tanna showed Rune where to stand—close to the big goon, who actually seemed like a nice guy now. Then she directed Rune, and he put his leg behind Stillo's leg, and she put Rune's right hand on Stillo's left shoulder and his other hand near the small of his back. It was a simple move, and Rune could easily see how it worked but he let Tanna show him, anyway. Then he pushed, and Stillo resisted because of course he didn't want to look too easy to knock down, and Rune let out a shout and pushed harder and they both tumbled to the ground.

Rune ended up on top of him. Tanna was laughing like she was having a great time. She thinks we're on a date, Rune thought. He got to his feet.

"I guess I need to practice," he said. "Or only do it on smaller people."

Stillo got up and laughed, and he pointed at Tanna. "She did it fine."

"Yeah, she's good at it," Rune said.

"It's true," Tanna said. Rune knew she was always happy with a compliment.

There was a moment of silence, and it was almost awkward, but then Rune said, "I'm tired. All that fighting wore me out. Maybe I'll go to sleep."

Tanna hesitated. "Okay," she said. "Think about what I said… I'll talk to you soon."

"I'll be here."

She looked at him, and she flashed her big eyes one last time, and she left. Stillo shut the door.

Rune opened his hand and smiled. He stared at the GoBug he'd stolen.

Chapter 39

Markla's eyes moved fast, searching the room. Maybe waiting for this guy was a bad idea. She would curse herself if she ended up tied and gagged on the floor again. But she couldn't leave with just the clothes on her back—no way. Her chance of survival would be zero.

It looked like she was in some kind of dining room, and it was mostly empty. There was an old wooden table in the center and a bunch of matching chairs, and her first thought was silverware—and maybe something she could use as a weapon. But there was nothing like that around.

There was a door that looked like it went to a closet. She yanked on the knob but it was locked. She ran over to the window and noticed it was made of glass. She'd been told the Basics didn't use any modern technology, and that they shunned outside materials—but unless they had a glass factory hidden out here in the woods, someone had purchased the materials for this window. Also, they had rifles, and they hadn't manufactured those, either. So the information she had concerning these people was wrong. Well, it wouldn't be the first time that rumors and gossip and news had turned out to be a bunch of lies.

She slid the curtain aside and peered out. It was early morning, and it was a sunny day, and all she saw were pine trees. She moved toward the door and it swung open.

She leaped backward and saw Ronelo standing there. His arms were filled with things—her things.

He grinned. "Were you leaving?" he said.

"Maybe."

He laughed. "I'm glad you didn't because you would've missed out on all your stuff." He carefully set everything down on the table. "You have some interesting things. You're a real outdoorsy girl, aren't you?"

Markla ignored his comment and rifled through the pile. She saw her backpack filled with food packets, the folded SuperSeal sleeping bag, her flute, her radio, her canteen, the denim jacket, the gun and ammunition, and her dagger—and everything else. Even the birth control pills.

She breathed a sigh of relief. "Thanks," she said and attached the dagger to her belt. Ronelo eyed her as she did this but didn't comment.

"So where are you going?" he said. "Are you looking for the Free Sparkla people?"

Markla was quiet. Exactly how much did these Basics know? Be cautious about what you tell them, she thought. But she always followed her instincts.

"Yeah," she said. "Do you know where they are? I've only got a general idea."

"Sure, we know. And you're not going the best way."

"I know that. The best way would be to take a hover-ship or maybe a train."

"True," he said with a grin. "We don't have trains or hover-ships but I can show you a better route. If you go west a bit you'll find a path through the woods. We use it all the time and it's a lot easier. I can take you there."

"No thanks. But if you could point me in the right direction, that would be great."

He laughed. "You're so hostile, Markla."

"You attacked me! You shot me with a dart and paralyzed me and tied me up."

"Yeah, but that was yesterday. Besides, that was a misunderstanding. Also, I get the feeling you wouldn't have been too friendly, anyway."

She started to respond but stopped. Okay, maybe he was right about that. Why was she so hostile? Because people were always messing with her—that was why.

"I'm sorry," she said. "Sort of."

"No, you're not," he said with a grin. "But I like you, anyway. Also, my mom wants to talk to you."

An alarm bell went off in Markla's head. "No way. I don't want to talk to her."

"Markla, she's fine. She's on your side now, and believe me, that's a good thing."

"Really? Does she have a magic spell that can turn me into a bird or something?"

Markla was going to continue with a whole "witch tirade" when the door swung open again and a woman said, "I'm not a witch. I'm just a keeper of the land."

It was her. Markla stopped talking and stared. Then she thought about how this woman really did look like a witch.

She was dressed in the same dark-colored animal skins Markla remembered from the forest. Her gray and black hair was longer than Markla recalled, and it hung halfway down her back. Her skin was smooth but weathered, and her eyes were green like the eyes of a wolf. There were also three other people with her—two shaggy-looking guys with beards and a young woman about ten years older than Markla. The woman was tall and sinewy with the same dark hair as the witch. She wore a necklace of colored stones like the one Markla was wearing. She also had a scar on her lower jaw.

Markla braced herself. She also kept herself from grabbing the gun—but she was quite aware of its location on the table.

The woman was smiling, and her teeth were quite white. "Hello, Markla Flash. My name is Monaca, and I'm Ronelo's mother. But I think he told you that already."

"Yeah. He mentioned it."

"I think he also apologized for our treatment of you."

Markla said nothing.

Monaca laughed. "You don't hide your anger well, child."

"I'm not a child."

Monaca focused her green eyes on Markla's face, and they were like a pair of lamps. "We guard this land from the poison outside," she said. "We evaluate the life forces of those who pass through, and we didn't know who you were or what you were doing. But now we know your purpose—and you're welcome here.You're not a poisoner. Let's sit down and talk."

Markla didn't want to sit down, and she didn't want to talk, and she didn't want to hear any more witchy mumbo jumbo. She thought about Rune, and how he was imprisoned because of her—and then she thought about what he'd do if he were here.

He would say it was going to be fine, she thought. *He would tell me to sit down and talk.*

They sat at the table, and then a few more people came in, a young boy and a girl. They brought food, and it was some type of grainy bread and oil, and Markla realized she was hungry.

Monaca introduced her to the two guys who had names Markla quickly forgot. The other witchy woman was named Rala, and apparently she was Ronelo's sister. She towered over Markla but she seemed friendly enough, and it didn't matter because Markla had no intention of hanging around, and how many times did she have to say it?

Monaca took a piece of bread and looked at Markla. "You lack patience," Monaca said. "And you're filled with rage."

Markla wasn't about to argue—obviously, she was a bit testy. Meanwhile, the bread was good.

Monaca kept talking. "What happened to you? Something terrible."

Markla shrugged. "Are you talking about last week, or when?"

"I'm talking about when you were younger. You were abused, badly abused, more than you've ever told anyone—including yourself. You have flashbacks, especially when you feel trapped or forced into a place beyond your control. Then you feel rage, and you can't control yourself… You've done unspeakable things— acts of extreme violence. There was blood, lots of blood."

Markla stopped eating. Who was this woman? The things she was saying—yeah, that's exactly how it was, and she wanted to hear more but she also didn't want to hear anything. She wanted to scream. She wanted to cry. She had to get up and leave the table.

She pushed away her food and stormed outside, slamming the door behind her. She didn't know where she was going but she was walking fast, and her chest was heaving.

Ronelo was behind her now. "Markla, wait!" he said. "Don't run away."

Markla spun around to face him. "I don't want to talk about it, okay? I just want to leave. I have something to do. Does your mother know about that, too?"

Ronelo sighed. "My mothers knows a lot of things. Maybe she's psychic, or maybe she's just a good guesser. I've never been sure. Anyway, come back inside."

Markla took a deep breath and noticed the sun shining down. The leaves on the trees were like a canvas of colors, and the birds were chirping—but it all seemed a little blurry.

Stay calm, she thought. *And stop acting like an idiot.*

"Okay," Markla said. "I need my stuff. And then I really am going."

"Sure, no problem."

She saw that the room she'd been in was part of a cabin, and there were other cabins nearby. They were not clumped together in any real pattern. They were spread out among the trees. These cabins were not much different from the one where Shala and Jerome lived. Markla paused at the door, took a deep breath and plunged back inside.

Everyone was still sitting and eating. Everyone looked up, and Monaca smiled. "I'm sorry Markla. I know you want to go. Ronelo will go with you. He'll show you the way."

Markla shook her head. There was no way she wanted some strange guy traveling with her. He seemed friendly enough—but no. Then Monaca said, "I know the idea makes you uncomfortable, so Rala will go with you, too. She's my daughter. So I'm lending you the best."

What? The warrior girl? Markla wondered if she was filled with the same witchy wisdom as her mom. No, thanks. But then Rala looked at Markla and said, "Don't be an idiot, Markla. We know this forest better than you ever will, and we can take you to the Free Sparkla people." Then she smiled and said, "We won't force you to take our help, but don't be stupid."

Okay, this girl did not speak like her mother. She was more relatable.

"I appreciate your offer," Markla said. "But some people were chasing me. I think they're gone now but they could send more, and I've already caused enough trouble for people trying to help me."

"We know about them," Monaca said. "But those people are poisoners who don't belong here. We'll deal with them."

Really? And now Markla wondered where this woman got her information. She acted mysterious and creepy but there was probably a more reasonable explanation. Maybe the Basics were a lot more connected to the world than the world believed, and maybe that was a good thing.

Markla turned to Ronelo and Rala.

"All right," she said. "Let's go."

Chapter 40

Rune worked fast. He ran into the bathroom of his luxurious prison suite and slammed the door. Then he slapped the GoBug behind his ear.

He knew the device wouldn't recognize him because it was configured for Stillo, but there was an option to connect using a different name, and he used his own because his personal account was still active. Stillo could trace this and see who was using his GoBug but Rune could fix that. Everything could be fixed—always. If his plan worked, no one would ever know he'd connected at all. He just needed to be quick, and he needed some luck.

And I've always been lucky, he thought. He switched to his smasher identity and called Gort.

Pick up! Pick up!

Gort appeared in front of his eyes. "Rune! What's going on? How are you calling me?"

"Gort! I need to reformat a GoBug fast, and I need a new account for the connection—and we need to make sure all the connection data gets deleted. Can we do it?"

Gort didn't hesitate. "Yes! I'll send the script to access the code. Then send it to me."

Every GoBug had a secret identity code registered with the government. But it could be found. Gort sent Rune a smasher script, and Rune activated it to reveal the code. Then he sent the code to Gort.

"Hang on," Gort. "Here we go."

In an instant, everything went black. Rune saw nothing—and then everything came back on, and the mindstreams of the world were glowing in front of his eyes. It was so fast that even Rune was surprised.

"What happened? How did you do that so quick?"

"I'm the best," Gort said with a grin. "Also, I've done it lots of times, and I've got a great script. All the connection data is gone—wiped out. And that GoBug no longer exists for whoever owned it. If he tries to trace it—nothing. As far as changing the account that's connected, it's no longer Rune Roko. I sent you your new connection info. It's an account paid for by Gin Xantha."

"Gin Xantha?"

"Yeah, he pays for his whole family, and he's got about twenty GoBugs. We smashed into his account the other day. Eventually someone might notice that his Uncle Zio has two GoBugs, but it might take a while. No one is safe, Rune—no one. The only way to have any privacy is to not connect at all."

Rune laughed, and he thought about Markla, and how she would say the same thing. And she would be so right.

"Have you heard anything about Markla? Is she okay?"

"She's doing fine. She's busy outwitting the country's finest commando squad." He quickly told Rune about the cabin incident, and how Markla and her brother had filled the world's mindstreams with Sparkla's humiliation.

Rune laughed out loud, but then he felt a flash of fear because she was still out there. And then he heard a sound. The door in the other room was opening.

"I have to go Gort! We'll talk soon!"

Chapter 41

Burno had a weapon, and he even had new clothes, curtesy of the pilot of the extraction ship. Of course, he'd slipped the pilot some money, and the guy was going to be flying back to Sparkla in his underwear, but people had done worse things for money. At least the guy had been about his size, and even his boots fit pretty well. So maybe his luck was turning around.

The weapon was a rifle that was on board the ship—another lucky break. There wasn't a lot of ammunition but he wasn't planning to get into a firefight. As far as he was concerned, he only needed one shot. Meanwhile, he still had the food and survival supplies because Markla hadn't taken those.

Interesting girl, he thought. *I can't wait to kill her.*

Burno had a plan. He'd asked the pilot to give him a ride farther south, and he'd agreed. Now they were ready to go. Red was standing next to the ship, and the engines were on, and the big sliding door on the side was open. Red looked at Burno and shook his head.

"You're crazy to go after her. If you don't spot her from the air, how are you going to find her? You don't have a tracker. She could be anywhere."

Burno set his jaw and scowled. "She's not going just 'anywhere.' She's following that stream—heading south. She's probably trying to find Stoke, right? What else would she be doing?"

"I don't know. Maybe settling down with a local guy, having a few kids… There are lots of things she could be doing."

"Yeah, but this girl's not doing those things. This girl's a soldier. She's going to find Stoke, and we already know where he is. He's not too far south of here."

"But we're not doing too well attacking his base."

"True, but that's not our mission. She's heading that way,

and that's where I'm going to have the ship land—farther south. I'll be waiting."

Red hesitated. "I'd go with you if I could."

"Forget it. Get your ankle healed."

Red stared at Burno now. "She's got weapons, Burno, and it doesn't take a big person to fire a rifle. You know what I'm saying?"

"Yeah, I know. I won't underestimate her again."

"You're sure?"

"I'm sure. Let's go."

They stepped into the hover-ship, and it took off and sailed across the sky.

Chapter 42

Ronelo made another stupid joke, and Markla almost smiled. They were hiking through the autumn woods, and it was cool but not cold and a perfect day to walk. Despite Markla's initial hostility, she had to admit she was glad to have company.

She often said she liked being alone, but was it true? Maybe I've been lying to myself, she thought. *No one really likes to be alone.* She couldn't deny it felt comforting to have other people with her, and she couldn't deny that Ronelo was amusing—even though he talked way too much.

But it was happy talk. He kept glancing at her and asking questions. The questions were silly but they didn't bother her. In fact, she was having fun giving sarcastic answers.

"Markla, were you always this small?"

"No," she said. "Last week I was huge, like a tree."

He laughed. "Are you sure you're sixteen?"

"Yeah. I guess around here someone my age is usually married, right? Probably to a cousin."

He laughed again. "I'd totally marry you. You'd be a great wife."

"Why? Is it all the guns and grenades?"

Rala shook her head. "Leave Markla alone, Ronelo. Stop bothering her."

"I'm not bothering her! She loves my questions."

"I don't mind," Markla said.

She actually liked the way Ronelo joked around. It gave her brain a break from all the serious thoughts that were always threatening to overwhelm her.

Rala stopped walking. "Listen!" she said.

Markla stopped, and she heard it—a hover-ship. They all scrambled to hide among the trees. Markla pressed herself against the trunk of a gnarled maple.

The ship didn't pass right over them. It was a bit to the west but it was close and heading south. It was gone quick and everyone relaxed.

Markla swore. "They're still after me," she said. "I know it. You two should go back and leave me here. You're going to get yourselves killed."

"No," Rala said. "This is our land. If those people are from Sparkla, they're making a big mistake."

"Those people have weapons."

"So do we."

"Rala, I don't want to be responsible for you getting hurt."

Rala flashed Markla a fierce look. "We know about your fight, Markla—and it's our choice. You only see a few of us here, but there are more, a lot more, so don't worry. We can take care of ourselves. Things will be fine."

Markla started to object again but she stopped. She got the feeling Rala might get insulted.

They resumed walking, and Rala said, "The people of Sparkla don't understand or respect this land. We have a government but it doesn't have much power. The Sparklans call most of us 'Basics' but we don't use that name. We live in clans, and we resist any bigger kind of organization. We have some, but it's minimal."

Markla shrugged. "It sounds good."

"It's good and bad. I won't tell you Narna is a paradise—it's not. But in Sparkla people worship technology, and they've let their GoBugs and LiveDreams take over their lives. We use some technology but most of the clans are determined to not become like Sparkla… We have just enough—for now." She sighed. "I'm worried it could all change. Eventually, the people here might get seduced by all the things that seduced the Sparklans."

Markla gave a short laugh. "Your mother doesn't seem ready to be seduced."

"My mother is part of the problem. She embraces lots of old ways but the younger people know about the rest of the world. They know it's out there because you can't keep it hidden. So my mother's ancient rituals and weird talk just sounds crazy to them, and there's a danger that they'll turn away and end up embracing all that other stuff. We need something in between—something honest, something that's based on education and reality, not ancient ideas or greed or just wanting to control other people."

Markla wasn't sure what to think of all this. Did Narna have a president? Markla got the feeling that Rala would make a good one. But then she thought about that hover-ship.

"Rala, has anyone in Narna embraced hover-ships?"

"No. I think that ship was from Sparkla."

"But it was heading south. That's where we're going. There could be some people on that ship looking for me."

"It's possible. But there's a clan where we're going, and they'll help us. And they know we're coming."

"How do they know?"

"My mother told them."

"Oh. Does she have some kind of psychic way to communicate?"

Rala smiled. "No. She has a radio."

Chapter 43

Diana looked at herself in the mirror. Natural blond hair was rare in Sparkla, and hers was especially lustrous tonight. But I still look tired, she thought. *My eyes always have those tired-looking rings.*

She knew she was about twice the age of the typical soldier in this fortress—but that was only because they were so young. She also noticed these young guys were still eyeing her when she walked by, so she wasn't dead yet. Well, if it helped get the job done that was fine.

She was wearing a short black skirt and an untucked white shirt with sleeves. Her legs were bare. She stepped back and studied herself in the mirror one last time. Don't kid yourself, she thought. *You can still turn a few heads.*

As she left her room, she thought about the pistol in the bottom drawer of the dresser. It had been Kalo's weapon, and she frowned. What had driven him into the arms of 20 Eyes? Had she done something wrong as a mother? Or maybe something right? Either way, she wasn't going to be using a weapon like that this evening. Then suddenly, for the thousandth time, she thought about that black dagger she'd handed to Markla—and she felt a little sick. She wanted to forget that moment but it kept popping up in her head. It was a wide-awake nightmare that wouldn't go away.

I knew that crazy girl was going to kill Aldo, she thought. *Why did I give it to her?*

She shook her head and told herself to forget it. She had something important to do. She walked out of her apartment and headed across an enclosed steel bridge that connected to another building. Along the way several scanners pointed at her face and allowed her to proceed through metal doors that slid open as she approached. Eventually, she got into the turbo lift and headed down to the main control center. This was an area she'd never visited before, and it was one of the only places she had left to see. Last night she'd visited the power station out beyond the landing field. When she stepped out she was in a brightly lit hallway. She saw cameras and a guard in black body armor holding an automatic rifle.

"Hello," she said with a smile.

He looked like a kid. He looked like Kalo had looked before he'd died—before he'd been killed by the police. Did he even shave yet? Yeah, but not much.

"You can't be down here, ma'am," he said.

"I have security clearance."

He studied her, and she remained still as the 'eye capture' feature of his GoBug scanned her face. She knew the data was now floating in front of his eyes.

"Yes, you do, ma'am,' he said with a grin. "You're one of the few."

"Good," she said with another smile. So her hack had worked. She wasn't a smasher but she was a teacher of technology, and this hadn't been too difficult. She already had a high level of clearance so bumping it up a few notches hadn't been too hard.

She looked around. "I need to check this space for a new piece of equipment. We need some place very secure."

"This area is secure. Down there is the War Room and the Electronic Brian that runs the whole base. This is the first checkpoint. There are two more."

"Have you seen the room?"

"Yes, ma'am," he said, and he puffed out his chest a bit. "It's right after the last checkpoint. I've done duty there a few times. There are always at least two security people in there, and there are always armed guards stationed outside the room. You can see it if you want to. I can take you there."

"That would be great."

He seemed eager, and he showed her everything. They went through the last checkpoint where there were two armed guards and then entered a sprawling underground bunker. The bunker was a cavernous room filled with glowing lights and glass consoles. It was also loaded with security. In addition to several more guards, there were eye scanners and DNA verification devices above each piece of equipment. Was all this really necessary?

The government is awfully scared of its citizens, she thought. It was the sort of thing Kalo would've said.

There were several people in the room, all of them military. They glanced at Diana but didn't say anything. Meanwhile, she recorded all of it on her GoBug using her own "eye-capture" feature. Then she left the area and said good night to her guide, and she wondered if he was watching her walk away.

When she got back to her room she slid into a chair and activated the dream station on her desktop.

She'd only met the Free Sparkla people once, right after Gin Xantha had asked her to take this job and move to this dismal place. They only wanted to know one thing, and she'd told them she'd help because Kalo had hated the government, and the government had tortured Rune.

Kalo was a 20 Eyes subversive, she thought. But maybe he'd been right about a few things. *He would've wanted me to hand Markla that dagger. He would've been proud of me.*

She told the Free Sparkla people that she didn't want to transmit information directly from a GoBug, and the information she had was too complex for a radio message. She said she'd transmit the information a different way.

She waved her hand and activated a LiveDream. It was a public dream, not encrypted or secure. It was a LiveDream that could be posted from an anonymous account to a free mindstream. The dream was called "Treasure Hunt." It was a horror dream where someone was chased by a demon. In the middle of the chase, the dreamer entered a vast complex of tunnels beneath a mountain. Eventually, the dreamer entered a long hallway and encountered other demons, and then finally discovered a room filled with treasure. The treasure was well protected but not invulnerable. The demons were relentless—but they could still be beaten.

This is what someone would see if they played the LiveDream under normal circumstances. But if they played the LiveDream using a special promotional code, they would see something quite different. They would see a complete tour of Fort Freedom.

Chapter 44

Rune closed the door to the bathroom. The door had no lock and it wouldn't matter much but it might buy him a few seconds. He was in a sweat as he scanned the tiny room.

Where could he hide a GoBug? The drain? No way. Under a towel? In the shower? He had to be quick.

He heard a voice booming in the other room. "Rune, where are you?"

It was Stillo. Rune swore and kept searching and now he saw a spot. On top of the sink was that small ceramic dish holding several pieces of colored soap. As the door to the bathroom swung open, he mixed the GoBug in with the soap pieces. He turned toward the door just as Stillo opened it.

"What's going on?" Rune said, trying to sound casual. "Another nightmare?"

Stillo scowled. "Where's my GoBug?"

"Your what?"

"Don't lie to me. I had it when I came in here, and now it's gone. You stole it when we were fooling around with that takedown move."

Rune shrugged. "I didn't take your GoBug. Maybe it fell off. Maybe it's on the floor somewhere."

"I didn't see it—get up against the wall!" Before Rune could move, Stillo grabbed him and threw him against the tiles. "Put your hands on the wall and don't move!" Stillo said.

Rune did as he was told and tried not to look at the soap. Stillo patted him down and made him turn his pockets inside out. Then Stillo stood back and scowled again.

"Okay, it's not on you. But it's in here somewhere, isn't it?"

Rune glanced sideways at the shower. Stillo leaped toward the shower and pulled back the purple curtain. Then he stuck his big head inside. Rune reached into the soap dish, grabbed the GoBug, and shoved it into his pocket.

Stillo checked the soap dish in the shower and checked the drain cover but it was firmly attached. Then he came over to the sink—and he looked in that soap dish, and he opened the medicine cabinet above the sink that had nothing in it but a toothbrush and some toothpaste. He examined the toothpaste and slammed the cabinet shut.

"Can't you search for it with an EB?" Rune said. "You can see exactly where it is."

"I didn't try that yet. I just came running in here when I noticed it was missing. Besides, you could take out the power crystal."

"Yeah, but if I put it back in and tried to use it, you'd see your account is active. You can also set up an alert on an EB or on another GoBug that will tell you when it's being used." Rune smiled. "I can show you how to do it." Then he smiled again because the alert would show nothing. From a digital point of view, Stillo's GoBug no longer existed. But Rune had a feeling that Stillo wasn't too tech savvy. Most people who get paid to stomp around all day and look mean weren't too enlightened.

Stillo stormed back into the other room. He was on the floor now, searching under the bed. He was rifling through the bedsheets and the pillows. He was searching in the empty closet. But he kept his eyes on Rune, too—and Rune realized he'd come in here alone. In fact, the door was probably unlocked, and why not just make a run for it?

Stillo stood up. "Don't even think about it. I'll sound the alarm."

"How? With your GoBug?"

Rune dashed toward the door—and yes, it was unlocked. He yanked it open and rushed into the hall—and crashed right into another guard. The guy grabbed him in two massive arms, turned him around, and tossed him back into the room.

Stillo shook his head. "How dumb do you think I am, Rune? Blort was right outside."

"Yeah, I see that."

"And I'm going to check the EB and see who has my GoBug. And it better not be you."

"It won't be," Rune said. "I guarantee it."

The two guards left and locked the door. Rune took a deep breath. Then he sat on the bed and laughed.

Chapter 45

The weather turned unusually warm for the time of year, and Markla decided to take a bath in the stream.

She wasn't shy but she didn't feel like being naked around Ronelo. Of course, she also had no idea how these people normally lived. Maybe they took baths together all the time. She mentioned this to Rala, who said it wasn't the case, and Rala sent Ronelo to scout ahead. Markla removed her clothes and slipped into the water—and yeah, this was a great idea.

The water felt cool against her skin but not cold, and the bottom of the stream was soft and silty between her toes. She thought about Rune, and she wished he were here, and she once again tried to bury her merciless feelings of guilt. It was something she often did with her worst thoughts. Ronelo came back as she was getting out of the water.

He was a bit downstream, and he stopped walking when he spotted her, but she could see him watching as she used a towel to dry off. He wasn't staring but did he glance a few times? What was he thinking? *Well, he's a guy and I'm a naked girl, so what would he be thinking?* She didn't want him checking her out but she couldn't deny feeling a little flattered, and she wondered about his history, and why he was paying her so much attention. She'd never considered herself to be overly attractive—but then again she seemed to attract some pretty good-looking guys—Dru, who she pushed out of her mind right away, and Rune, who was the best, and now this guy Ronelo who'd been joking about marrying her all morning.

Back in school I was the crazy girl, she thought. *But now I'm Markla Flash, man magnet.* She laughed to herself.

Before she could get her clothes on the radio beeped. It was lying on the ground beside her pants.

" 'Hiker one,' are you there? " 'Hiker one' can you hear me?"

She seized the device in a tight grip. "Yes! I'm here! What's happening?"

Rala came over and stood nearby. There was lots of static but they could hear Jerome on the other end.

"Your mother was released and she went home," he said. "The commandos were called back, too—but there's still one guy chasing you. That's all I know."

"What about Rune?"

"He's okay. He's not hurt."

"Can you get him a message?"

"No. But he's all right. That's all for now."

Jerome disconnected, and Markla stood staring at the radio in silence.

Her mind felt like a pot boiling over—so there was no real news about Rune, and there was still someone chasing her, and she wanted to throw something, or punch something, or maybe just scream. But then Rala put an arm around her shoulder and squeezed her a bit, and suddenly Markla felt better.

"You two should leave," Markla said. "You're going to get hurt because of me."

"We've already covered this, Markla. We're here because we want to be."

Ronelo joined them now, and Markla realized she was still only wearing a towel. But Ronelo didn't make any jokes. Instead, he said, "We don't want Narna to turn into Sparkla. We want to help you. Let's go."

So Markla got dressed and they started walking again. There was less talk now, and everyone seemed more serious. They walked all day, and Rala told them it wasn't much farther but it was getting dark. Was it safe to sleep with that commando guy out there?

"I'm sure they gave him more stuff," Markla said. "He probably has night vision gear. He could have a tracker or those rover things. He'll find us while we're sleeping."

Rala looked around at the dense forest. "This is when my mother would say 'don't worry, the land will protect you.' "

"Your mother's not here."

"Yeah, I know. That's why we need to take turns keeping watch."

"I'll go first," Markla said. She never slept much anyway, and she suspected this wasn't the night she'd suddenly start. She also noticed that both of her companions had SuperSeal sleeping bags—more proof that these Basics weren't so basic. She mentioned it, and Rala laughed.

"It's a philosophy and a lifestyle," Rala said. "But we're not stupid. We don't want to be cold."

Rala and Ronelo went to sleep, and Markla wrapped herself in an insulated blanket. In her hand was the weighty pistol she'd brought from Rune's house. She also had a small heating orb but she didn't use it. She stayed out of sight near a mossy tree and surrounded herself by other leafy things. She stared into the darkness.

She gripped the gun while her mind reeled with thoughts. What was Rune doing, what was Tommi doing, how had she ended up here? She thought about her mother stumbling around drunk, and her four cats—especially Raz, the gray female with a few battle scars who was always getting into trouble. How was Raz doing without her?

Meanwhile, the forest was filled with the noise of leaves rustling, insects humming, and the gurgle of the nearby stream. After a while she heard another noise—and she turned quick and saw Ronelo.

He was grinning in the darkness. "It's my turn," he said.

"No, it isn't. I haven't been out here that long."

"Yeah, but I couldn't sleep. So you go ahead."

"I won't be able to sleep, either."

"So I guess we'll just sit here together." He dropped down beside her with his own blanket. "Hey, I saw that flute in your backpack," he said with a smile. "Maybe you can play me a song."

"I don't know any songs."

"Then what do you play?"

"I just play what's in my head."

He laughed. "That must be a pretty wild song."

She started to scowl at him but then she laughed, too—because he had no idea. "Sometimes it helps me sleep," she said. "But right now I want to stay awake."

"Yeah, and I'm staying awake, too. Someday, this will be a fun story to tell our kids."

Markla rolled her eyes. "Ronelo, I'm not the best girl for you. Besides, I have somebody, and you know that."

"And I'm sure he's a great guy. But if you ever get tired of him, you know where to find me."

"Yeah, out here in the middle of nowhere."

"You'd like it out here, Markla. I think Rune would like it, too. Seriously, when he gets out, you two should come live with us."

"You don't know us. You've only known me for two days, and for part of that time I was tied up and gagged."

"It's easier to get to know someone under extreme circumstances. I think it speeds things up. Anyway, I know you think I'm joking, but I'm not. I really like you."

He looked at her, and all the humor was gone. For an instant, her heart beat a little faster.

She looked off into the darkness. "That's nice, Ronelo—but there's a lot you don't know about me."

"You mean all that stuff my mom was saying?"

"Yeah, that's part of it, and I don't want to talk about those things. I never do, okay?"

"Okay. But in time, those things will fade."

"I don't think so. They'll always be there, plus a lot of other stuff. The list keeps getting longer."

Now under the blanket, she felt his hand touching hers—and she jerked away from him.

"What are you doing?" she said.

"What? I was trying to make you feel better."

She was giving him a sharp stare now but not speaking. Did he mean any harm? Probably not. But did she want him doing that? No.

"Ronelo, I like you, and I appreciate your help. But don't touch me."

Her tone sounded like a reprimand, and she kind of regretted it. But he didn't seem offended.

"You like me?" he said with a smile. "I guess you don't know me, either. Maybe someday." He turned away from her gaze and stared into the darkness. "I'm sorry. I shouldn't have done that… You should get some sleep."

"Yeah, maybe I'll try and do that."

He gave her a sideways glance and laughed. "I guess you're not going to give me a goodnight kiss."

She hesitated, and she actually considered it—on the cheek, of course. Because she felt bad about her sharp tone, and because he'd been so nice, and he'd been helping her a lot. Also, she couldn't deny that under different circumstances she would totally go for him.

Instead, she just smiled. "Good night, Ronelo. Wake me up if someone attacks."

A minute later she was crawling into her SuperSeal sleeping bag. She closed the top and shut her eyes. But she was still awake.

Chapter 46

Tanna plopped down on her new bed in Fort Freedom, and she frowned. Why was her mattress filled with stones? Was that some kind of military thing? She was trying to adapt to this awful place but obviously the people who'd built it didn't understand her life of luxury. Back home she lived in a glittering palace and had a shoe closet bigger than this stupid bedroom. She rolled her eyes and sighed. Well, she was the one who'd wanted to get involved.

I'm so spoiled, she thought. *I need to be tougher—like Markla.*

She frowned again because it infuriated her to have this thought in her head, and she didn't want to have another thought about Markla Flash ever. But a few seconds later she was on her GoBug, bringing up pictures of this girl she despised.

She'd seen these pictures before but she was looking again, and this time she was looking more carefully, trying to see something—anything—that would offer a clue as to why Rune liked her so much.

Okay, Markla wasn't really ugly, and some people might even say she was cute. Maybe she was the cutest killer in Sparkla. But she doesn't have a rocking body like mine, Tanna thought, and her sense of fashion was terrible. Loose flannel shirts, cat hair all over the place, no makeup, and the hair on her head was a total disaster. Spilt ends, tangles—does this girl own a brush? *Why have long hair if you're not going to take care of it? Does she use any kind of products—ever?* But Tanna noted with satisfaction that Markla's untamed locks were midnight black, just like her own. So that was one thing they had in common.

It's not her looks, Tanna thought. *I've got her beat by a long shot.* So what is it?

Maybe Rune just has a thing for sociopathic killers. *Well, she definitely has me beat there.* But there was also a great chance that Rune would never see Markla again. Hopefully, Markla would be dead soon, with her brains splattered all over the forest—and when that happy day arrived Rune would need some consoling, and then he'd move on. It was probably going to happen. So why didn't this feel right?

Tanna recalled seeing Markla's house—and reading her profile, and her history of abuse. *She survived all of that, and do I want to be responsible for her death?* Now the image of Markla stared back at her, and Tanna looked away, and then she felt a twinge of something strange—was it guilt? She swore and switched off the image. And then there was a knock on her door.

She leaped up and ran into the living room to answer it. Stillo stood there smiling.

Tanna's eyes opened wide. "How did it go?" she said. "Come on in."

Stillo was still smiling as they sat at the kitchen table. "It went great," he said. "Rune put the GoBug in a soap dish and then stashed it in his pocket while I was searching the shower."

"Perfect! I thought we blew it the first time. Why didn't it fall off when you were wrestling with him? I thought that was the plan, to just let it fall and pretend not to notice."

"Yeah, well, it didn't. But that's because he stole it first, and that worked out even better because now he thinks it was his idea. And after my great performance in his room, I'm sure he has no clue that we set this up. He'll be using that thing soon."

"You always were a good actor. By the way, how's that going?"

Stillo was involved with theater. Despite the popularity of LiveDreams, people still liked real theater. Because the people seemed more real.

He shrugged. "I can't do much stationed up here. When I go back, I'll do more. They always want me to play a big dumb guy."

"Well, you are big."

He grinned. "I guess. So, what happens now?"

She laughed. "Rune thinks it's an ordinary GoBug but it's not. Since it's not showing up on the EB, I'm guessing he's already reformatted it, probably with help from the same person who smashed into the grid. But he only reformatted a shell of the real GoBug, an electronic facade. The real GoBug is still active... Unfortunately, the call he used to do the reformatting can't be traced. That info was lost when it was reformatted. But when he initiates a new connection from the new identity, we'll be able to trace it. I'm guessing he'll connect to an encrypted mindstream for smashers, and I'm sure the person on the other end has all kinds of encryption to hide their identity—but Rune's GoBug has a special script that can crack it. At the very least, we'll locate the GoBug, even if we don't know the identity of the user. Then we'll send a squad and make the arrest. So hopefully he'll connect soon."

Stillo raised his eyebrows. "Nice," he said. "Did your boyfriend set this up?"

"No, I asked another script writer working for my dad. I didn't tell Jorro anything."

"Really? I thought he was helping you?"

"He was supposed to be but he hasn't been doing much. So I gave it to this other guy, and we'll see what happens." She smiled. "I hate guys who can't get the job done."

Stillo cocked his head. "Are you and Jorro breaking up? Because you know I'm available. And I get it done."

She laughed again. She'd known Stillo since they were about ten years old, and he'd been making these types of comments for years. But it was all fun talk. Nothing had ever happened between them.

"I don't think so."

"One of these days you'll come around, Tanna. And you'll never go back."

Tanna hesitated. Then she said, "Maybe. But it won't be today."

Chapter 47

What Rune wanted more than anything was to talk to Markla. He wanted to know she was alive. He wanted to hear her voice.

He knew someone could bring up a display that would show every active GoBug in the fortress. So even though this one wasn't registered to him, someone could still see a blip that would show there was a GoBug active in this room. But that was only if they were specifically looking for one.

Of course, Stillo was looking, so Rune had to be careful. He decided he'd only use it for brief time periods, and only at odd hours—like 3 a.m. It was still risky but it was better than nothing.

He watched the time, and the minutes seemed like hours, but finally he put the GoBug behind his ear and called Gort. Rune guessed Gort would be sleeping but he might have an alarm set for certain kinds of calls and messages. In less than a minute, Gort appeared in front of Rune's eyes. He didn't look that sleepy.

"Rune! You still have the GoBug!"

"Yeah, for now."

"So, what's been happening?"

"I'm being interrogated by Tanna Xantha. But MindCore isn't working, so she's using regular LiveDreams."

"Why isn't MindCore working? Do you have help inside?"

Rune started to tell Gort about Diana—but he stopped. There was no reason to get her involved.

"I don't have any help," Rune said. "It just doesn't work. And the interrogation is getting strange because Tanna seems to like me."

"It's not that strange, Rune. You're a likable guy. But she's devious so don't trust her."

"You know her?"

Gort hesitated. "I'm familiar with her. And if she likes you, play along. It might lead to an opportunity."

"I might do that," Rune said. "But really, I don't care about Tanna. I want to talk to Markla. Is there any way to make that happen?"

"She has a GoBug but it's got no power. She probably removed the crystal."

"She might have smashed it. Smashing GoBugs is one of her hobbies."

"Okay, well, she also has a radio but I haven't been contacting her. I've been contacting a friend in Narna who relays messages to her. He calls her 'Hiker One.' Hey, I can probably call her directly on my radio, and you can hear her voice through my GoBug. Then I can patch the GoBug through some speakers in the room, and she could hear you on her radio. So yeah, it's possible. It's a little dangerous for both of us, and you can't talk long. I mean it has to be really quick. Plus she's probably asleep."

"I'd give anything to talk to her for even a minute. Do it!"

"I'll give it a try."

Rune's stomach filled with butterflies. This was an amazing idea! Please be awake, he thought. *Please, please!* He knew Markla was a light sleeper. In fact, he wouldn't be surprised if she was up. As he heard Gort calling out across the airwaves, Rune felt his heart pounding.

"Hiker One, are you out there? Can you hear me Hiker One?"

There was silence.

"Hiker One, can you hear me? Are you there Hiker One?"

Rune realized he was holding his breath—and suddenly there was some static, and then a voice said, "Hello? This is Hiker One."

Rune felt like his heart would explode. It was her.

"Markla!" he said. "It's me, Rune!"

There was more static. Then she said, *"Rune? Rune, is that really you? Where are you? Are you okay? What's going on?"*

"I'm okay! I'm in a fortress, and I'm fine. How are *you?*"

"I'm all right! I'm out here in the middle of nowhere, and I wish you were here with me. I worry about you all the time… How are you talking to me?"

"I stole a GoBug, and Gort has a radio. It's a long story, but we can't talk much. I really miss you."

"I miss you, too… Rune, don't do anything stupid trying to escape, okay?"

"I won't. I met Tanna Xantha. She's pretty evil but she's not that smart. I'm just playing a game with her, waiting for my chance."

"Be careful, Rune. She's sneaky."

Rune laughed. "She thinks she is—but I'm only worried about you. I heard there were people chasing you through the woods."

"They're not going to catch me. I can't wait to see you again."

"I can't wait, either."

Suddenly, Gort's voice cut in. "I hate to interrupt, but that's probably long enough."

"I have to go," Rune said. "Markla, I love you."

"I love you, too. A lot!"

Gort disconnected the call. Rune sat staring into the darkness. It was quiet, and he could hear himself breathing hard.

Chapter 48

Burno crawled out of his SuperSeal bag before the sun came up. The air was cool, and he stared at the fading stars and wondered about his adversary. Was she awake yet? He knew that she was. All the best ones were early risers.

He'd walked a long time yesterday, looking for the perfect spot to kill her, and now he was standing near a riverbank. It was an endless forest, and Markla could come from many directions but he was pretty sure she'd be coming here.

She'd been following that stream, and the stream led to this river and a place close to where Stoke had set up a base. But Stoke was not in Narna. Stoke and his people were across the river in Sparkla, and there was only one way to cross the river without a boat, and Markla didn't have a boat. Not yet, anyway. That girl was full of tricks. But she probably had no boat, and so she'd need to cross this bridge.

The river was wide, and the bridge was long and spindly. It was also narrow and made of wood and not meant for vehicles. It occurred to him that someone must be maintaining the bridge—but who?

He heard a sound, and he jerked his head around fast, scanning the trees. Was someone watching him? No, it was just a breeze. Why did this seemingly deserted place make him feel so nervous? He'd heard stories about some fierce people living out here, and he didn't want any trouble. Really, he couldn't wait to get back to Sparkla because they had real stuff in Sparkla, like GoBugs, grocery stores, and shopping centers. Of course they also had grandstanding idiots telling constant lies on mindstreams, and LiveDreams filled with more lies and misinformation, and military leaders who took orders from self-serving government scumbags.

Maybe it's not so bad over here.

He'd spent his whole life fighting for people who rarely appreciated it. Maybe Markla Flash had a point, and in a way it seemed like a shame to kill this young warrior girl who was so much smarter and braver than the imbeciles and cowards who ran the world. But that's the way it usually went—it was always the best ones who had to die.

I need to get out of these woods, he thought. *I might turn into a real rebel.* And now he laughed, because really, he'd always been a rebel.

Right about here, he thought. This was a perfect spot to wait. This is where it would end.

Chapter 49

Markla was hopeful, and her heart felt light as a butterfly. Rune was alive, and the sun was rising again.

They were camped at the top of a slight hill covered with piney trees. The water from the nearby stream was colder today but Markla didn't mind as she waded into it. She got out and dried herself off and put on her clothes, and then she saw Ronelo coming out of the woods. He didn't see her at first—but then he did, and he grinned.

"Markla, you get up so early."

"Yeah. I want to avoid people watching me take a bath."

He laughed. "I didn't know you were here. I couldn't sleep. I guess I missed everything."

"You didn't miss much."

"Why do you say that? You're really pretty."

She stared at him and decided it was a harmless remark.

"No, I'm not," she said. " 'Cute' is the best I ever get."

"Well, you're cute and pretty. Rune's a smart guy."

Now she laughed. She was glad he'd mentioned Rune. She started drying her hair with a towel. "I hear we're meeting up with the River Clan today."

"Later this morning. Your hair is really wild."

"Yeah, but not in a good way… My mom wanted it to be short, and that's why it's long—and that's why it's always going to be long." She paused. Why was she telling him this? Maybe because he seemed so interested in her.

He hesitated. "Your mom had no clue… Do you want breakfast?"

They went and found Rala, and together they ate some bread. It was tasty, with a grainy texture and a variety of nuts mixed in. Rala said they'd meet up with the River Clan and then go to a certain bridge. On the other side of the bridge was Sparkla and Stoke. There was also some fighting going on near there so they had to be careful.

Suddenly, Markla was worried, and she put down her bread crust. "What about that hover-ship we saw? Someone is out there waiting for me. If it's the same guy from before, I'm an idiot. I could've killed him, but I let him go, and now he's still out there, and he's going to try and kill me and maybe shoot one of you."

Suddenly her good mood was gone. Rala reached out and grabbed her hand. "Markla, it's going to be fine. You've got friends here—and you're a warrior."

"I'm not a warrior!" Markla said, and she felt her voice shaking with anger. "I'm tired of hearing that. You have no idea what's in my head." She took a deep breath and suddenly found her eyes tearing up. She wiped them a bit, and when she spoke again her voice was soft. "I'm sorry. I didn't mean to yell… Actually, what's in my head is a lot of crazy stuff. Sometimes I don't handle it too well."

"I think you handle yourself fine. Just do the best you can and know there are people who care about you—because that's what really matters."

Markla didn't respond but now she thought about Rune, and Tommi—and even Rala and Ronelo. And once again she had a feeling of hope. "Everything is always so difficult," she said. "I wish that just once something would be easy."

Rala smiled at Markla, and then her radio crackled. She picked up the device.

"Hello," she said. "This is Rala."

"Rala? This is Loro."

"Loro! We're close to you. What's happening?"

"We captured a Sparklan soldier. I think he's after your friend."

Markla's head jerked upward. *What?*

Markla leaned close to the radio and grabbed the transmission button. "Who is he?" she said. "What happened? Did anyone get hurt?"

There was some static and then Loro said, "He's some kind of commando. No one was hurt. A hover-ship dropped him off and we followed him for a bit and then he fell into a hole-trap."

Markla paused—and now she laughed out loud. This guy sure did like falling into holes.

"What do you want us to do with him?" Loro said. "We can get rid of him."

"No!" Markla said. "He has a wife and a daughter, and I have a better idea."

"Okay. We'll keep him here."

Markla looked at Rala and Ronelo, and now they all laughed. The day was off to a great start.

Chapter 50

Two goons chained Rune's hands and feet and shoved him down the hall. He knew he was headed to the nightmare room.

Rune had hidden the GoBug inside the bolla drum. It wasn't the greatest hiding spot but it was less obvious than sticking it under the mattress, and it seemed like a luckier place to put it. Even if they found the GoBug, it wouldn't be so bad now. He'd talked to Markla, and she was alive, and the sound of her voice had been thrilling—and he would see her again. He just had to find a way out of here.

Tanna was behind the console, looking sexy as always in her black leggings, and Rune let his eyes linger on her longer than usual. The trick was to keep her happy but not too happy. She stared back at him and shook her head.

"Hi, Rune. You haven't told me anything. Do you see how that's a problem?"

"It's really not a problem for me, Tanna."

"Yeah, but it could be, and I don't want that. Anyway, we'll see how things go."

A bad feeling descended on him like a dark cloud. She didn't seem too friendly today, and he recalled Gort's words about how she was always scheming.

Rune decided not to say anything. Yeah, he'd let her do the talking. But she didn't say anything else.

One of the goons strapped him into the chair and placed the GoBug behind his ear. Tanna glanced at him and started the nightmare. For an instant everything went black, and then he was somewhere else.

***

He was standing on a rocky mountaintop, and he shivered. There were no trees, and the wind was cold, and the sky was ash gray. It was a high mountain, and in every direction he saw more jagged mountains. About fifty paces in front of him, perched on a cliff, was an ancient-looking castle made of blueish stone. There were two towers on either side of a massive wooden door.

Despite the cold, he started to sweat. A castle was a common nightmare trope and not very original. But Tanna wasn't overly original with her dream writing, and scary things often happened inside these LiveDream castles. Was this Tanna's idea of a date? The thought made him uneasy.

She might know he'd stolen that GoBug. Sure, Stillo might not have said anything because it would be embarrassing to report it—but what if he had, and what if she knew? Despite her recent attempts to seem nicer, she had a sadistic streak.

Rune considered waiting outside in the chilly air but it would be pointless. She could make him enter, so he might as well enter. As he approached the door it opened. He stopped and listened, and he tried to peer inside, but he saw and heard nothing suspicious. He took a few steps forward.

He found himself in a dimly lit room with a gray stone floor, stone walls, and a vaulted ceiling supported by heavy wooden beams. There were narrow windows high on the walls that allowed a smattering of light, but not much. He searched the shadows, looking for any kind of threat. He took two steps, and it popped up in front of him—an assassin! He gave a shout and leaped backwards. But then he stopped and stared, and he shook his head. In front of him stood a clown-faced manikin dressed in black. The fake guy had a plastic axe in his hand, and he was grinning through broken teeth and shaking his phony weapon. The "killer" gave a high-pitched laugh and then vanished.

Rune gave a grim smile. Was Tanna trying to be funny? The

absurdity might be part of the plan so he needed to stay alert. Then he heard some noise, and he noticed a door set into the wall, and he realized the noise was coming from there. Okay, I guess I'm supposed to open it, he thought. So he did, and he walked into a completely different world.

Through the door was a restaurant. It was bright and sunny, and a chorus of happy voices greeted his ears. Polished oak tables were filled with people laughing and eating, and steaming food was piled high on silver plates. Meanwhile, wide windows showed a bustling city street outside complete with pedestrians and hover-cars. There were no castles or mountains in sight.

This place seemed more real than the castle, and Rune was impressed. Then he felt a tap on his shoulder. He turned, and there was Tanna.

Rune caught his breath. She was wearing a tight red dress with a slit on the side, exposing one of her shapely thighs. Her hair was untied, tumbling down like a gorgeous black river. On her feet were stylish shoes with straps and high heels.

Okay, maybe she does like me, he thought, and he recalled Gort's words. *This might be my way out.*

She laughed. "Hi, Rune. How did you like my castle?"

"It was very realistic," he said, and he waved his hand at the room. "Are the king and queen in here eating dinner?"

"Not yet," she quipped. "But we can sit down if you like."

Naturally, there was a table free near the window. So Rune followed her to it and sat down across from her. He ran through a quick checklist of what to say. Mainly, don't mention Markla, he thought. He knew she hated that.

Tanna laughed. "Rune, my castle was terrible. I didn't create that. I just took it from a dreambank. I thought it might be fun to watch your reaction."

"Oh. And what was my reaction?"

"You weren't too impressed. You thought it was stupid and unoriginal."

Rune laughed. "That's not true. I wasn't sure what to think. I'm still not sure. Did you bring me here to eat dinner?"

She hesitated. "I'm supposed to be torturing you. But that was getting dull."

"Yeah, I agree."

"So, how do you like my dress?"

"I like it."

"That's it? Don't I look nice?"

Rune smiled. "You *do* look nice, Tanna. But this is a LiveDream. Anyone can look nice."

"Oh, and I don't look nice in real life?"

He was quiet for a second. Then he said, "Actually, you look nice in real life, too."

He was still thinking about how to escape, and he was wondering what she had planned. They could do anything in a guided LiveDream—anything, and no one would see it or know about it. But she could not physically feel anything. Only he could feel, and this image of Tanna was just a character she was manipulating. It was like she was watching a puppet of herself.

"Do you want something to eat?" she said. "You can get anything here, and it'll taste great." She waved her hand. "I didn't create this, either. I'm just doing the guiding. I told you, I'm not a very good dream writer."

"That's not true. That last one was pretty good."

"Thanks. But it's not my calling."

"And what's your calling?"

She sighed. "I'm trying to figure that out, Rune. I do a little of this and a little of that but I'm all over the place. My father thinks I'm good at everything but he's wrong. I'm *okay* at everything but not really great at anything. I'm pretty, and I've got rich parents, and that's about it."

She paused, like she was waiting for him to say something.

"That's not it," Rune said. "You're smart, too."

"You think I'm smart?"

"Yeah, you're smart."

She smiled again. "Are you just saying that to keep me happy?"

"No, I'm not."

"You hate me, don't you?"

"No, I don't."

She leaned toward him a bit and lowered her voice. "Do you think under different circumstances we could be friends?"

"Maybe."

"What about right now?"

She reached across the table and put her hand on top of his. "We're in a LiveDream, Rune. Anything can happen, and no one will know about it but us."

He hesitated. "But you can't feel anything."

"Do you want me to feel something?"

Now Rune felt himself starting to sweat again. This wasn't going quite the way he'd planned—but he'd never had a plan, just a vague idea, and he was starting to realize that for his vague idea to work he might need to do a few things he didn't want to do.

Just keep stalling her, he thought. "I don't know," he said. "Maybe."

He guessed this answer would annoy her but it didn't. Then the restaurant vanished, and they were on a sandy beach.

Whoah! Smooth transition!

He scanned the scene fast, and it looked like the same sandy beach they'd been on before. But this time it was evening. The moon was full and the stars were like a hundred winking diamonds. A tropical breeze was blowing in from the sea and there was no one else in sight.

They were sitting on a blanket. She was beside him, and she was no longer wearing the red dress. She was wearing a two-piece bathing suit, and she was so close to him. Meanwhile, he was also in a bathing suit, with no shirt, and she was touching his thigh.

She put her mouth near his ear. "Kiss me," she said.

Rune froze—and a swarm of thoughts blew through his head.

He didn't want to kiss her but what would happen if he didn't? What would happen if he did? Did it matter anyway because none of this was real? And most of all, what would Markla think?

I should pull away, he thought. Or maybe pretend I'm kissing Markla. Or maybe not do anything at all.

While he was thinking, Tanna kissed him. She twisted around and kissed him hard on the lips. She practically climbed on top of him.

Rune was stunned. Markla was the only girl he'd ever kissed, and she was a great kisser—but so was Tanna. This wasn't even real, and yet Tanna's kiss was filled with passion. It was a long kiss, too, and she poured herself into it, and Rune was trying to think of a way out—but she was right up against him, and her body felt so warm and full of life, and her kiss was electric and thrilling, and it was hard to think.

It's like I'm drowning, he thought. *I need some air!*

He pushed her away. He took a breath and said, "You're using me."

"What?"

Rune frowned. "You're pretending to like me so you can get information from me."

Now it was her turn to seem stunned.

"No, I'm not."

"Yes, you are."

She sat back and shook her head. "Do you really think I'd do that? I'd whore myself out for information?"

"Why not? It's a clever plan. After all, this isn't real, and you said it yourself—no one will ever know what happens in a guided dream. Meanwhile, you don't even feel anything, so you're not whoring yourself out. It's a brilliant idea, Tanna, and I almost fell for it."

She hesitated. Then she said, "That would be a brilliant plan, Rune. But it's not my plan." Then she stared at him with those gorgeous brown eyes. "Rune, I really like you."

This is so crazy, Rune thought. And in the farthest corner of his mind, for just an instant, he thought that maybe she wasn't all bad. But then he laughed.

"No, you don't," he said. "You're just being clever."

"I'm not that clever, Rune. Well, sometimes I am. But not this time."

"I think you should end this dream."

"I don't want to end it."

"I don't want to do anything. If you really like me, you'll respect that."

Rune was feeling pretty good. She seemed unsure of herself now. But then she narrowed her eyes and said, "Rune, do you like me?"

His heart beat fast while his mind groped for a reply.

"I didn't like you at first," he said. "But you have a lot of good qualities. Maybe you're okay."

"What are my good qualities? Besides my looks. I already know about that. Everyone tells me all the time."

"Right. Well, I think you have a good sense of humor, and you're fun, and you're intelligent."

"You said I was mean."

"Sometimes you seem that way, Tanna, but maybe that's just a first impression. I think you have another side that's kind of sweet. Maybe people don't see a lot of things about you because they mostly notice how great you look."

That's enough, Rune thought. Hopefully, that was what she wanted to hear.

She smiled. "All right," she said. "I'm ending this dream."

There was a moment of blackness, and then Rune was back in the nightmare room.

He took a breath and looked around. Tanna was standing behind the console but there were also two security people in the room as well. Rune was glad to see them. He didn't want to be alone with her.

Meanwhile, she was looking at him. She wasn't smiling but when she spoke she seemed happy.

"Unstrap him," she told one of the guards. "Take him back to his room." Then she smiled again and said, "Rune, I think we'll continue the interrogation in real life, where I can feel things. I'll see you soon."

Chapter 51

Markla wasn't sure what to expect from the River Clan. Rala said there would be no problems but Markla had heard overly optimistic talk before. She planned to stay alert.

Rala also said that her clan and the River Clan had been friendly for centuries but they didn't have too much contact with each other. Apparently, it was like that with all the clans in Narna. They believed in cooperation but minimal interaction.

It didn't take long to find them. Three members came to meet them in the woods, and as they emerged from the trees Markla stopped short. There were two men and a woman, and while they were dressed in similar clothes to Rala's people the style was more warlike. They all had paint on their faces—spidery black lines, and the woman wore a necklace made from some creature's teeth. Also, they were all huge. Had they sent the three biggest people they had, or were all these people giants? They were scary-looking but Markla held her ground and kept her face blank.

One of the men had a rifle, and Markla thought about the pistol in her backpack, and how she should really put it in a more accessible place. I'm a great warrior, she thought. *If I'm attacked, I just need a few minutes to rummage around and find my gun. Hang on, please! It's in here somewhere.*

Markla relaxed a bit when Rala grinned and lunged forward to embrace the man with the rifle.

"Loro!" Rala said. "It's been a while."

Loro had darker skin and longer hair than the others. Even though it was cool outside, his arms were bare and muscular.

"Too long," he said. "You should come down here more often."

"So, who's this soldier you've captured? Are you sure he's alone?"

"We're sure. We took his weapons and his GoBug, and we cut that device out of his arm—the one they use to call for help."

"What?" Markla said. "He had a device in his arm?"

"It's a button imbedded just below the skin but I don't think he used it. I don't think he was planning to call anyone."

Markla recalled the tracker she'd cut out of her arm after escaping from the Dream Prison. The toads were so sneaky.

"Did he say anything?" Rala said.

"He swore a lot. But he mostly seemed to be cursing himself."

"Can you take us to him?"

"Sure. Maybe he's in a better mood now."

Markla didn't want to meet this guy. After all, she'd blown up that cabin and killed his friends, and then she'd taken all his weapons, so it was bound to be a hostile situation. She vaguely wondered if he might have some kind of hidden weapon he could use against her. She decided not to get too close to him.

The River Clan people lived in simple log cabins similar to the ones used by Rala's people. Like Rala's Red Forest people, the cabins were scattered without any real pattern. They were close together but there was nothing resembling a street. It was like someone had thrown them down randomly from the sky.

As they approached one of the cabins, Loro pointed and said, "There he is."

Markla looked, and she instantly felt better. She remembered this guy, but now he wasn't looking so dangerous.

Burno Blivi was sitting on the ground, tied to a heavy pole with his hands behind his back. Markla got the feeling that the pole had some other intended use—like maybe to hang laundry. But either way, this guy wasn't going anywhere.

She saw a bloody bandage on his forearm. She also noticed that his clothes didn't seem to fit very well.

He stared up at her with narrow eyes, and she guessed what

he was about to say. Here it comes, she thought. *You're so young. You're so tiny. You look like a little girl.*

But he didn't say those things. Instead, he gave a nod of his head. "So you're the mighty Markla Flash," he said. "You did a great job out there. I wish I had ten warriors like you."

Markla hesitated. She'd never been susceptible to flattery, even when it sounded sincere.

"I'm not a warrior," she said.

He laughed. "Sure you are. You're the best kind of warrior."

"Why is that?"

"Because you find a way. When all the great plans from all the big brains turn into crap and chaos, the best ones find a way to get it done. And that's what you do, Markla. You're a natural."

She shrugged. "I was only trying to keep you from killing me."

"It was nothing personal," he said with a shrug. "I just follow orders."

"So does an idiot."

He laughed again. "You're right about that. And you're looking at an idiot." He shook his head and was quiet.

Loro said, "You're only alive, Burno, because these people have some kind of plan for you."

Now Burno grinned. "Well, I appreciate that, and I can't wait to hear it. I hope it involves a nice long vacation and then a new career."

Rala turned to Loro. "I called my mother," she said. "She's sending a few people down here to get him. Meanwhile, Markla needs to cross the bridge. What's happening over there?"

"There was some fighting last week," Loro said. "But now they seem to be at a stalemate. The government can't destroy the rebels, and the rebels can't destroy the government, and we're not getting too involved." Then he grinned and added, "But you know most of us don't like the government of Sparkla. Anyway,

I guess they're both scheming. We can contact the people there and take Markla across the bridge, as long as she remembers us some day when she's running the country."

Markla gave a soft laugh. "I don't think so. I can barely run myself."

"So where am I going?" Burno said.

"You're going for a walk," Rala said. "And since we don't have hover-ships, it's a long walk. But you seem healthy enough. Hopefully, you won't fall into any more holes."

Chapter 52

Tanna smiled and admired herself in a full length mirror. What should she wear to Rune's next interrogation? It would be happening soon over at his place.

She was tingling in all the right places. Stay calm, she thought. But she felt like she was floating. Maybe Rune really would fall in love with her when Markla was dead—or maybe he'd fall in love with her even if Markla stayed alive. Wouldn't that be amazing?

She stepped back from the mirror and struck a few dramatic poses. She thought about the provocative dress she'd been wearing in the LiveDream but she didn't actually own that dress, and it wouldn't be appropriate, anyway. Rune wasn't a formal guy—and really, she wasn't all that formal herself. She wanted something that was casual yet sexy because that's what she usually wore. She tried on a few other options but didn't like any of them. She swore and wished she had access to her vast wardrobe back in Liberta.

There was a knock on her door, and she frowned. She wasn't expecting anyone but she opened it—and there was Jorro.

She stared in silence. Then she said, "Jorro, what are you doing here?"

"Hi," he said with a smile. "You're always dropping in to visit me, so I thought I'd drop in and visit you."

She tried to not seem annoyed. But it was difficult.

"Yeah, but you live in Liberta," she said. "And you're a student. This is a fortress, and it's a long way from your apartment."

"I'm part of the team, remember? It was your idea. And I can take all my classes using a GoBug. Anyway, I'm here for a meeting about the grid security. I could've done that by GoBug, too—but I thought I'd use it as an excuse to see you. It's only a little over an hour away by hover-ship."

He leaned forward and kissed her. She did her best to not seem disgusted.

He stepped back and cocked his head. "Tanna, are you all right? What's going on?"

"Nothing!" she blurted and turned way. "I just wasn't expecting you. So I'm a little surprised."

"Yeah, I wanted to surprise you. I guess you don't like surprises."

Actually, there was some truth in his words. She hated surprises—especially this surprise.

"It's just that I'm busy, Jorro."

"Oh, what are you doing?" He motioned to the various articles of clothing tossed on a nearby chair. "It looks like you're trying on clothes. Do you have a date?"

He laughed, and she forced herself to do the same.

"I'm meeting my father for dinner," she said.

"I can come back later."

"How much later?"

"As late as you want. How's your interrogation of Rune going? Has he told you anything yet?"

With real effort, she kept herself from screaming. She didn't want to talk about Rune with Jorro—not at all. But then her GoBug sent her an alert. The device was behind her ear, and the alert was inside her head, and Jorro didn't hear it.

"Hang on," she said. "I have a message."

She answered, and who was this guy? Oh wait, this was Turin, the guy who was tracing Rune's GoBug. How could she have forgotten about that?

"Jorro, can you give me a minute? I need to take this."

"Sure," he said, and he smiled again. She walked into the bedroom and shut the door. The visual was on a private mind-stream and could only be seen by her, but she wanted total privacy.

"Hi, Turin," she said. Turin was about 25 years old, and he

looked like a rat. He was smart, though, and seemed like a nice guy. It was a real shame about the rat face.

Turin smiled. "Hi, Tanna. We've traced the GoBug. There was still some encryption involved but we've got it now. We also retrieved the conversation Rune had when he last used it. I just played it a few minutes ago."

"Really?" Tanna felt her pulse pounding. "So, what do we know?"

Turin stopped smiling. "There's good news and bad news," he said. "The good news is that we know who the mysterious smasher is. He calls himself 'Gort.' We don't know his real name but we can trace the location of his device. The bad news is that based on the conversation I just heard, he might be someone you know. And the GoBug is inside the fortress. I'm looking at the location right now."

"What? Where is it? Send a security team!"

While he was talking to her, he was staring at another display. "I just sent them… But Tanna, it looks like this is in one of the bedroom suites. Where are you located? What is your room number?"

"What?"

She suddenly felt light-headed as the possibilities began to click in her head—but it couldn't be. There was no way.

A buzzer sounded. Someone was at the door. She raced out of the bedroom and saw Jorro standing in the living room, and she stopped and stared at him. Then she yanked the door open, and there was Stillo—along with three other guys. She turned back to Jorro.

"You!" she said. "You!"

"What?" He was looking uneasy.

"You're the smasher!" she screamed. "I can't believe it!"

Jorro hesitated. "What are you talking about? How can you say that?"

She walked over to him and pulled the GoBug from behind his ear. Then she looked back at Turin, who was still connected. "Is this it?" she said. "Is this the one?"

"Yeah, that's it."

Tanna was having trouble breathing. But she recovered quickly.

"How could you?" she said. *"How could you do this to me?"*

Jorro hesitated again, and then he sighed. "It wasn't about you, Tanna. It was about bigger things. Maybe you should think about some of them."

"Lock him up!" she shrieked. "I never want to see him again!"

He started to object but then he got quiet. Stillo grinned and grabbed Jorro while another guy put on a pair of handcuffs. "Let's go, traitor," Stillo said. Then he added, "Tanna, I'll see you later." Jorro didn't look at her as they led him out of the room.

Tanna collapsed into a chair. She felt like she'd been punched hard in the gut. She felt overwhelmed, like she was drowning.

Her brilliant plan had uncovered the smasher. It had also revealed how she'd been sleeping with the enemy—literally. She'd never felt so betrayed because she'd never been so betrayed. She couldn't think.

"Tanna, are you okay?"

She realized Turin was still there.

"No, Turin. I'm not." She wiped a tear from her eye and then tried to regain her composure. "You said you retrieved the conversation he had with Rune. I want to hear it."

"Sure, I'll send it to you. It's really two conversations. Rune talks to Markla, too."

She took a few deep breaths and tried to prepare herself. But she suddenly felt empty inside—and alone. She'd never felt so alone. Did she really want to play this recording? No, but it had to be done.

She disconnected from Turin and played the call, and when she heard Rune's words, she wanted to curl up into a ball and die.

He thinks I'm evil and stupid! He's humoring me and waiting for an opportunity! And he's totally in love with Markla!

She turned off the GoBug and sat for a while just staring into space. Then she took another deep breath and called her father.

Chapter 53

As Markla brushed her hair, she found herself pulling at the tangled spots with more violence than usual. She could tell the River Clan people liked her, and it made her uneasy. They're confusing my desperation for bravery, she thought. But she wanted Rune to be free, and if they could help her it was all fine.

It was a short walk from the clan settlement to the river. When they arrived, Markla stared at the scene and caught her breath.

The Dive River was wide and deep, and the bridge above it was long and narrow and resembled a line of skinny boards standing on stilts, and anyone who crossed the rickety-looking structure would be an easy target. Markla scanned the trees on the opposite bank and looked down at the murky green water. She wondered if she could jump from the bridge and swim if necessary. But she'd be an easy target in the water, too. Really, the best thing to do was to cross this scary bridge as fast as possible.

Along with Markla, Rala, and Ronelo, there were three River Clan people. By necessity, everyone walked single file across the bridge, and they moved fast.

Loro and his people were in the lead. Markla was behind Rala and in front of Ronelo.

Markla said, "Rala, how do these people know Stoke? How are they going to know not to shoot us?"

"Stoke was born in Narna. He's what they call an 'X-er.' His parents left at a young age but he has roots here. Loro is directly in touch with him."

I'm trusting these people a lot, Markla thought. But there was no other way.

It didn't take long to find the Free Sparkla people. As soon as they crossed the river, Loro sent out a message on his radio and two people appeared, a man and a woman. These were not people who lived in the woods. These were soldiers, and they carried rifles and wore black body armor.

They greeted Loro and the others, and then they greeted Markla. They were warm and friendly, and they seemed to know who Markla was, and it felt strange.

"So you're Markla Flash," the woman said. "We've heard a lot about you."

"Hi," Markla said. Then there was an awkward silence as she silently cursed all the mindstreams of the world. She'd never wanted to be a celebrity.

Rala and the other clan people said they'd be returning to the Narna side.

Markla embraced Rala. "Thanks so much for your help," she said. "Tell your mother I said thanks, too."

"I'll do that. We'll see each other again, Markla. I know it."

Ronelo gave Markla a big hug, too. He squeezed her hard but she didn't mind.

"Come back, Markla," he said. "Come back with Rune. You can stay with us."

"Goodbye, Ronelo. Thanks for everything."

Then Markla walked through the woods with the two soldiers and they told her the situation.

Rune was being held in Fort Freedom in northern Sparkla, and that was exactly the place that needed to be captured. Unfortunately, it was well defended by a massive system of automated weapons that would obliterate anyone who came near. The air defenses were also automated and were impossible to penetrate. Anything that came remotely close would be shot down, including something as small as a bird. Meanwhile, the Free Sparkla people had the same kind of defenses in a captured fortress nearby, where Markla was heading, and both sides were now staring at each other from a distance, trying to break the impasse. Markla listened to all this with some interest—but really, her mind was dominated by one thought.

How can I get Rune out of there?

Soon enough they encountered more soldiers, and then they came to a clearing, and in the clearing was the Free Sparkla fortress. It was a typical fortress, featuring ominous gray walls, tooth-like towers, and a multitude of guns sprouting from everywhere like the hairs of a giant monster. The walls were a bit battered, with a few chunks missing and some burned splotches—but overall it seemed to be in reasonable shape. She wondered how it compared to the place where Rune was imprisoned. Then the wide gate opened, and they all went inside, and Markla was led to a room with a large table that showed a three dimensional map of Sparkla. It was glowing like something from a LiveDream story. She was taken into an office, and there was Stoke.

He was a tall dark-skinned guy and she once again remembered that moment when he'd offered her and Rune a ride away from the Dream Prison—and she'd refused.

I should have said yes, she thought. *One more bad decision.*

Stoke rose from his chair and shook her hand. He was about two heads taller than her, but that was true of many people. "Hello, Markla," he said. "We meet again. I'm glad to see you're still alive."

"I need to free Rune!" she blurted. "I know it sounds crazy but that's why I'm here. Can you help me? I'll do anything."

He stopped smiling. He gave her a sober look and sat back down. He said, "What we really need to do is shut down the defenses of that fortress. We have hover-ships and troops ready to go but we can't get past those automated defenses that can destroy anything that gets close. When we attacked the Dream Prison, we had lots of people inside, but they've rooted out most of them now. The military streams are far more secure, too; we can't smash into them like your friend did at the police station. If we could shut them down we could get in there and free Rune. In fact, if we capture that fortress the whole government will probably fall."

"If the government falls, then no one will be chasing me, right?"

"Yeah. But right now they're still there, and they've got a lot of interest in you."

"I know."

He shifted a bit in his chair. "After what you did, you can't expect them to stop looking for you anytime soon."

"I know," she said again, and for an instant she felt overwhelmed, like she was being crushed. "Maybe I shouldn't have done it. But I just snapped." She wiped a tear from her eye. "I don't want to cause trouble for anyone else, and now I've hurt Rune, and I need to fix that."

Stoke sighed. "First of all, don't feel so bad. Aldo was a terrible guy, and so is Gin and his whole family. When you're fighting people like that, you do what you need to do. But I have some bad news… They just sent us a message. In fact, it came in right before you arrived. I hate to play it for you, but it wouldn't be right to keep it from you, either."

Markla braced herself. "What is it?" she said.

Stoke handed Markla a GoBug. She tried to keep her hand from shaking as she put it behind her ear. She knew it was going to be something horrendous. In an instant, she was connected to a secure mindstream, and she was seeing the message. But it was all dark. There was no image.

Just when she thought it wasn't working, there was a low noise, like someone murmuring, but she couldn't make out the words. And then there was a scream, a horrible scream of agony. Someone moaned, and said, "No! No! No!" and Markla felt her blood go cold—it was Rune. Then there was more screaming, and some wailing, and then a sound like someone gagging. Then it seemed to repeat, only with even more horrific shrieks of pain. She could barely breathe. It was the most frightening thing she'd ever heard.

She grabbed onto her chair. She was filled with nausea, and she started shrieking.

"Turn it off!" she said, and she yanked the GoBug from behind her ear and smashed it down on the desk. "Turn it off! I don't want to hear it!"

She leaped up and walked over to the wall and slammed her fist against it. Suddenly she was sobbing, and her chest was heaving, and her mind was whirling.

"It's all my fault!" she said. "All my fault!"

How much time went by? She wasn't sure, but she suddenly felt like collapsing onto the floor—but then she didn't. She had another thought. Would they let Rune go if she died?

She took a few deep breaths. Why hadn't she thought of this before? There was a dagger strapped to her belt, and she knew she could do it. She reached down—and then she felt Stoke's hand on top of hers, stopping her. And then his other hand was on her shoulder.

"You don't want to die, Markla," he said. "No one here wants that. Rune doesn't want that."

She pushed his hand away. "I'm causing Rune all this agony. It's all because of me."

"No. Other people are causing the agony, and if you die he'll feel more agony. Stay calm and think about that day when you'll see him again."

She started to yell at him—and stopped. She thought about seeing Rune, and for one second she felt a spark of hope. Then she thought about the people who were torturing him, and how much she hated injustice, and then a few horrible memories flashed across her mind, and suddenly she felt cold, like a stone. But it wasn't a feeling of despair. It was rage.

She stopped crying. "Is there more to the message?"

"Yes, but it's just text."

She turned to face him. "Read it to me."

" 'Markla Flash can end Rune's torture by giving herself up. If she does that, we'll let him go.' "

"I'm doing it," she said.

Stoke shook his head. "Markla, like I just said, dying isn't a plan, and if you give yourself up they'll kill you, and they probably won't let Rune go, anyway. I like Rune, I do. He's Blog's son, and Blog was one of my best friends. But throwing away your life won't accomplish anything."

"I'm not going to throw away my life. You said you need to shut off those defenses. Maybe I can do it."

"No, you can't," Stoke said. "It's all controlled by an Electronic Brain deep underground, in the War Room, and they're not going to take you there. And even if they did, you won't have a weapon and the security is extremely tight." He sat back down behind his desk. "I know what you've been up to, Markla. I know all about you and the things you've done, and it's all very impressive—but this is different. If you go in there, you're going to find yourself in an impossible situation."

Markla was quiet. For some reason, she felt more relaxed now. She felt determination filling her with strength. She sat down in a chair across from him.

"Do you know the layout of the place?" she said.

"Yeah, we do. We have a key person inside, and she's been very helpful. We know every nook and cranny of that fortress."

"So I guess she can't turn everything off?"

"No. I told you, it's way too secure. Besides, our contact isn't a fighter. She's a dream writer."

"Are you talking about Diana Drogo?"

Stoke hesitated. "Yes," he said. "She was your teacher, right? Does she like you?"

"She thinks I'm a psycho. But she loves Rune. You need someone to get in there and do this, so I'll give myself up, and I'll be inside. I'll turn everything off and you can attack."

Stoke gave her a long stare. Was he trying not to laugh? No, she didn't think so. He finally said, "We have nothing to lose by letting you try. But they'll scan you before you're brought in. They'll take any kind of weapon, and they'll lock you up quick. They might beat you up pretty good, too. You're smart and you're tough, Markla, but that might not be enough. I think people tend to underestimate you because you're young, and you're small, and you're a girl. But at some point they're going to stop doing that."

Markla shrugged. "What can I say? I'm young, and I'm small, and I'm a girl. And I'm going in there. I can do it. I'll find a way."

He hesitated again, this time for quite a bit longer. Then he reached across the desk and handed her another GoBug. Markla looked in his eyes as she slapped the device behind her ear and immediately found herself staring at the complete layout of the fortress.

"This is from a LiveDream," he said. "Diana posted it, and this is what you see if you use a special promotional code. But there's one thing we don't understand. Does this mean anything to you?"

In the LiveDream, on a stone wall inside a small room, some words had been sprayed with paint. The letters were in the style of graffiti, and they said, "LiveDream, Arena, event trigger, fly away, disconnect."

Markla studied the message and nodded her head. "Yeah," she said, and she recalled her days studying LiveDream writing that hadn't actually been too long ago. "An 'event trigger' is a phrase inserted into a LiveDream that will make something specific happen regardless of what the script or the dream guider says. I think Diana's telling us that someone wants to use a LiveDream called 'Arena,' and she's inserted an event trigger that might be useful. That's a common one."

"You don't want to end up in MindCore."

"I know. But it will probably happen."

She returned to the images again—and at some pictures of the nightmare room, and the chairs where people could be strapped in place. She zoomed in closer to study the chairs.

"I have an idea," she said.

"Is it something risky?"

"Probably. Do you have any surgeons here?"

"We have a few."

"Good. I need to see one of them."

Chapter 54

Tanna was sitting alone in the nightmare room. She heard a beep from the GoBug behind her ear and saw it was her father. She sighed and connected, and there was Gin grinning at her.

"I just got the news," he said. "Markla Flash is going to surrender, and my little girl is brilliant."

Tanna frowned. "I'm not that little anymore. They're flying her to the fort, right?"

"Yes," Gin said. "You'll finally be able to meet your nemesis." He paused. "What's wrong?"

Tanna was quiet. She should be feeling wonderful about this but she wasn't. For some reason, she found herself fidgeting at the thought.

"I don't know," Tanna said. "Maybe I don't want to meet her."

"You don't need to. But really, she's a problem. We can't just execute her because everyone knows she's here—the Free Sparkla people have loaded mindstreams with a story about how she's giving herself up to free the love of her life. So she's very popular; in fact, her approval numbers are much higher than mine. We'd either need to make it look like an accident or a suicide, or maybe get someone from 20 Eyes to kill her in prison. Yeah, that's probably the best plan, the old prison death squad."

"I don't want her dead. I changed my mind—at least for now."

"Right! We need to still make it look like Sparkla is a land of justice, and so she needs to serve her sentence. She'll spend the rest of her life incarcerated. Hopefully, when we emerge victorious in the war her popularity will fade. So you win, honey."

"Yeah. I win."

He smiled, and then crinkled his forehead. "Why aren't you thrilled? What's wrong, Tanna? Is this because of Jorro? Everyone makes mistakes when it comes to love. That's why I always try to avoid it… Anyway, I never liked Jorro. Besides, you caught him, didn't you?"

"I don't care about Jorro."

"Is it Burno on the mindstreams?"

Early this morning, Burno had arrived at the capital of Narna as a prisoner of some primitive clan of Basics. He was a huge embarrassment to the Sparklans—a real live commando captured in their territory after the country denied anyone was still there. And now he was on some major mindstreams talking about how dumb the government was and how he wanted to open a restaurant.

"I don't care about him, either," Tanna said. "Look, I'm fine. I'm going to do an interrogation of Markla when she arrives—as soon as we fix this MindCore thing. I'm going to do Markla and Rune together."

"Great! I'm sure you'll get it working. Keep me posted."

"Yeah, I'll tell you everything."

"Cheer up! Things are looking good."

Tanna shook her head and disconnected the stream. *Markla's giving herself up for Rune,* Tanna thought. *Would anyone do that for me? Would I do that for anyone?*

It was infuriating. It was inspiring. And it was so beautiful.

Her eyes wandered to a dagger sitting on the console, and she picked it up.

The weapon had been taken from a captured member of 20 Eyes, and now she imagined killing Jorro with it. The violent scene filled her with euphoria—but then she felt the sharpness of the blade and grimaced. Who was she kidding? She could never kill someone with this thing. She could do it in a LiveDream but the idea of doing it in real life filled her with revulsion. *And Rune thinks that I'm the mean one? I don't think so.*

She turned her head as the door opened, and Stillo came strolling in. He was grinning.

"You wanted to see me, Tanna? Hey, what are you doing with that? Are you going to join 20 Eyes?"

Tanna tossed the weapon onto the desktop. "No, but I suppose I do need a new way to meet people."

He laughed. "Who do you need to meet? You've got me. I've been waiting a long time."

She looked at him and smiled. "Stillo, you could do better than me."

"You really think so?"

"No chance. But right now I need your help."

"That's why I'm here. By the way, you look amazing."

She rolled her eyes. "Stillo, stop talking—because flattery will get you everywhere, and I have things to do."

"Okay. I'll stop telling you how incredibly hot you are but only for a minute. What do you want from me?"

She stood up and handed him a GoBug. "I want you to put this behind your ear and go into MindCore."

"MindCore? I thought it was broken. I thought that woman was fixing it."

Tanna scoffed. "Diana's about as useful as Jorro. But then again, she's a teacher, not an engineer. So we're going to see if we can fix this thing without her help."

"Sure, why not? Hey, what's going on with Rune? Did you listen to his conversations?"

She shook her head and tried to keep her voice from shaking. "Yeah, and he thinks I'm stupid, even though he's the one locked up in a prison cell. Meanwhile, I caught the smasher. It's too bad he happened to be my boyfriend but that's not the point— and guess what? I'm going to catch Markla, too, after the great commando team totally failed. So we'll see who's stupid."

"Why does he think you're stupid?" Stillo said. "You're the smartest person I know."

Tanna eyed him for a second before responding. "No, I'm not," she said. "But I'm not stupid, either. Anyway, we sent out a recording of Rune being tortured, and supposedly Markla heard it and now she's going to give herself up to save him."

"You tortured Rune?"

"No. The recording is fake, and Rune doesn't know about it. But it's a digital construction using sound samples from his actual voice, so it will register as real if they do an analysis."

"That's pretty clever! Like I said, you're so smart. You're just as smart as you are gorgeous."

"Stillo, really—stop talking. I just arrested my boyfriend, okay? I need a cooling off period after that kind of thing. And then I'm still going to say no. Now get ready for MindCore."

"Hit me with it, honey."

Tanna smiled. Stillo was actually cheering her up. She'd been studying Aldo's notes, and now she touched a few buttons—and whoah, what was this?

"Do you feel anything?" she said.

"Yeah," he said with a frown. "It's weird, like there's something crawling around inside my head. I don't like it."

She caught her breath. So this is how it worked when it wasn't being blocked.

She was using the GoBug in conjunction with the console, and she saw the three dimensional images in front of her eyes. She assumed they were memories—but they were so vivid, it was like she was there. She made an adjustment, and now she was a little farther from the action. And there was a lot of action.

"Stillo, who is this girl?"

"What?"

Tanna knew one of the problems with MindCore was that it didn't have a practical way to search through the memories, and it didn't show them in chronological order. In this sense, it was a reflection of the human brain. A brain tends to remember things based upon their significance. The typical mundane events of any given day are discarded, while events of significance are given top priority. Obviously, Stillo's significant events involved a girl Tanna had never seen before.

"What are you looking at?" Stillo said.

Tanna flipped to another memory, and the same girl was there doing the same things with him. No one was overly dressed.

Tanna was suddenly feeling a little warm. She knew she shouldn't be watching but the girl was obviously enjoying herself, and Stillo definitely knew what he was doing, and it was hard to look away. It was certainly memorable, and now Tanna wondered about her own memories, and what would be the first thing someone would see? She quickly flipped through some more images. Now she saw random moments with people she didn't know, quick glimpses of people and places. And wait—here was an interesting one.

Tanna was staring at herself. She remembered this day. She was talking to Stillo about her father, and how she didn't want to disappoint him, and it was strange to see herself stored inside someone else's head. She also felt touched that he'd remember this moment right beside his other more intense activities.

She wondered if it was possible to do a simple search, not by date, but by some other information. She tried using the word "Tanna"—and a whole slew of images appeared. Hey, she remembered that dress. She'd worn it at a formal party, and her father had been there, along with Stillo and his parents. Yeah, she'd looked great that day—and he had, too. And he'd been so sweet.

"What are you doing?" Stillo said. He sounded agitated now. "What are you seeing? I want to get out of this thing."

She turned it off. He was giving her an odd look, like he knew he'd been violated in some way.

Tanna wasn't sure what to say. "So, who was that girl?" It was the first thing that occurred to her. "There were some memories of you with a girlfriend."

"I don't have a girlfriend."

"Don't be mad at me. I didn't know what was going to come up."

"I'm not mad. What did you see?"

"A lot. This thing is unbelievable… But we're not done yet. Now you need to try and block it by filling your mind with a strong emotion—like anger."

"I'm not angry. But I don't want you looking at any more of my brain."

"Then be angry, and we'll see if it doesn't work."

"No. I'm not doing it again."

"It doesn't have to be anger. Rune was using love. Are you in love?"

He hesitated, and now he grinned. "Maybe I'm in love with you, Tanna. But I'm still not doing it."

"Stillo, I need your help."

"No. Nothing is getting me back in there… Hey, why don't you go into the machine, and I'll see what's in your mind? It doesn't look like it's too hard to operate. Besides, you're angrier than me."

"I am?"

"Sure. I'm never really too angry." Then he laughed. "You're in a rage all the time."

"No, I'm not!"

"You're in a rage right now."

She scowled and swore. "Give me that GoBug. Get over here and I'll show you what to do. Tell me if you see anything."

They switched places.

"Are you ready?" Stillo said. "Are you angry? Let's make sure. Think about Markla Flash—you hate her, right?"

"I guess so."

"Yeah, you do, because Rune likes her better than he likes you, right? You think you're so sexy and amazing, and she looks like a wild animal—but she gets all the love, and you can't stand it because you're spoiled! Because you grew up with everything and she grew up with nothing and now she's more famous than you! And you don't appreciate the people who do care about you because you only care about yourself!"

She cursed at him. "Stop talking and hit the button!"

"I did."

"And it's not working?"

He hesitated. "No, it's working great. This is amazing… I see lots of your memories… Who is this guy? This isn't Jorro… Hey, I know this guy. He used to work at that restaurant on 7th Avenue—you and him? Really? Are you serious?"

"It was just one time!"

"Well, all these other images are interesting, too. You won an award, you won a contest, you yelled at a few people. Those are your memories. One encounter with a sleazy cook and lots of you, you, you. How come I'm not in here?"

She yanked the GoBug from behind her ear and tossed it across the room.

"He wasn't that sleazy," she said. *"And MindCore doesn't block anything!* It must be some kind of trick." She put another GoBug behind her ear, and she gave Stillo a sideways glance as she called Turin.

"Hi, Tanna," Turin said with a smile.

"Turin, I need you to look at MindCore and tell me what's wrong with it—or what's not wrong with it."

"I'll see what I can do."

"Thanks."

Stillo returned her glance. "I'm sorry," he said. "I was just trying to make you mad."

"It worked."

"I didn't mean all that stuff."

"Yes, you did, and it's okay because it's all true. In fact, it's even worse than that." She stared at the floor for a few seconds, and then she sighed and looked up. "You've been in my thoughts lots of times, Stillo. MindCore doesn't read thoughts—only memories."

"Oh. So maybe we need to make some memories."

She hesitated. She was still burning with anger but she didn't want to think or talk. She stepped toward him. He gave her a quizzical look, and then she kissed him on the lips. He immediately kissed her back, and now it was a long kiss, and he wrapped his arms around her. They hugged each other hard.

Chapter 55

Markla looked at the time. She had about ten more minutes of freedom.

She felt surprisingly calm, and she wasn't sure why. She was in a hover-ship heading for Fort Freedom, and her mind was crowded with thoughts—yet they weren't overwhelming her. She was getting organized, and she was going to be ready for this, and it wasn't just about Rune anymore. It was bigger than that.

I'm going to find out who I am.

She'd been 14 years old when Dru had recruited her to join 20 Eyes. She'd been working in his family's greenhouse for two years, and she couldn't believe how he'd seemed to like talking with her, and she'd looked forward to it every day. He was older than her, and very sexy, and he'd been filled with ideas. Maybe it was true that she'd seen 20 Eyes as a surrogate family but she'd also seen them as people fighting for something she believed in. Did she still believe in those things? Yes, she did.

She glanced at the time again. Maybe eight minutes left.

She ran through a list of her crimes, and they were numerous, and some would say horrific. Did they give her feelings of guilt? Yes, every one. Would she do them again? Yes—every one. They'd been done for good reasons.

They'd called her a subversive and a murderer, and maybe that's what she was—or maybe she really was a fighter, a soldier, a warrior. It was all a matter of perspective. She blinked at the bright sun and stared out the window of the hover-ship as it skimmed low over the trees. She imagined how things might unfold.

They might shoot her on sight but it was unlikely because they'd want her to suffer first. That was the way justice was handled in Sparkla—and yeah, that was why she'd wanted to fight the toads in the first place.

She took a deep breath. She'd been in trouble before but this was going to be worse, much worse. She looked at the time once more and guessed she had about five minutes remaining.

The Sparklans had been notified about this hover-ship, and they said they wouldn't shoot it down. But the ship would land before it was in sight of the fortress because Stoke didn't trust the automated defense system, and neither did Markla.

There was to be no exchange of prisoners. The Sparklans didn't want any dramatic rescue attempts, and so the situation was very one-sided. If Markla gave herself up, Rune would no longer be tortured, and they'd let him go. If she didn't they would keep sending her recordings. Would they let Rune go if she died? Maybe at some point. After all, his only real crime had been helping her. So here she was, and what was her plan? It was risky and vague at best.

With a jolt, Markla felt the ship stop moving forward, and now it was descending. She had no more time, and she felt her heart racing. I'm not afraid, she thought, but it was a lie. *Okay, I'm afraid but I'm going to do it anyway. Maybe that's what it means to be brave.*

I'm strong, she thought, and that wasn't a lie. She'd seen enough of the world to know she was stronger than most people— her mother, who was a hopeless drunk, and her father, who'd run off, and all the people in 20 Eyes like Dru who'd talked so tough but had run like rats from the Dream Station and left her behind. She was different, and she was proud of it.

The ship was on the ground now, and Markla said goodbye to the pilot and walked into the woods alone. She was unarmed. She'd also removed the necklace Jerome had given her. She'd get it back when she returned.

She found the meeting point, where a squad of heavily armed soldiers appeared like a pack of wild dogs and started barking instructions, and then it was a haze of shouting and shoving, and she stared with a blank expression as they searched her and scanned her and pushed her to the ground and chained her hands behind her back and forced her to stand and slapped her a few times and made some crude remarks and then tossed her into the back of a hover-car.

She said nothing, and she didn't resist. Not yet.

Chapter 56

What was going on? Something had changed. Rune had a bad feeling, and he was lying on the bed in his prison suite, and he couldn't get comfortable and kept squirming around. Was it a sixth sense? Or was it because sooner or later his luck was bound to run out?

He smiled. No, that wasn't it. *My luck never runs out.*

He considered making another call to Gort on his stolen GoBug but then the door opened and three big goons came stomping in. One of them was Stillo, and the wide smile on his face was unsettling.

"You're going to get your wish, Rune," Stillo said. "You're going to see Markla again."

"What?" Rune leaped from the bed. "Where?"

"In the nightmare room. Let's go. No more questions."

Rune felt lightheaded as they chained his hands and feet. So Markla had been captured! He felt his heart sink with sadness—but then he felt some relief, too. At least she was alive! *And I'm going to see her!* Then the goons started pushing him down the hall, and despite their instructions, Rune had questions.

"What's going on, Stillo? Is she really here? Where's Tanna?"

Stillo shrugged. "I don't know much. I just know that Markla gave herself up to stop you from being tortured."

"You mean the dream in the desert? She saw that?"

Stillo laughed. "No, this was a lot worse… You should've heard the recording Tanna made. You were screaming and crying like a baby. Hey, be glad it wasn't real. She cut you a break."

Rune's jaw dropped as he took in the information. For a second he struggled to breathe but then he clenched his fists. They weren't going to get away with this. No way.

They reached the MindCore room. The lights were dimmed,

and the console was lit up, and there was one person there, a skinny rat-faced guy Rune didn't know. Rune also noticed a 20 Eye's dagger lying on the desk beside the MindCore console. Then he was shoved into a chair and strapped down, and the door opened and three more soldiers appeared—along with Markla.

Rune's eyes went wide.

"Markla!"

She tried to run to him but they held her. Her hands were bound behind her back, and she thrashed and twisted. There was some yelling, and one guy slapped her in the face and knocked her to the floor.

"Stop it!" he said. "You'll be together in a few seconds."

Rune shouted and cursed at him. Then Markla looked up from the ground, and when she spoke her voice shook with rage.

"You were supposed to let him go."

"Maybe that will happen," Tanna said. She was gliding into the room. "But we have something to do first."

"That wasn't the deal."

"The deal is whatever I want it to be, Markla. So try and behave. I know it's hard for you."

Markla stood up, and Rune studied her while she looked around. He once again felt some relief. She was a little beaten up but didn't seem badly hurt. Markla turned to Tanna and did little to hide her contempt. Meanwhile, Tanna stared back at Markla but almost seemed frozen. It was like she was mesmerized.

"So you're Markla Flash," she finally said. "You're so small."

Markla rolled her eyes. "I'm as big as I need to be."

Tanna hesitated. "You killed my uncle."

"Your uncle was a toad who tortured me and Rune, and I doubt you're much better."

"But he didn't kill you!" Tanna said. Then she paused. "You'd probably kill me too, wouldn't you?"

Markla shrugged. "I don't think we're going to be friends."

Tanna frowned at Rune. "Rune, you think I'm so stupid, right? I heard every word you said on that stolen GoBug because it was all part of a plan—I plan that I created. So who's the stupid one now?"

Rune hesitated, and suddenly it felt like the room was spinning. Was she telling the truth? Then he looked at Stillo and saw him grinning, and he knew it was true.

Rune paused, trying to think. Then he swore to himself. He'd underestimated this girl.

"I don't remember what I said, Tanna. But if I insulted you, it's not a reason to abuse Markla."

Tanna laughed. "Maybe that's true, but luckily there are plenty of other reasons to do it." Then she smirked at Markla and said, "That torture recording was a fake. While you've been scrounging around in the wilderness, Rune's been living a life of luxury. It was just another plan of mine, and here you are—so how stupid am I? Strap this little girl into the chair."

Markla showed no expression and didn't struggle as they secured her in place. Then Tanna did something unexpected. She turned to the rat-faced guy and said, "You know what to do, Turin? You're not guiding, you're just watching."

"I know," Turin said and took a place behind the MindCore console while Tanna sat in another chair beside Rune. She didn't strap herself in but she placed a GoBug behind her ear.

Stillo shook his head. "Tanna, why do you need to do this? You found the smasher, so why not just turn Markla over to the police and send her back to prison? You don't need to prove anything to her—or to Rune."

"I want to do it, Stillo. Try and understand."

"Yeah, I understand just fine," he said, and his face got a little red. "But I'm not going to watch. I'll be outside the door. Call if you need me—you're good at that."

Tanna sighed. "Stillo, be serious. It's not like that."

"I see exactly how it is, Tanna."

He turned and stomped out of the room. For an instant, it looked like Tanna was going to call out to him but then she didn't. Instead, she turned to Rune and Markla. "I'll see you two in MindCore," she said. "We'll sort this out once and for all."

Rune glanced over at Markla. She seemed less angry now. She looked at him, and she didn't say anything—but she almost smiled.

Suddenly, his heart felt lighter. Then the lights in the room were turned down even more, and someone flipped a switch, and everything in Rune's mind went dark.

***

Rune opened his eyes. He was in a desert, but it wasn't the same desert Tanna had used before. There was no endless wasteland of sand. This was a more hospitable place, in a little valley between two rocky red hills, and all around were cactus plants higher than his head. Scattered across the ground were low scrubby bushes. The orange sun was hanging in the hazy sky, and it was warm but not hot.

Tanna was standing about ten paces in front of him. She was dressed in tight black athletic clothing, and her hair was tied in a ponytail. In her hand, Rune saw something he recognized—a black 20 Eyes dagger.

Rune shuddered. This was MindCore. Everyone was in the same dream together, and everyone could feel everything that happened. He knew this was only a dream but the thought of Tanna using that dagger to cut Markla to pieces filled him with dread. Markla would feel every cut like it was real—but then again, so would Tanna. So why was she doing this?

Standing a few paces to Rune's right was Markla. She was watching Tanna with a blank expression on her face. If she was afraid, she hid it well.

Tanna smiled. "This is a LiveDream called 'Arena' " she said. "We could do this for real, outside of the dream—but then it would only happen once, and you deserve a lot worse. I haven't had any scripts written for this dream and nothing is prearranged. Whatever happens isn't controlled by me, do you understand? Turin is watching but not guiding. I'm just another player in the game." Then she held up the dagger. "Do you recognize this, Markla? In a way, you have an advantage—you're the only one here who's actually murdered someone. But we'll see how well you do today."

Tanna gave them both another smug smile. Then she took a few steps back, and with a shout she starting performing intricate fighting maneuvers. She moved fast, and she used quick footwork followed by precise lunges and slashes, and Rune caught his breath. He couldn't deny it looked intimidating but he showed no expression on his face.

I'm not scared, Rune thought. *I can handle a little pain and agony.* But what about Markla? *She can handle even more.*

With another shout, Tanna finished her exhibition and looked pleased with herself. Then she bent down and stuck the dagger into the sand and stood in a place where she and Markla were approximately an equal distance from the blade.

Tanna pointed at the knife. "You and I are going to fight, Markla. If you don't fight, that's fine, but I'll stab you and kill you and it will hurt. If you do fight, it will go the same way, believe me. I want to find out how tough and clever and amazing you really are—I want to see it for myself, and I want Rune to see it, too. And then you'll go back to prison where you'll be killed another thousand times, and you'll never see Rune again."

So this was her plan, Rune thought. She wanted to demonstrate her superiority before sending Markla back to the Dream Prison to suffer.

Rune clenched his jaw a bit but continued to show no emotion. But his brain was boiling at this unnecessary attempt to hurt and humiliate the person he loved more than anyone. Then he looked at Markla, and he was struck by surprise. He'd expected to see some barely concealed fury but instead she still gazed at Tanna with a blank stare and said nothing.

Tanna's face flushed with anger. "Don't you have anything to say?" Then she was quiet, like she was waiting for a response. Markla turned to Rune, and there was a look in her eye, a look of cool defiance. "Event trigger," she said softly. Then she spoke in a louder voice. "I think you and Tanna need to spend some time together, Rune—a little time, that's all I need. Right now I'm going to *fly away.*"

There was a flash of light, and Markla turned into a bird.

It was a tiny bird—blue and white, and it looked friendly. But it screeched like a demon as it flew at Tanna's head. Tanna swore and ducked down. The bird let out another screech and headed through the valley. As it flew it grew larger, and it rose higher, and its image continued to grow even as it got farther away. By the time it reached a distant cloud its wingspan was enormous. And then it was gone.

Tanna watched the bird's journey with a look of confusion on her face. Meanwhile, Rune was thinking fast. Markla needs some time, he thought. *To do what?* He didn't know, but he had to do his part.

"Tanna, is this your plan? I don't think that bird's coming back."

Tanna scowled with anger. "That's not right. She can't do that! What did you do, Rune? *What did you do?*"

Rune laughed. Tanna had supposedly studied dream writing—but obviously, she'd never really studied.

"Wouldn't you like to know?" he said. "I'll tell you—if you fight me."

He lunged toward the blade and yanked it from the ground. He grinned and pointed it at Tanna, who still looked bewildered.

She didn't leap into any sophisticated fighting stance. She made no attempt at self-defense. She just shook her head.

"Would you really kill me with that thing?" she said, and she looked at him, and her big brown eyes were suddenly watery, and she seemed so sad.

Rune hesitated. "This is a LiveDream, Tanna. You won't actually die."

"But even so, would you do it?"

Rune gazed at her for a few seconds, and then he sighed and dropped the weapon.

"I don't want to hurt you, Tanna—even in a dream. But I'll do whatever I need to do to keep you from hurting Markla."

She was quiet for a few seconds. Then she looked up at the sky and said, "Turin, get me out of this place. I'm done here." Rune said nothing more, waiting for her to vanish. But it didn't happen. "Turin, can you hear me?" she said, and her voice rose with anger. "Get me out of the dream!" But Tanna still remained.

It was Rune who vanished.

Chapter 57

Markla opened her eyes. She was back in the nightmare room. Diana's script had disconnected her from the LiveDream but Markla knew this was unseen by whoever was monitoring. She was sure the script created the illusion that she was still a bird flying around in the dream.

Her heart was pounding; she had to move fast. Diana's LiveDream had shown that the straps on the chairs were not metal but were instead made of something that could be cut—and that's why she'd had a surgeon implant a tiny blade in her wrist. It was retractable when she flexed a certain way, and she flexed her wrist now and started cutting. Her efforts were choppy and frantic but still effective.

She sliced through the strap quickly. Hopefully, Rune could stall Tanna. It probably wouldn't take long for Tanna to put an end to the dream.

Her wrist was free! She fumbled a bit but undid the other strap and slipped out of the chair. Was that 20 Eyes dagger still on the desktop? She'd spotted it when they'd brought her in, and hopefully it was still there. Luckily, they'd turned the lights way down in the room to set a nightmarish mood—and the guy who was monitoring the LiveDream was busy watching the screen, staring at the images that interfaced with his GoBug. Markla was quick and she was quiet—and yeah, the dagger was still there, and then it was in her hand. She snatched the GoBug from behind the guy's ear, tossed it on the floor, and wrapped her arm tight around his chest. With the other hand, she put the blade against his neck.

"Don't move," she said.

He sucked in his breath. "What?" he said, and his voice was shaky. "How did you get out? I don't want any trouble."

"Well, I'm a lot of trouble—and if you don't do what I say I'm going to kill you." She poked him a bit.

"I believe you, Markla!" he said with a yelp. "I'll do whatever you want."

"Okay, we're going over to the nightmare chairs." She held his collar and pushed him toward Tanna, whose eyes were closed. She was still in MindCore, oblivious to the real world.

"Strap her in," Markla said. "Do it fast, and do it right! If those straps are loose I'm cutting your throat."

"Okay!" Turin said. "Please! They'll be tight." He quickly secured Tanna's wrists to the chair.

"Good," Markla said and pointed with the blade toward another chair. "Now have a seat." There were five chairs in the room, and Markla shook her head. It's a regular theater of horrors, she thought.

He sat down in the empty chair. Markla pointed the blade at his chest and made him secure one of the straps. Then she strapped his other hand down fast and ran to Rune and yanked the GoBug from behind his ear. He opened his eyes.

For a second he seemed dazed. Then he said, "Markla, you turned into a bird."

"Yeah, I know." She unstrapped him and he stood up.

"It was a pretty bird."

He lunged forward and kissed her hard, and she kissed him back. They didn't have much time, but it was a beautiful three seconds. She pulled away and spoke to Turin.

"Why is Tanna still in the dream?" she said. "Can't she free herself?"

"No," Turin said. "She doesn't have an exit script. She went in there like anyone else. She needs someone to disconnect her."

Markla scowled and said, "I should disconnect her permanently. But I won't." Instead, she stabbed the blade into the chair just above Tanna's head. The chair was cushioned, and she sliced the cushion in an outline down past Tanna's ear. Then she said, "Rune, there's a guy outside the door. We need to get his gun."

"Right!" Rune said. "I'll get behind the door and grab it when he comes in."

"No! Just open the door."

Markla stayed beside Tanna and put the blade at her throat. Rune hesitated and then ran to the door and opened it. Stillo was just outside, and he turned as the door slid aside, and he looked at Rune with surprise. Then Markla spoke. "Put your hands up and don't use your GoBug. Do it now or Tanna dies."

Stillo froze for a second, taking in the scene. "Don't kill her," he said. "Please!" Then he raised his hands and Rune quickly grabbed the gun from a holster on his hip. He also snatched the GoBug from behind Stillo's ear.

"Good," Markla said. "We've got a chair for you. Get in here and sit down."

Rune kept the gun pointed at him as he walked to the chair. Markla said, "I'll hold the gun, Rune, while you strap him in." He gave it to her, and she kept the weapon aimed at Stillo while Rune strapped him in place.

She wasn't taking any chances. She loved Rune but he was a little too nice, and if this big goon tried anything she was going to shoot him. *I hope Rune doesn't think I'm a monster,* she thought. *But we need to do what's necessary.*

She took a breath. "All right," she said. "I suppose they'll get out of here pretty soon, but do we have a way to gag them?"

Rune spotted a closet, and inside were some tools—and a roll of tape. "How about this?"

"Perfect. Do it!"

Rune wrapped the tape around everyone's mouth. Then he removed the power crystal from Stillo's GoBug and put it in his pocket along with the device.

Markla frowned. "What are you doing?"

"We might need it."

She hesitated. "Okay," she said. Because Rune was good with GoBugs.

They went over to the door and he spoke to her in a soft voice. "Do you have a plan?" he said. She gave him a sarcastic look, and he laughed. "I just thought I'd ask."

"Actually, I do have a plan," she said. "Stoke and I studied the layout of this place, and I know it pretty well, and we came up with an idea. But we'll need to improvise a bit. We're going to turn off the auto-defense system."

"Great! Let's do it!" Then he hesitated and said, "Where is it?"

"I'll explain but don't take any stupid chances."

"But that's what we always do."

"Yeah, I know. But I don't want you getting hurt because of me."

"Markla, if we die, we die together, okay?"

"Is that a promise?"

He looked into her eyes. "Yes."

She smiled. "Okay, let's go."

Chapter 58

Rune followed Markla as she raced down a narrow hallway and into an office. There was a dream station on a desktop, and an open closet door, and some clothes inside the closet—as well as some weapons, a pair of eye scanners, a radio, a backpack, and what looked like a bunch of camping supplies.

This must be Diana's office, Rune thought. So she was still helping them, although she wasn't here right now. But it was good to know she was on their side.

Markla pulled a shirt from the closet, the kind worn by the Sparklan military. "Rune, this is for you. Put it on. But I've never really cared for a guy in a uniform."

Rune smiled and grabbed it. "That's because I've never worn one."

There were two helmets in the closet, and Rune shoved his long hair under one of them and vaguely wondered if his father would've been proud. Overall, he thought he made a decent-looking soldier. Meanwhile, Markla was a problem because she was so small. There were no boots for her, so she'd need to keep her moccasins. But there was a uniform, and it actually fit.

Markla shook her head. "Where did Diana find this? What do you think?"

"I think you're the smallest soldier in Sparkla. Small but fierce. What are we doing next?"

She tied her hair back and stuffed it under her helmet. Then she picked up a pistol and checked to see if it was loaded. She rummaged through the camping gear and took something that looked like a long metal bolt dangling from a small chain. Rune was about to ask her what it was when she said, "The EB that controls everything is underground. There's no way we're getting in there. Too many guards, and even if we got in, it would be impossible to access anything—face scans, eye scans, voice recognition, DNA check—there's just no way."

"So then how are we going to do it?"

"Well, they've made it hard to turn off just one thing—but maybe we can turn off everything. We're going to kill the power to the whole fort. That's the plan. By the way, Stoke has a few people inside who might be able to help when things start happening." She gave him a sober look. "Rune, this might involve some shooting, and this is real ammo. Are you okay with that?"

His eyes went wide. "Of course!" he said. "I've been fighting with you all along."

"Yeah, but you haven't really hurt anyone."

Right. He knew this was true, and of course she'd noticed. He hadn't killed anybody. Was he ready to do it now?

"I'm sure they'll be shooting at us," he said. "And I'm going to shoot back."

Markla hesitated. Then she handed him the gun they'd taken from Stillo. "Take this," she said. "I'll use Diana's… Let's go."

She stuffed their previous clothes into the backpack along with some of the other gear. Then they stepped back into the hall—and the air exploded with the sound of an alarm, and a voice boomed throughout the fort:

"Escaped prisoners, section twenty-two. Escaped prisoners!"

Markla swore, and they started running, and Rune felt his heart pounding. But Markla seemed to know where she was going, through a glass door and down a flight of stairs and outside into the vast landing area.

It was night, and a forest of floodlights shined down. But while they were bright on the landing field, in other areas it was dark and ghostly—like the nearby yard filled with vehicles. A siren started to wail, and Rune looked around at scores of hover-ships and other transports, and now he remembered this area from his arrival. Then Markla pointed and said, "The power station is this way."

Rune followed her as they sprinted through the darkness, hiding behind one parked vehicle before quickly moving to the next one. Then searchlights started scanning the yard, and Rune saw one coming their way.

"Look out!" he said.

They dove to the ground and slid under a hover-ship, right near the landing gear. Rune held his breath. The light was like a blazing eye but then it passed, and they sighed with relief. Then they got back on their feet and moved on. Finally, they were behind a massive transport of some kind, staring across a wide stretch of the landing area. In the gray distance was a low concrete building that was all lit up. It was located behind a metal fence topped with razor wire. Markla studied it through the eye magnifiers.

"That's it," she said. "But it looks like there are tiny automated guns built into the walls, and on the roof, too. Stoke and I didn't see those on Diana's recording. There's no way we can shoot our way in, and I'm pretty sure if we ring the doorbell they're not going to be too friendly."

"So we need a new plan," Rune said. "Hey, this is a fort. There are lots of weapons lying around. If we could steal a hover-ship and fire a few missiles at the building, that would work, right?"

"Maybe. But do you know how to fly a hover-ship and launch missiles from it?"

"No."

"Neither do I. But you just gave me an idea. Come on."

She started scurrying around among the vehicles, and soon she was on the back of a flatbed hover-truck, waving her hand.

"Rune—look!" she hissed. "What are these?"

Rune leaped onto the back of the truck and examined what

she'd found. "They look like a couple of missiles," he said.

"Right. Do you think these could blow up that building?"

"Maybe. It looks like they're on some kind of launcher. It's probably controlled by a GoBug script. If we had the script, maybe we could figure it out."

"A script? I was thinking we'd use fire. If we set these on fire, they'll explode, right?"

"Hey—yeah! That could work, too."

"Okay! We'll drive this thing through that fence and smash it into the building and light these on fire. We just need something flammable. Then while it's starting to burn we can run. So, what can we use?"

None of the vehicles on the landing field were powered by liquid fuel. That was all part of ancient history. They needed something else.

"Over there!" Markla said. She was pointing across another part of the landing field to a multi-story building. In the corner of the building were some thin windows but they looked mostly dark. "Those windows in the corner, that's an officer's club. I noticed it on Diana's recording… It's a bar, Rune—a place full of alcohol, and I remember my mom used to light her drinks on fire with her boyfriend. They thought it was fun. It needs to be the strong stuff."

"This looks like a place where the drinks would be strong."

"Yeah. But we'll need a way to carry it. And we'll need to do it without being seen."

"There are lots of vehicles here," Rune said. "Let's go shopping. How about this one?"

It was a hover-scooter with two saddles bags mounted on either side of the rear tire. It was the most primitive kind of vehicle but that was fine since it didn't require any special access code. Rune hopped on and Markla got behind him. He planned to stay in the shadows near the edge of the yard but he still knew they'd be a lot more visible.

"Do you feel lucky, Markla? We're going to need it."

"Yeah, I know," she said. And then a bomb went off.

It was somewhere inside the fortress—maybe a grenade. It was followed by two more explosions. Rune didn't know what was happening but he was sure it was good. It might distract anyone looking for them out here.

"What's going on?" he said.

"I don't know, maybe Diana or one of Stoke's inside people—but go! Go!"

Rune revved the motor and they took off.

The sirens were still wailing, and somewhere inside the fortress another bomb exploded. But they made it to the door of the club without incident. Markla hopped off the scooter and grabbed the door handle. She looked surprised to find that it was open.

She turned to Rune. "Remember, we need the strongest stuff."

They walked into the pub. The room was small and had red walls, a mirror behind the walnut-colored bar, and soft pinkish lighting. The place was also empty except for a bartender. But he wore a soldier's uniform, and as they walked in he looked at them with narrow eyes.

"Hey, everyone went on alert," he said. "I was just about to close."

"Yeah, we're on our way," Rune said. "But we need a drink first. Something with a lot of kick."

He eyed them with suspicion, and then Markla pulled out her pistol.

"Put up your hands," she said. "We want the strongest stuff you have. Where is it?"

His eyes got wide. "So you're the escaped prisoners. Take it easy, little girl. We've got plenty to drink… We've got the seventy-five percent stuff. It's practically pure alcohol. It's right here in this cabinet."

He pointed to a cabinet near his feet, and then he bent down to open it. Rune was watching him—and suddenly the guy was whirling fast, and in his hand was a pistol.

Markla shot him in the chest. He gave a grunt and crashed backwards into a shelf filled with bottles. But he was still standing, trying to raise his weapon, and she fired again—and the bullet struck him in the throat, and now he tumbled to the floor. Rune caught his breath. Stay calm, Rune thought. *Stay calm!*

It was quiet. He looked at Markla.

"What kind of bottles are in there?" she said.

Right—the bottles. Rune jumped over the bar and tried not to look at the dead body as he pulled a fat bottle out of the cabinet. His heart was racing as he read the label.

"McGregor Group Seventy-Five."

"Perfect," she said. "One of my mom's favorites."

The cabinet was full of bottles but they estimated they could only carry seven—three in each saddle bag and then one that Markla could carry on her lap. They loaded up the scooter and headed off into the dark.

Chapter 59

Markla sat behind Rune on the scooter as they moved through the darkness. She had a bottle of McGregor on her lap, and she had her arms wrapped tight around his body.

I'm going to hold on to him forever, she thought. *I mean if we don't get killed tonight.*

She wondered if he was thinking about the incident in the bar, and how she was a cold-hearted killer. But she wasn't—at least she didn't think so. She'd done what she had to do. More and more, she could see this was a pattern, and maybe it wasn't such a bad thing. After all, it had kept her alive, and it was going to keep Rune alive, too. She was going to make sure of it.

They arrived back at the flatbed truck and started unloading the bottles. Then they climbed up into the truck and starting pouring the alcohol on top of the missiles.

Rune swore. "How are we going to light it on fire? I didn't see an igniter in Diana's stuff. It seems like a small detail but we don't have a way to light this stuff up."

"Yeah, we do, Rune." Markla dangled the chain with the bolt-like thing attached that she'd taken from Diana's closet. "This is a fire rod, and that's what it does. It's made of different metals. It's a common survivalist thing."

He cocked his head and laughed. "Well, you're a real survivor. Let's do it."

Markla emptied the last bottle and they climbed into the cab of the truck. She didn't want to drive, so she was happy when Rune got behind the wheel. But now she saw a true problem. Unlike the scooter, the truck required an eye scan in order to power up the engine. She slammed her fist against the door.

"This stupid toad machine! I should've known we wouldn't be able to start it."

But Rune was calm, and he was reaching into his pants pocket. "We can start it with this," he said, and he pulled out a GoBug along with the power crystal. "This is the one I took from Stillo. He was the guard in the MindCore room."

Markla shook her head. "But he's probably got an alert on that thing. The second you connect, using a guest ID or whatever, they're going to know where we are."

"Who cares? They're going to know where we are anyway the second we blow up that building. Just watch me."

She watched as Rune put the device behind his ear. Meanwhile, she stared across the shadowy yard and saw lights flickering in the windows of the pub.

"Rune, someone's in the pub. They're probably checking all the outside cameras right now. They're probably going to find us quick."

"Don't worry. We'll be fine."

But she was worried. "Hurry up!" she said. "How much longer?"

Rune shook his head. "Stillo doesn't have access to these vehicles. So I'm signing into my smasher account and getting a script."

"Are you crazy? We don't have time for that!"

"Markla, trust me. My account is still active… This is going to work. I'm fast."

She kept looking out the window—and now she saw several hover vehicles coming their way, and she saw the silhouettes of people with rifles leaping out and running into the yard. Meanwhile, Rune was talking.

"Signed into my account," he said.

Markla gripped the gun and leaned out the window.

"Searching for the script," he said.

Markla saw a few people looking at her. Someone was pointing.

"Found it," he said. "Trying it now."

Someone fired a shot.

"Almost there…" Markla gritted her teeth.

The truck started up. Rune gave a whoop as he retracted the landing gear—and in an instant they were shooting out of the yard and onto the landing field.

A storm of shots hit the rear of the vehicle, shattering a few tail lights. But they kept going. They didn't need to go far. The power station fence was right across the field. It was getting closer and closer.

"Hang on!" Rune said.

Markla braced herself. The truck smashed into the fence and she was thrown forward. Then she heard Rune swear. The truck hadn't gone all the way through the fence—it was stuck half way.

"Hit the accelerator!" Markla shouted.

"I'm trying! We're stuck. It won't go through!"

"Keep doing it!"

He kept trying but the truck wouldn't move.

"It's not going to work!" he said. "We need to do something else!"

"Like what?"

He put the truck in reverse and it sprang free of the fence. Then he swung the vehicle back out toward the landing field.

"What are you doing?" Markla said.

"We need more speed to get through."

She started to yell again but stopped—maybe he was right.

He gunned the vehicle all the way down the landing field, much farther away from the power station. They were near the wall now, and Markla looked up and saw the big guns on top of the towers, staring down.

"Rune—the guns!"

"We'll be gone before they notice."

Markla took a deep breath. This might be true—they weren't set to target things inside the fort. But they could be told to do it pretty easily, and then they'd have no chance.

Rune once again revved the engine. And once again the truck shot down the landing field.

The hover-truck was surprisingly fast. The buildings were a blur as they headed back to the power station. Through the darkness, Markla saw other vehicles coming toward them.

"Look out!"

"I see them!"

They almost hit one but Rune swerved at the last second, and they passed right by it, and here was the station once again—and here was that spot in the fence.

They hit it much harder this time. There was a loud crash as the windshield shattered. Was it from the impact or a bullet? Markla was holding onto the dashboard, and she didn't know—but she looked up and they were through the fence and heading toward the building. Rune aimed for the main door and the truck smashed right through it.

Sirens were screaming. People were shouting.

"Markla, are you all right?"

"Yeah," she said. "I'm fine."

Actually, she felt dizzy, but it quickly subsided—and she was glad the windshield was broken because the truck was stuck half inside the building, and the doors were pinned shut against the walls.

She pulled out her dagger and used it to clear away the rest of the broken glass.

"I'll light the fire," she said. She scrambled out onto the hood, and then over the top of the cab and into the back of the flatbed.

She heard shots and people running, and then she saw two soldiers coming toward the truck. They were already through the fence, and now she realized her pistol was still on the front seat. She cursed and braced herself—but then two gunshots rang out, and she saw Rune on top of the cab. He'd shot them both.

"Go!" Rune shouted. "Go!"

He's going to get himself killed, she thought. *We're both going to die!*

But they would go out in a ball of fire. She had the fire rod in one hand, and the 20 Eyes dagger in the other, and she noted that her hands were steady. She swiped the blade across the silvery metal—and there was a flash of light, and a shower of sparks, and flames erupted in the back of the truck.

She heard Rune fire two more shots, and then he was there beside her, and they had to get out of the vehicle, and he was grabbing her arm. "This way!" he said.

They leaped to the ground. They were outside the building now and they ran back toward the fence because that was the only way out. But there were at least two groups of soldiers nearby, and they were coming out of two trucks, and there was no way they were going to get through that fence without being shot. And then the air crackled with gunfire, and Markla braced herself once again, waiting for the impact, waiting to die—but instead she saw a bunch of soldiers fall.

Someone else was shooting from across the landing field, someone with a high-powered rifle. Was it Diana or one of Stoke's other people? Either way, their timing was good, and Markla and Rune dashed through the mangled fence. "This way!" Markla said, and they raced along the fence away from the power station and away from the soldiers. They had to get as far from the station as possible, and they had to do it quick, and she'd never run so fast in her life. They reached the wall, and they kept running toward the far tower—and then there was a thundering roar.

Markla was thrown to the ground. She skidded on her stomach, and she heard pieces of the building raining down around her. She covered her head for an instant, and then she looked around, searching for Rune. He was on the ground beside her, and he was smiling.

It was dark. The entire fortress was dark.

"We did it," Rune said, and he laughed. "We did it!"

"Yeah," she said, and she laughed, too. Then she got up on her knees and reached for the radio that was somehow still with her.

"What are you doing?" Rune said.

"I'm sending a message to Stoke. The base is a long way from here but he has a couple of teams nearby. I'm going to tell him where we are—near tower three, so they don't shoot us. In fact, we should take these uniforms off. And then we try to hang on until they get here."

He reached out his hand, and she grasped it. The radio crackled and they waited together in the dark.

Chapter 60

Rune heard lots of shouting but the sirens had stopped. Firefighters were visible through the smoke and haze, drenching the power station with water. People dressed in bright yellow suits and helmets were combing the rubble, searching for survivors.

Rune felt a pang of guilt at what he'd done, but what would his father have said? Would he have been proud? Probably. *But am I proud? Yeah, I am.*

It was dark but not totally black. There were no clouds tonight and the gold-colored moon was almost full. He peered into the shadows and saw that they were lying on a grassy area near the stone wall, close to one of the towers. There were also a few willowy trees and some benches, and it was like a mini park. There were several buildings nearby, but they didn't see any people entering or leaving.

Rune looked over at Markla. "How long will it be?"

"Soon," she said. "A commando unit is coming in ahead of the main force. Stoke said without the defenses, they could destroy this place with low-flying missiles but he wants all the equipment. He wants to capture as much as possible, so there's going to be an invasion. But the main base is a long way from here. We should really get out of these uniforms." She ripped off her backpack and pulled out her original clothes.

"Wait!" Rune said. "Maybe we should still try to blend in."

"I'm done blending, Rune."

Despite the serious situation, Rune laughed. It was true, Markla wasn't much of a "blender." Besides, they didn't want to get shot by the people on their own side. They quickly ditched the uniforms and got back into their original clothes. Then from a dark corner of the landing field, Rune saw a flash of light and watched a small hover-ship take off.

"Look!" he said. "Someone is leaving."

Markla also watched but said nothing. Then they heard a few noises, and they looked up—and people were coming over the wall.

They were dressed in black, and they were dropping from ropes like spiders. Markla pushed a button on the radio and waved at one of them who came running over.

The commando was a muscular guy, heavily armed and wearing night vision goggles. "Markla Flash?" he said.

"Yeah. I can fight."

"We don't have any gear for you. Besides, we're here to get you out."

"What do you mean? I have a gun. We can help until the main group gets here."

As Markla spoke there was a roaring sound, like the sound of a thousand mighty engines, and the commando looked up at the sky.

"We're here," he said, and through the moonlight Rune saw the outlines of hover-ships—lots of them. They turned the dark sky black with shadowy shapes.

"What?" Markla said. "How did you get here so fast?"

"When you gave yourself up, Stoke started moving everyone into position." The guy smiled. "I guess he thought you'd get the job done."

Rune couldn't believe the number of ships. It was an enormous force, and a vast symbol of the unpopularity of the Sparklan government.

"Come on!" the commando shouted. "Move!"

Rune and Markla looked at each other, and they dashed toward the wall. Another soldier secured a harness around each of them, and within a few seconds they were being lifted through the air, out of the fortress, and into a hover-ship. It was just in time.

Rockets and weapons from the ground started blasting—but it was obvious they were no match for the force above. Without the automated defenses, the fortress was thrown into a state of chaos, and now the swift attack caught them by surprise. The hover-ships were equipped with automated systems that easily targeted the location of any attack and instantly returned fire. The fortress had been designed to keep people out but now it was a monstrous death trap.

Rune and Markla scurried into the cramped cockpit of the hover-ship. A couple of people slapped them on the back. The pilot gave them a big grin and it occurred to Rune that they were going to be treated like heroes. But at the moment he felt no elation. He only felt numb. He put his arm around Markla and they watched as the entire inside of the fort lit up with explosions and flames. The sound was deafening and the fire was blinding. Many of the buildings inside the fortress were struck by missiles and gunfire, and some were blown to bits, and the troops on the ground trying to fire hand weapons were easy targets. No more Sparklan hover-ships lifted off—if they tried, they were destroyed instantly from the air.

Rune sucked in his breath. Then he looked over at Markla and wondered what she was thinking. She hated the Sparklan government but she was quiet and showed no expression.

Rune thought about Diana, and he felt a little sick. Was she being killed right now? The hover-ships targeted the towers, the guns, and the troops on the ground but many of the main buildings were not hit—and he knew there was a vast complex underground. She was resourceful and smart, and hopefully she was safe.

After a short time, the gunfire from the ground stopped and some of the hover-ships started dropping down into the fortress. Free Sparkla soldiers started pouring out.

"I should be down there with them," Markla said.

Rune started to respond but he stopped himself. He felt fine to be up here. They'd done their part.

Chapter 61

Tanna had never flown a hover-ship before but she had a script that could do it. She and Stillo skimmed low over the trees while she stared into the night.

She was still feeling stunned about waking up in the nightmare room and being strapped in place. She was still in shock thinking about what Rune and Markla had done.

"I feel like a coward," she said. "I should've stayed."

"Why?" Stillo said. "You couldn't have done anything. They escaped, and the fort is under attack. If a couple of people hadn't come looking for me you'd still be in that dream. Just be happy you're alive."

"Oh, I'm thrilled!" she snapped. "I'm so happy Markla didn't cut my throat!"

"She could've done it pretty easily."

Tanna started to yell again—but she stopped, and she recalled the outline that had been cut into the chair around her head. Yeah, it was true.

"How did she escape?" Tanna said.

"I don't know. She cut the strap somehow. How did she get out of the dream?"

"I don't know."

In the distance, they heard explosions coming from the place they'd left behind.

"I should've stayed," Tanna said. "I can fight!"

"No, you can't. Your father wanted you out of there, and he was right."

"I deserve to be blown up. I'm the one who caused all this."

"What are you talking about?"

She banged her fist down on the dashboard. "I brought Markla into the fort! My obsession with Markla and Rune destroyed everything! I wanted her dead, and then I just wanted to hurt her, and it was all so wrong and stupid—and the whole government will probably come crashing down because of me."

She slumped in her seat and started crying. It wasn't something she did often. "I'm a loser," she said, and she was sobbing now. "I'm such a loser."

Stillo shook his head and put his arm around her. "That's not true at all," he said. "You didn't start the war. All the fighting was caused by other people. You're a great girl, and no matter what happens I love you."

She stopped crying, and she spoke in a low voice. "You're always joking about that."

Stillo smiled. "Yeah, but it's never been a joke. I've been in love with you ever since we met." He laughed. "I guess I was ten, and you were so pretty—and so smart. You're still the smartest person I know. "

She wiped her eyes. "Really?" she said.

"Yeah, really. But I guess you could check my brain in MindCore and see."

Tanna frowned. "I don't want to check anything in MindCore. I'm done with all that, and I want to do something new with my life. I'm tired of trying to impress my father. I need to get out of his stupid shadow."

"Great! Maybe I can help."

She kissed him on the lips. He kissed her back, and then they did it again. Then she pulled away and looked at him, and she felt something strange. Yeah, her body was tingling a bit but it was more than that. Was this real love? It was hard to say.

Chapter 62

Markla felt sick in her stomach.

It was early morning, just before daybreak, and she was back at Fort Liberty. She was standing on the breezy roof of an observation tower high above the dense forest, where she could see across the colorful tapestry of leaves all the way to the snaky river that divided Sparkla from Narna. She was near a metal railing, beside a wooden bolla drum that Rune had purchased from a soldier and lugged up here so he could happily bang notes into the open air. They'd been here for two days.

By most accounts things were wonderful. She'd been talking on the radio to Tommi, and he was fine, and she'd be seeing him soon. He'd heard all about what she'd been doing—sort of. She'd need to give him a different perspective, but it had been thrilling to hear his voice and to know he was okay. Meanwhile, Diana had not been harmed in the attack. She was still at Fort Freedom, working with some of Stoke's people, and this made Markla happy. More than anyone, she'd helped Rune and Markla stay alive. Jorro was also unharmed, and he'd been released. Stoke and his fighting force had captured Fort Freedom and all the equipment inside, and a huge part of the military had defected. An hour ago, it was reported that Gin Xantha had fled the country. Supposedly, his daughter Tanna had gone with him.

A new government was going to be elected, and the mind-streams and GoBugs were exploding with news, and most of the news was true. Everyone was intently watching the streams. Unfortunately, many of the streams were focused on Rune and Markla.

Markla took a few deep breaths and tried to focus on the pink horizon. At least I don't have a GoBug, she thought. Because it would be buzzing like a beehive.

The Free Sparkla people who'd been broadcasting had turned their story into a phenomenon. Had someone decided the movement needed a couple of heroes? Or had the story evolved organically? It was hard to say. But either way, everyone wanted to talk to them, and everyone wanted more information about how two teenagers in love had helped bring down the government. So Markla was still in the fort, hiding in a high tower. And she was feeling sick.

She saw Rune coming out of the lift and running toward her. He had a small burlap bag in his hand, and he was grinning, and it looked like he wanted to tell her a million things at once.

"Markla, guess what? I just talked to my mother on a GoBug, and I can't believe she's awake this early. We've changed the world! Anyway, she wanted me to give you a message. She said, "Tell Markla she did a great job.""

"Oh, yeah?" Markla gave a little smile as she remembered her promise to Maya. At least that had worked out.

Rune was still grinning. "I was on e mindstreams, and you really need to see what's going on."

"I know what's going on, Rune. It's a circus, and we're a couple of clowns."

"We're not clowns. We're superstars!" He took her in his arms. "Okay, I know you're not happy about being a celebrity but you're hugely popular! Everyone is saying that the new government will pardon you for everything you've done because the old government made up so many lies. Do you hear me? We could stay here! We don't need to leave."

Yeah, she'd heard about this possibility. Everyone she'd seen for the last two days had told her about it. She pulled away and leaned on the railing, and a cool breeze blew through the chaos of her hair.

"Rune, do I deserve to be pardoned?"

His eyes flashed. "Of course you do! There are things worse than death, and that's what they were doing to you. That's what Aldo wanted to keep doing to you."

She shook her head. "I've been thinking a lot about who I am, and I'm not a celebrity or a superstar. Nobody knows what's inside my head, and I don't want anyone to know, and I'm not interested in talking to people."   She gave him a sober look. "Rune, I'm a soldier. I've been denying it, but it's true. I'm not saying I want to spend my life running through the woods with a rifle in my hand, but I want to stand up for things I believe in. That's why I joined 20 Eyes, and that's why I've done a lot of other things—even when I was a little kid. That's who I am. I'm a fighter."

Rune laughed. "Yeah, I know," he said.

"You do?"

He shrugged. "I've always known. It's kind of obvious." Then he paused and added, "But that's not who I am. My father would hate to hear it, but I'd still rather write a LiveDream than fight another battle."

"You fight when it matters," Markla said. "And you don't want to write LiveDreams that torture people or turn them into slaves. Your father would've been proud of you."

He hesitated. "You don't think I should be more of a warrior?"

"No," she said. "You're fine the way you are. But then again it doesn't matter because you *are* a warrior. You're just doing it a different way." She paused and gave him a sideways glance. "But what about me, Rune? Do you think I should be different? Someone less…crazy?"

Rune laughed. "You're not crazy, Markla. But if you are, I don't care. I love my little crazy girl."

Now they both laughed. Then there was a moment of silence. Finally, Markla said, "I talked to Rala on the radio. She said they'd be happy to have me in Narna. They also need people who can learn technology and help them use it in a responsible way. They have a small university in Camarillo, and her clan has friends there, and she said we could go there, if you want to do that." She paused again. "But if you want to stay here, I'll understand."

She held her breath, waiting for his response. She could hear her heart beating.

He smiled. "You know I'm going with you, Markla. I'll always go with you." Then he hugged her, and her heart leaped—and he reached into the bag he'd brought with him. Inside was her wooden flute.

Rune handed it to her. "Let's play," he said. "Finally, me and you. Whatever you want."

She stared at Rune, and she smiled back at him. She didn't know any songs. She liked to pick her own notes. It made her feel calm.

She started to play, and then the drum joined in, and they watched the sun rise.

The End

About The Author

Joe Canzano is a writer and musician from New Jersey, U.S.A. For the latest news about Joe's books, subscribe to his newsletter. You can find it at www.happyjoe.net, where you'll also find more information about Joe than you'll ever need.

He invites you to email him at happyjoe800@gmail.com

Thanks for reading!

Novels by Joe Canzano

MAGNO GIRL
SEX HELL
SUZY SPITFIRE KILLS EVERYBODY
SUZY SPITFIRE AND THE SNAKE EYES OF VENUS
RUNE AND FLASH
ESCAPE

For more information check happyjoe.net.